W9-CNO-168

APR 2 8 2014

DECEPTION COVE

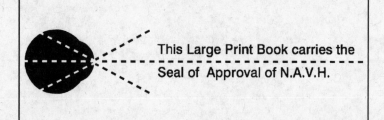

This Large Print Book carries the
Seal of Approval of N.A.V.H.

A RAINSHADOW NOVEL

DECEPTION COVE

JAYNE ANN KRENTZ
WRITING AS JAYNE CASTLE

THORNDIKE PRESS
A part of Gale, Cengage Learning

GALE
CENGAGE Learning·

Detroit • New York • San Francisco • New Haven, Conn • Waterville, Maine • London

GALE
CENGAGE Learning·

Copyright © 2013 by Jayne Ann Krentz.
Thorndike Press, a part of Gale, Cengage Learning.

ALL RIGHTS RESERVED
This is a work of fiction. Names, characters, places, and incidents either are the product of the author's imagination or are used fictitiously, and any resemblance to actual persons, living or dead, business establishments, events, or locales is entirely coincidental. The publisher does not have any control over and does not assume any responsibility for author or third-party websites or their content.

Thorndike Press® Large Print Core.
The text of this Large Print edition is unabridged.
Other aspects of the book may vary from the original edition.
Set in 16 pt. Plantin.

LIBRARY OF CONGRESS CATALOGING-IN-PUBLICATION DATA

Castle, Jayne.
    Deception Cove : A Rainshadow Novel / By Jayne Castle. — Large Print edition.
      pages cm. — (Thorndike Press Large Print Core)
    ISBN 978-1-4104-6534-4 (hardcover) — ISBN 1-4104-6534-9 (hardcover)
    1. Large type books. I. Title.
PS3561.R44D425 2014
813'.54—dc23   2013037746

Published in 2014 by arrangement with The Berkley Publishing Group, a member of Penguin Group (USA) LLC, a Penguin Random House Company

Printed in the United States of America
1 2 3 4 5 6 7 18 17 16 15 14

This one is for Houdini.
When it comes to a vanishing act, no
other magician does it with more style.

A NOTE FROM JAYNE

Welcome back to Rainshadow Island on the world of Harmony.

In the Rainshadow novels you will meet the passionate men and women who are drawn to this remote island in the Amber Sea. You will get to know their friends and neighbors in the small town of Shadow Bay.

Everyone on Rainshadow has a past; everyone has secrets. But none of those secrets is as dangerous as the ancient mystery concealed inside the paranormal fence that guards the forbidden territory of the island known as the Preserve.

The secrets of the Preserve have been locked away for centuries. But now something dangerous is stirring . . .

I hope you will enjoy the Rainshadow novels.

CHAPTER 1

The two low-rent thugs were waiting for Alice when she left the darkened theater through the stage door. She sensed their presence as soon as she started walking toward the street. They were hiding behind the large garbage bin in the middle of the alley. They were not the subtle type.

"I do not have time for this," she said to the dust bunny perched on her shoulder.

Houdini chortled enthusiastically and bounced a little. At first glance he looked like a large wad of dryer lint that had been decorated with six paws and two baby blue eyes. He had a second set of eyes — they were a very feral shade of amber — but he only opened them for hunting or when he sensed danger. He was still wearing the elegant red satin bow tie that Alice had put on him for the night's performance of the Alien Illusions Magic Show.

A born ham, Houdini adored the limelight. He was always up for a performance. Somehow he sensed that they were about to give one here in the alley. True, it would be for an audience of two, and neither of the lowlifes had purchased a ticket, but he wasn't particular about the size of the crowd and the concept of money was lost on him. He took a more pragmatic approach to finances. Pizza worked for him.

"I'm glad you're enjoying yourself," Alice said. "We've got an empty refrigerator waiting back at the apartment and a mean landlord who will be expecting the rent tomorrow, remember?"

She did not have the money for the rent. The Alien Illusions Magic Show had folded without notice tonight. That kind of thing happened in show business, but in this case she was pretty sure she knew why the owner of the theater had cancelled all future productions. He had been bribed to dump the act.

She was now towing a wheeled suitcase crammed with costumes, wigs, stage makeup, and everything else she had been able to salvage from her tiny dressing room. A large blue tote filled with props was slung over her shoulder.

It had not been a good day, and the night was turning out to be worse. Not only was

10

she once again unemployed, she'd been experiencing the all-too-familiar edgy sensation for the past several hours. During the past year she had learned the hard way that the icy little jolts of warning were coming from her intuition. Someone was watching her. Again.

And now a couple of street creeps were about to try to mug her.

"Really, how much can any woman be expected to take?" she said to Houdini.

Houdini chortled again, eager to go on stage.

One of the thugs emerged from behind the far end of the garbage bin. His head, which had been shaved to better display the tattoos on his skull, gleamed in the light cast by the fixture over the stage door. He had a knife in one hand.

The second man popped out of hiding and moved toward her along a parallel trajectory. He wore a stocking cap over his long, straggly hair. The blade of his knife glittered in the light.

"Now what's a nice girl like you doing out here all alone at night?" Tattoo Head asked. "Didn't anyone tell you this is a dangerous neighborhood?"

His voice was high-pitched and over-rezzed with the sort of unnatural excitement that indicated he had been doing some serious stimulants earlier in the evening.

"Get out of my way," Alice said. She adjusted the weight of the tote on her shoulder, tightened her grip on the suitcase, and kept walking. "I'm not in a good mood."

"Now why you wanna go and talk like that to a couple of guys who just want to party?" the man with the stocking cap crooned. "We're gonna show you a real good time."

"A real good time." Tattoo Head leered. "What's that thing on your shoulder? Some kinda fluffy rat?"

Alice ignored him, closing the distance between the three of them as she trudged toward the alley entrance. No doubt about it, a really bad day was turning into a really bad night.

"Listen up, bitch," Stocking Cap snarled. "Stop right there. First, put that big purse down on the ground. You hear me? You're gonna take out all the money you got inside, and if my friend and I like what we see, we'll all have some fun. If we don't like what we see, why then, you're gonna have to give us a reason not to cut you up a bit."

Alice ignored the threat.

"Hey, my buddy told you to stop," Tattoo Head hissed.

Alice continued walking. She felt Houdini's little claws grip her shoulder. He was no longer chortling. He growled a warning and sleeked out, his scruffy gray fur flattened against his small frame. He opened his second set of eyes and watched the knife-wielding pair closely. He was ready to rumble.

"There's an old saying about dust bunnies," Alice said to the thugs. *"By the time you see the teeth, it's too late.* Turns out Houdini and I have our own little twist on that bit of wisdom. *If you can't see the teeth or anything else, you're in trouble."*

"What do you think you're doing, you stupid woman?" Stocking Cap said. He skipped and danced across the pavement, closing in on her. "You asked for it. I'm gonna have to cut up that face of yours to teach you a lesson."

"Oh, for pity's sake," Alice said. "I've got some real issues at the moment. You shouldn't mess with a woman who has issues. Never say you weren't warned."

She jacked up her senses and pulled hard on her talent. She had never met anyone else with the same kind of psychic ability that she possessed — light-talents of any kind were rare. Those strong enough to do what she could do were considered the stuff of fairy tales.

She cranked up her aura and used the energy to bend the wavelengths of normal-spectrum light around herself and Houdini. The process was similar to the way a rock diverts water in a stream. To all intents and purposes, she had just gone invisible to the human eye.

She pushed a little harder and extended the shield to her tote and suitcase. It took a lot of power to bend light around not only herself and Houdini but the objects she was touching as well. She figured she wouldn't have to do it for long. She had learned over the years that people tended to freak out when they realized that, in her case, going invisible was not merely a magic trick.

As paranormal talents went, the ability to vanish for a short period of time was not nearly as useful as one might think. Career options were limited. Having concluded that she was not cut out for a life of crime, she had tried various other professional endeavors ranging from the food-and-beverage business to a job as a clerk in a museum gift shop. The last one had nearly gotten her killed.

This past year she had tried her hand at the magic business. It seemed like the perfect career for a woman with her skill set. As it happened, however, any halfway-

14

experienced magician could routinely make objects disappear on stage. The fact that she used psychic energy to achieve the effect did not impress anyone in show business. She was a one-trick wonder.

Still, the ability to disappear at will, along with whatever she happened to have physical contact with at the time, did have its benefits.

"Shit," Tattoo Head yelped. He halted abruptly and stared at the place where Alice had been seconds earlier. "Where'd she go?"

"I don't know," Stocking Cap said. He was clearly jittery. "This is too weird. Maybe that last dose of green dust was bad, man. Gotta find a new dealer."

"It's not the dust," Tattoo Head said, edging back toward the entrance of the alley. Fear shivered in the atmosphere around him. "Maybe that magic act of hers is for real. Maybe she's a witch or something."

"No way. Are you crazy? No such thing as a witch."

Alice hurried toward the alley entrance. She could not remain invisible for long, not now. She had used a lot of energy on stage. Psychic energy was subject to the laws of physics, just like any other kind of energy. Use a lot of it and you needed time to recover. But she was sure she would only have to bend light for another minute or two. Stocking Cap and Tattoo Head were starting to panic.

On her shoulder Houdini chortled gleefully. The sound echoed eerily in the night. So did her footsteps and the rattle of the suitcase wheels on the pavement.

"Shit, I can hear her," Tattoo Head said. "It's like she's a ghost."

That proved too much for Stocking Cap.

"I'm getting out of here," he said.

He whirled and fled toward the alley entrance. Tattoo Head was hard on his heels. They nearly trampled Alice in their haste. She got out of the way, hauling the suitcase to one side, and she stood with her back to the brick wall as the pair thudded past.

They did not get far. A man materialized in the shadows at the front of the narrow passage. Moving with the swift, efficient speed and agility of a specter-cat, he did something fast and ruthless to Tattoo Head and Stocking Cap. Alice could have sworn that she saw a spark of dark paranormal lightning flash in the night, but it winked out before she could be certain.

She blinked and saw Tattoo Head and Stocking Cap were on the ground. Neither moved.

The newcomer walked to where his victims lay and collected their knives. Then he crouched and went swiftly through the pockets of the unconscious men.

Just when you were convinced that a day could not get any worse, Alice thought. She stood frozen, her back to the alley wall, suddenly afraid to make any noise. She held her breath and struggled to keep the invisibility shield wrapped around herself, Houdini, and her burdens.

For his part, Houdini no longer appeared concerned. He was alert and watchful but he was back in dryer-lint mode. She was not sure what to make of that. On the one hand, it was reassuring to know that he did not sense another threat. Then again, maybe he was simply relishing the extended performance.

Evidently satisfied with his search, the man who had taken down Tattoo Head and Stocking Cap rose easily to his feet and started walking toward her.

As he came into the full glare of the alley door light, she saw that he was wearing wraparound, mirrored sunglasses.

Mirrored sunglasses. At midnight.

She just had time to realize that the stranger looked somewhat familiar before it dawned on her that he was looking directly at her.

"You must be Alice North," he said. "Your great-grandfather and mine were partners in a seafaring business a long time ago. My name is Drake Sebastian."

That explained a lot, she thought, including the sunglasses-at-midnight thing. The Sebastians kept a low profile, but given her personal interest in the family, she paid attention when a member of the clan occasionally appeared in a rez-screen video or in the newspapers. Drake was the heir to the corporate throne — the man slated to take over the helm of the family empire — so lately he had been showing up more than any of the other Sebastians.

Drake was never seen in public without his mirrored glasses. They were his trademark. According to the media, he did not wear them for effect. The unique mirrored lenses had been developed specially for him in a Sebastian company research lab. It was no secret that following a lab accident three years earlier he had developed a severe sensitivity to light from the normal end of the spectrum. Now, without his special sunglasses, Drake was even blinded by a low-watt lightbulb.

For the past year there was only one thing

Alice had feared more than her obsessive ex-mother-in-law's unrelenting harassment. Her worst nightmare for months was that the powerful Sebastian family might figure out that something very bad had happened on Rainshadow Island a year ago and that she was responsible.

Now it appeared the clan had, indeed, sent someone to track her down — and not just some low-ranking security agent. It was the next president and CEO of the family empire standing here in the alley. And he was looking straight at her even though she was bending light with all of her talent.

No doubt about it. *This is officially a really, really bad night,* she thought.

"You can see me," she said.

The overhead light glinted on Drake's mirrored glasses. His mouth curved in a mysterious smile, an edgy combination of masculine satisfaction and anticipation that sent shivers of awareness across her senses.

"Oh, yeah," he said. "I can see you, Alice North."

"Crap."

"Nice to meet you, too."

CHAPTER 2

Alice lowered her senses. No point wasting any more energy, she thought. She was close to exhaustion. It was clear now that she was going to have to make another run for it soon. In the meantime, she needed to conserve her talent.

She called on her other talent, the kind she used to conceal her emotions on stage. She was pretty good when it came to acting. She had learned the art early in life. It was one of many useful life lessons she had been schooled in at the orphanage. Rule Number One: *When in doubt, brazen it out.* The corollary of which was, *Fake it 'til you make it.*

"Got some ID?" she asked coolly.

It didn't seem likely that one of Ethel Whitcomb's minions would take the enormous risk of using the Sebastian family name as a cover. But when it came to Ethel you could never be sure. Revenge was a powerful drug for some people, and Ethel was a true addict. To get a fix she would take any chance, pay any price — even if that price meant pissing off a powerful business rival.

Drake didn't miss a beat.

"Driver's license or Sebastian, Inc. ID?" He smiled again, gravely polite this time.

"Company ID," she said. "Fake driver's licenses are ten bucks apiece anywhere here in the Quarter. But a Sebastian, Inc. ID card would be a little harder to come by."

"What makes you think you'll know a piece of genuine Sebastian, Inc. ID?" he asked, reaching inside his leather jacket.

"Give me a break. Everyone knows that Sebastian, Inc. is in the high-tech security business, among other things. I'm betting their ID cards are very hard to forge."

She was on thin ice and she knew it. How would she recognize a false ID when she had no way of knowing what the real thing looked like?

But Drake merely nodded once in approval and opened his wallet to remove a card. She took advantage of the brief moment to examine him more closely in the glare of the stage door light. Her first impression had not been wrong. Sleek as a specter-cat, and a lot more dangerous because she was very certain that, unlike the big cat, he didn't operate entirely on primal instinct. The mirrored glasses made it impossible to read his eyes, but she could sense the mag-steel control that electrified the atmosphere around him. Her intuition told her there was only one reason a man would need to develop that kind of self-mastery — to control a powerful talent or powerful passions. Or both.

Everything about him looked as if it had been honed for the hunt. His dark hair was cut in a short, crisp, no-nonsense style. The hard, unyielding planes and angles of his face could have landed him a role as a professional assassin in the movies — or in real life. The fact that she could not read his expression because of his sunglasses only served to heighten the aura of power and danger.

He handed her the ID card. It showed a photo of Drake complete with the glasses. In addition to a brief personal description and a phone number to call for verification, there was a small sliver of amber embedded in the plastic. The amber was hot. It resonated faintly when she touched it with her fingertip. It wasn't absolute proof that the document was authentic, of course. She had been in show business long enough to know that, for a price, you could buy fake verification chips as easily as mag-rez guns in any of the Old Quarters. Still, it seemed unlikely that one of Ethel's private investigators would risk carrying a document that could get him locked up for a very, very long time.

Besides, she thought, there could not be two men in the world who looked like the man in the photo. Drake Sebastian was definitely one of a kind.

"You can call that number if you've got any doubts," Drake said. "It goes straight to the security department at company headquarters."

"That won't be necessary." She handed the card back to him. "I've seen you in the media a few times. You're Drake Sebastian and, according to the business press, you and your family are still in the pirate business. The only difference these days is that you do your plundering legally."

He startled her with a wicked smile that sent another disturbing frisson across her senses.

"You know, Alice, you aren't in any position to insult my ancestor," he said. "Your great-grandfather was Harry Sebastian's business partner out there in the Amber Sea. They did their pirating together."

She raised her chin. She had known noth-

23

ing about her family history until last year, but now that she finally had some knowledge of her roots she was fiercely determined to protect the North family honor. She was, after all, the last of the line.

"They were partners in a shipping business," she insisted. "But somehow, when the partnership ended, your ancestor came out of it a rich man. My great-grandfather got screwed."

"We can argue about ancient history later. It's modern history that we need to talk about tonight. If our conversation goes the way I'm hoping it will, I'll have a business proposition for you that I think you'll find interesting."

Well, at least he wasn't threatening to have her arrested for theft and/or murder, Alice thought. And evidently he was not in the employ of Ethel Whitcomb. Instead he had specifically used the words *business proposition.* But that still left a lot of questions. She did not know whether to be somewhat relieved or downright scared.

"Damn it, I knew someone was watching me today," she said.

"Took me a lot longer to find you than I thought it would." Drake sounded impressed. "You do a good disappearing act."

"I've had some practice."

"A few days ago I traced you to a magic act here in the Quarter, but when I got to that theater I discovered that you had vanished again. Took me another three days to figure out that you hadn't left town like everyone seemed to think. Instead, you changed your name again and set up your own show here at this theater."

"*Alien Illusions* closed tonight. Mind telling me why you've been following me around?"

"It's a little complicated. Why don't we go someplace where we can talk? Don't know about you but I'm not keen on holding a serious business discussion in an alley in the Old Quarter at this hour of the night."

"Where do you suggest we have this business chat?"

"I vote for your apartment."

"Forget it," she said. "If you want to talk, we'll do it in public. There's a tavern a couple of blocks from here. I'm hungry and I could really use a drink."

"Okay, that works for me." Drake studied Houdini. "Does the local Board of Health allow dust bunnies into food-and-beverage establishments?"

Houdini chortled encouragingly, clearly aware that he was the topic of discussion. Alice took heart from the realization that he

25

was not showing any indication that he viewed Drake Sebastian as a direct or immediate threat. Houdini's instincts were reliable when it came to that sort of thing. He had saved her from a close encounter with more than one Whitcomb investigator during the past year.

"In this neighborhood, the restaurant owners aren't too particular," Alice said. "Besides, everyone at the Green Gate knows Houdini. We always drop in for a bite after the show."

She started toward the alley entrance again, towing the suitcase.

"I'll take that," Drake said.

He gripped the handle of the suitcase and deftly slipped it out of her grasp before she could decide whether or not to accept the offer. Then again, it hadn't exactly been an offer, she thought. More like an order. Nevertheless, the suitcase was heavy and she was tired. It had been a very long night and it wasn't over yet. She released the suitcase without further argument.

"I guess you probably aren't going to steal a bunch of costumes and props," she said.

"Probably not," Drake agreed.

She glanced at the two men on the pavement. "What did you use on that pair? I thought I saw a little flash of dark lightning."

"I used a gadget that came out of one of the company labs. It's still experimental. We're calling it a light spear. It uses ultralight to temporarily freeze the target's senses — all of the senses, normal as well as paranormal."

"Sounds useful."

"Not yet. It was designed as a law-enforcement weapon but it's still in development. There's a major hurdle that has to be overcome before we can go into production."

"What's the problem?" she asked.

"Currently only someone with our kind of talent can activate a light spear."

She gave him a searching look. "You're a light-talent, too?"

"Yes."

"I've never met another light. I've heard there aren't a lot of us around."

"No," Drake said. "There aren't. To further complicate matters, no two light-talents are the same, so each spear has to be individually tuned to the person who will use it. I'm the only one who can operate this particular spear. Once I've exhausted the charge it will have to be re-tuned."

"What happens to those two guys that you took down?"

"I don't know and I don't give a damn.

27

I'm not here on a mission to clean up the Old Quarter. I've got other things on my to-do list tonight."

"Clearly you are a man who knows how to prioritize," she said.

He ignored the not-so-veiled sarcasm. "That pair just happened to get in the way. Sorry I got here a bit late." Drake looked at the two men without much interest. "Not that you weren't handling things just fine all by yourself."

"My version of light-talent isn't good for much, but occasionally it comes in handy."

"I noticed," Drake said. "Same with my version."

She shot him a quick sidelong glance, trying to read his unreadable face. "You could see me when I did my invisibility thing. I've never met anyone who could do that."

"My version of the talent is as rare as yours." Drake's mouth quirked in a brief, humorless smile. "But not nearly as useful. It would be handy to be able to become invisible once in a while."

She pondered that for a moment. "I'm not so sure that yours is less useful. You see things that other people don't see."

"There is that," he agreed.

He did not add the obvious, she noticed, which was that ever since the lab accident,

28

he no longer saw things the way other people did. She wondered how the world looked to him.

"Perpetual night," he said.

Startled, she gave him another swift, searching glance. "You read minds, too?"

"Sadly, no. That would be another useful talent. But it was a good bet that you were wondering what the world looks like to me."

"Oh. Sorry. I didn't mean to get so personal."

"Don't worry about it. You're not the first person to be curious."

"Perpetual night, huh? So the world is always dark for you?"

He smiled slightly. "I said it was always night. I didn't say it was always dark."

"I don't understand."

"The night is illuminated with a million shades of paranormal energy," he said quietly. "I see light from that end of the spectrum the same way you see light from the normal end."

"What kind of light-talent are you?" she asked.

"Still trying to figure that out," Drake said.

They moved out of the alley and onto an empty sidewalk. Like all of the Old Quarters in the four major city-states on Harmony, the Colonial section of Crystal City dated back two hundred years to the era of the First Generation settlers from Earth. The founders had built the first towns around the ancient walls that surrounded the ruins of the large Alien cities.

The para-archaeologists estimated that the Aliens had vanished at least a couple of thousand years before the colonists from Earth had arrived, perhaps even earlier. But the unique green quartz the ancients had used to construct most of their urban sites as well as the vast array of underground passages that honeycombed the planet was virtually indestructible. And all of it glowed with an eerie green radiance that was noticeable to the human eye only after dark. There was no need for street-lights in the Old Quarters. The massive walls that surrounded the ruins cast an otherworldly radiance over the human-built scene.

In addition to the glow, the currents of psi that emanated from the towering walls and wafted up from the underground catacombs infused the Quarter with a little paranormal heat. Most people, even those with a low level of talent, found the sensation to be a bit of a rush. Alcohol and music enhanced the sparkly, slightly euphoric buzz. The background energy in the atmosphere was one of the reasons why many of the trendy nightclubs were located in converted warehouses and other Colonial-era buildings near the walls. But in spite of the clubs and theaters in the vicinity, the Crystal City Quarter, like all of the Old Quarters in the city-states, had a distinctly seedy atmosphere.

Drake surveyed the shuttered windows and graffiti-splashed buildings around them.

"Rough neighborhood," he observed in a very neutral tone.

"Also a cheap neighborhood when it comes to rent," Alice said. "And I don't need a car. My apartment is only a few blocks away."

"Very economical. Do you always leave the theater through that alley entrance?"

"Yes. But this is the last time I'll be using that door."

"Because of what nearly happened in the alley?" Drake asked.

"No, because the owner of the theater told me tonight that he has decided to cancel my lease. *Alien Illusions* closed this evening after only three performances."

"Why did the owner cancel your lease?"

"He gave me the usual reason: low attendance. The magic business is very competitive. A new show, *Catacombs of Mystery,* opened here in the Quarter last week and it's getting all the attention. Very high production values. *Alien Illusions* didn't have the financial backing needed to compete. Actually, it didn't have any financial backing at all."

"That must have made things difficult."

"Sure. Still, we were getting by, starting to draw bigger crowds." She reached up to pat Houdini. "Thanks to the star of the show here. The audience loved Houdini. We were doing some very cool vanishing acts. I think we could have made it. I'm pretty sure the real reason the show got cancelled was because Ethel found me again and bribed the manager to shut me down. I'm certain she made it worth his while."

"In the course of tracking you down, I did discover that your ex-mother-in-law has spent a lot of time and effort making your life miserable this past year," Drake said.

"She thinks I murdered her son. In her position, I'd probably be obsessed with revenge, too. Just wish she'd focus on the real killer."

"Assuming there is one," Drake said quietly. "According to the police report, Fulton Whitcomb died of natural causes."

"Ethel isn't buying that opinion."

"What about you?"

"I didn't buy it, either. But since I'm the

most likely suspect, I figure my best bet is to keep a low profile."

The lights of a beer sign hanging in a dark window sparked on Drake's glasses when he turned to look at Houdini.

"You said the dust bunny was the star of *Alien Illusions*?"

"Right. He's the magician. At least that's how we billed him. I thought it made the act sound more interesting."

"If you gave Houdini top billing, what did that make you?"

"Me?" She smiled. "I'm just the box-jumper."

"What's a box-jumper?"

"Old Earth word for a magician's assistant. Comes from all those tricks that involve putting a woman into a box and making it look as if she disappeared or got sawed in half or pierced with knives."

"Got it," Drake said, sounding satisfied. "The box-jumper is the only other person on stage who knows the magician's secrets."

CHAPTER 3

Drake was a little sorry to see the sign above the entrance of the Green Gate Tavern. He realized that he had been savoring the combination of the psi-rezzed night and the woman at his side. He could have walked with Alice through the Quarter until dawn.

Viewed through his mirrored-quartz lenses, the light of the illuminated sign was a sharp, bright green. He knew it was also the wrong shade of green, or, at least, not the same shade that Alice saw. He no longer saw colors the way other people did. There were limits to the technology of his lenses.

He was fine with the psi-lit atmosphere of the Quarter. The energy that emanated from the Dead City Wall was mostly in the paranormal range, the part of the spectrum that he could see clearly. True, the glow of the ruins looked different to him than it did to most other people — he could detect a much broader spectrum of colors in the

34

wavelengths generated by the ancient green quartz, for one thing — but it wasn't painful to look at.

A simple tavern sign, on the other hand, like the light over the stage door, would have temporarily blinded him if he had attempted to view it without his glasses. When it came to sunlight, he might as well have been a vampire. True, the light of day wouldn't kill him but it literally dazzled his senses, rendering him blind.

Alice stopped in front of the door. "This is the place I told you about. We can talk inside."

He studied the entrance. "Inside where you have friends."

She gave him what he was pretty sure was a fake smile. But it looked good. He would take any smile he could get from Alice North.

"Exactly," she said.

"I have no problem with that. Doesn't matter where we talk."

He really needed to keep reminding himself that he had a goal here in Crystal City and that time mattered. Normally he had no difficulty maintaining his focus on whatever objective he had set for himself. Various members of his family, including his mother, claimed he did that to a fault. But something about Alice was proving to be distracting.

He was well aware that she did not trust him. He was almost certain she was not just wary of him but flat-out scared, although she hid it well. She had every right to be nervous. He knew from what little he had found during the course of a hasty background check that she had been on her own ever since leaving an orphanage at seventeen. She had managed to survive and make her way without family ties in a world where family was the most important building block in the social structure. Among the descendants of the colonists, family was everything.

Life could be very hard for those unfortunate enough to find themselves utterly alone. For the past year life had been especially harsh for Alice. It was bad enough to be stranded in the world without any family connections. To be alone and on the run from the wrath of a powerful woman like Ethel Whitcomb would have been a thousand times worse. A lot of people, male or female, would have been crushed by the experience.

He opened the door. The deep, throbbing rumble of a heavy rez-rock tune playing on a cheap sound system spilled out into the otherwise silent street. Houdini chortled, clearly excited.

"He's a fan of rez-rock," Alice said. "He also loves the bar snacks and pizza here."

Drake heightened his senses a little as Alice slipped past him into the shadowy tavern. She was so close that she brushed against him. She seemed unaware of the brief physical contact but he got a hot, heady thrill that left him on edge.

He told himself that he was still gathering information about Alice, still analyzing the situation and evaluating possible strategies. Maybe, on some level, that was even true. But he knew that in reality he'd been fascinated from the moment he had seen her illuminated in a thousand shades of paranormal light, hauling a suitcase through an alley while she out-maneuvered two knife-wielding assailants.

In that moment he'd seen everything he needed to know about her — she was the kind of woman who would never give up, regardless of the obstacles. No matter what life threw at her, she would just keep going.

That inner fire marked her in subtle ways. There was a fierce, vibrant energy about her that called to his senses. She was striking rather than beautiful; intriguing rather than glamorous; strong-willed rather than flirtatious. She radiated an interesting mix of innocence, irrepressible optimism, and savvy, street-smart intelligence. Her dark brown hair was caught in a ponytail. Dressed in a sleek, long-sleeved black turtleneck, black jeans, and black sneakers, she looked like a cat burglar heading out for an evening's work.

He followed her into the moderately crowded tavern. The khaki-and-leather gear worn by several of the men occupying barstools identified them as members of the local Ghost Hunters Guild. They were drinking beer and Green Ruin whiskey. A man and a woman sat in a nearby booth. The man looked as if he was trying to convince the blonde to go home with him. The blonde looked bored.

Another booth was filled with a gaggle of young women dressed in flirty little dresses — *expensive* flirty little dresses — and stilettos. *Definitely not from around this neighborhood,* Drake thought. The women were drinking colorful drinks and trying to look as if they weren't aware of the ghost hunters at the bar who were eyeing them in turn. It was a familiar ritual in the Old Quarters. Taverns like the Green Gate were popular destinations for bachelorette parties, coeds out for a little fun, and ladies from the more affluent suburbs who wanted to party.

The large, middle-aged woman working behind the bar was busy filling a beer glass. She looked up when Alice walked in.

"Hey there, Alice, you're early tonight," the bartender called in a hearty voice. "What happened?"

"The act closed, Maud." Alice plunked her tote down on a seat in an empty booth and slid in beside it. "The owner of the theater cancelled me. Houdini and I are now unemployed. Again."

There was a low chorus of commiserating responses from the crowd at the bar.

"Ah, now that's just too damn bad," one of the hunters said.

"Real sorry to hear that," another added. "You gonna be okay?"

"Oh, yeah, I'll be fine," Alice said. "This is the way it goes in show business."

"Maybe you could get a job at that new magic show that opened up a few blocks from here," someone offered. *Catacombs of Mystery.*"

"Maybe," Alice said. She did not sound optimistic.

Houdini was the only one who appeared unconcerned by the sudden reversal of fortune. He chortled and bounced down to the floor. He scampered across the room, bounded up onto an empty stool, and from there hopped onto the bar. Several of the hunters greeted him.

"Lookin' good, Houdini," one said. "Nice tie."

A hunter pushed a bowl of bar snacks toward Houdini, who made happy sounds. He surveyed the offering, made a careful selection, and munched with enthusiasm.

Maud set the glass of beer in front of one of the patrons and wiped her hands on a towel. She looked at Alice with concern. "The usual for you and Houdini?"

"Yes, please," Alice said. "I'm really hungry tonight. And Houdini is always hungry."

Maud turned toward the open door at the far end of the bar and raised her voice to call to someone in the small kitchen. "Alice's usual."

A man garbed in a dingy apron and a yellowed cook's hat peered back through the opening.

"Coming right up," he promised.

Maud scrutinized Drake with a vaguely suspicious air. "Who's your friend, Alice?"

"He's not exactly a friend," Alice said. "More like a new acquaintance. We met outside the stage door a few minutes ago."

Maud raised her brows.

"The name is Drake Sebastian," Drake said.

"You're not from 'round here, are you?" Maud said.

"No. Just visiting."

"They wear sunglasses after dark where you come from?" Maud asked.

"I do."

"Huh." Maud did not look impressed. "What can I get you?"

Drake sat down across from Alice. "I'll have a beer."

Maud looked at Alice, awaiting direction. The ghost hunters followed suit. A distinct hush fell over the small crowd. Everyone was suddenly watching the booth where Drake and Alice were seated. There was a little hum of energy in the atmosphere. Drake wondered if he was going to find himself in the middle of a barroom brawl. He, too, looked at Alice, politely waiting for her to decide if there would be a fight.

"He's okay," Alice said. She wrinkled her nose. "At least for now. He helped me deal with a couple of low-lifes who were waiting for me in the alley behind the theater to-night."

"Damn," Maud said. "Are you all right?"

"I'm fine," Alice assured her. "But we left a couple of unconscious thugs back there,

41

thanks to my new friend."

There were murmurs of approval from the hunters.

"Huh." Maud looked satisfied. She turned back to Drake. "What kind of beer?"

"Whatever you have on draft is fine," he said.

Maud selected a glass. The ghost hunters at the bar went back to leering at the giggling young women. The energy level in the room went down.

Drake looked at Alice. "Thanks for the character reference."

"You've got five minutes to convince me you are not going to be a problem for me," she said.

"The thing is, I probably am going to be a problem. But on the positive side, I may be able to help you with your current unemployment situation."

She sat back and watched him warily. "You need a box-jumper?"

He thought about it and then smiled. "That's as good a description as any. A couple of very important items have disappeared. We need to find them, and fast."

"We?"

"Let's start at the beginning."

"Where is that, exactly?"

"The last time you were on Rainshadow Island."

Alice went very still. She got a little blurry around the edges. It was suddenly hard to focus on her. Drake was pretty sure it was not deliberate. Her instinct to disappear when she felt threatened was a natural aspect of her talent. He jacked up his senses a bit so that he could see her clearly once more and waited.

She took a sharp breath and snapped back into focus. Her expression gave nothing away, but it didn't take any psychic talent to know that her anxiety level had spiked.

"What does this have to do with Rainshadow?" she asked, her voice unnaturally even.

Before he could answer, Maud bustled around the end of the bar with two glasses in her hands. She set the beer in front of Drake and the white wine in front of Alice.

"Eggs and pizza will be out in a minute," she said to Alice.

"Thanks." Alice gave her a grateful smile.

Drake waited until Maud was out of earshot.

"Eggs and pizza?" he asked.

"The eggs are for me. The pizza is for Houdini."

"Got it," he said. "All right, to get back to

43

our business. You do know about the Sebastian-North legend, I assume."

"I do now." Alice took a small swallow of the wine and lowered the glass. "But I had never heard about it until a year ago."

"A year ago?"

"That's when I found out that I was descended from a certain Nicholas North."

That stopped him for a few beats. "I know you grew up in an orphanage, but didn't you know anything about your family history?"

"Nope." She drank some more wine. "The most that anyone at the orphanage could recall was that I arrived there at about age three after my mother was killed in a car accident."

"What do you mean, that was all anyone could recall? There must have been some records when you were taken in."

Alice shrugged. "There was a fire in the records office at the orphanage when I was four. What little information there was relating to my family history was lost."

"What about your father's people?"

Alice gave him a cold smile. "Nothing. The general theory at the orphanage was that I was the product of a one-night stand or a short-term affair in which neither party had kept current with their anti-pregnancy shots."

Drake said nothing.

Alice raised her brows. "They do happen, you know."

"What happens?"

"One-night stands between two people who don't take precautions."

He realized he was flushing a little. "I'm aware of that."

"Society and the legal system do everything possible to make sure no one grows up without a family, but kids still get orphaned." She paused. "I realize that sort of thing doesn't happen in the Sebastian family world, though."

"No," he said, refusing to let her sarcasm get to him. "It doesn't. We take care of our own."

Alice gave him a cool smile. "How very traditional."

"Moving right along, how did you find out about the connection to Nicholas North?"

"Long story. Involves my dead husband." Alice drank more wine. "I don't like to talk about him."

"We're going to have to discuss him at some point because I think he's linked to this thing."

Alice eyed him coldly. "What *thing* would

45

that be?"

"The treasure that North and Sebastian buried on Rainshadow. It's gone missing."

She narrowed her eyes. "You think I stole it, don't you?"

He watched her closely. "Did you?"

"No." She held up one hand, palm out. "And before you ask, no I can't prove it."

"Do you know who did steal it?"

"Uh-huh." She studied him over the rim of the glass. "Fulton Whitcomb."

"Your husband."

"Dead husband. And it was just a Marriage of Convenience so it doesn't really count. Death results in an automatic dissolution of the marriage. The surviving spouse does not inherit any property. She has no legal or financial obligations pertaining to her husband's estate. It's like the marriage never happened."

"Unless there are children from the union," Drake said softly.

Children changed everything. The birth of a child into an MC automatically converted what was otherwise a dressed-up romantic affair into a full-blown Covenant Marriage. Dissolving a Covenant Marriage was a legal, financial, and social nightmare. His brother, Harry, had discovered that the hard way.

"Yes, well, there were no children," Alice

said coolly.

"Because both of you kept current with your vaccinations?"

"I certainly kept mine up-to-date. Not that it mattered."

Drake heard a tiny mental *ping* warning him that this was important. "Why didn't the shots matter?"

"Because getting pregnant would have been biologically impossible under the circumstances." Alice drank the last of her wine and set the glass back on the table. "Fulton and I never had sex."

Maud came out of the kitchen carrying two plates. She set the pizza down on the bar. Houdini waved ecstatically and chortled.

Maud chuckled and carried the platter of eggs, toast, and potatoes to the booth where Alice and Drake sat. Alice looked at the repast as though it were a diamond necklace.

"Thanks, Maud," she said. "This is just what I need."

Maud went back to her work behind the counter. Drake folded his arms on the table and watched Alice dive into the eggs. It occurred to him that she was hungry because she had used up a lot of energy that evening with the magic act and then defending

47

herself in the alley. She was probably exhausted.

She swallowed a bite of eggs and began munching on a slice of toast. She paused mid-munch, glaring at him.

"What?" she said around a mouthful of toast.

"Nothing," he said. "I know you're hungry. I've been there. Go ahead. You can tell me your side of the story when you've finished. I'll tell you mine while you eat."

She nodded and went back to her eggs.

"Here's where things stand on Rainshadow," Drake said. "The treasure, which consisted of three dangerous Old World crystals of unknown properties, was stolen sometime during the past eighteen months. Recently one of the crystals was recovered deep inside the Preserve on the island."

Alice ate some of the potatoes. "Just one?"

"The other two crystals are still missing. We believe they are also on Rainshadow."

"We?"

"My family."

Alice frowned. "Well, that's weird. I wonder why someone took them back to Rainshadow after going to the trouble of killing Fulton and stealing the stones."

"Is that what happened?"

"Uh-huh."

"Not to get too personal, but why would you enter into an MC with Whitcomb if you didn't intend to sleep with him?"

Alice raised her brows. "Because I was an idiot."

"I'm guessing there was another reason."

"Nope, I'm pretty sure that was the actual reason. I told myself that I was falling in love with him. He was so charming, so much fun. I thought that eventually I would want to sleep with him. I explained that I was attracted to him but that the relationship was moving too quickly. I said I needed some time to be sure of my feelings for him and his for me. Believe it or not, he claimed he wanted a full Covenant Marriage."

"Fulton asked you to enter into a CM?"

Alice grimaced. "Hard to believe, isn't it? You know, I think it was his insistence on a CM that made me uneasy. It all seemed a little too good to be true. A fairy tale in which the handsome, charming, wealthy prince whisks the little clerk from the museum gift shop off her feet and asks her to marry him."

"You don't believe in fairy-tale endings?"

Alice shrugged again. "I grew up in an orphanage, remember? You learn a lot about real life in an orphanage. Deep down, I sensed that there was something wrong with the perfect picture that Fulton painted. Regardless, I admit I had a few hopes and dreams. But I wouldn't go for the CM. I did, however, let him push me into an MC."

"Even though you weren't ready to sleep with him."

Alice frowned. "You're really fixated on that aspect of the thing, aren't you?"

"Just curious," he lied. He was fixated, damn it.

"Fulton said he wanted some kind of commitment between us while I got to know him better. I'm pretty sure he figured that he'd talk me into bed fairly quickly. He was probably right. After all, he had dazzled me with a gift that no one else had ever given me."

"An expensive piece of jewelry? A car?"

She smiled wistfully. "None of the above. Fulton Whitcomb gave me something far more precious — a piece of my family history."

Drake experienced the sharp, edgy whisper of understanding. "He was the one who told you that you were Nick North's descendant."

"Yes. He was really into the antiquities market. He said he had a line on Nick North's diary. He promised to find it for me —" Alice broke off abruptly, as if she was not sure how much more she ought to say. "Along with a couple of other interesting North family documents," she finished a little too smoothly. "My turn to ask some questions. How did you find me?"

"You could call it a form of reverse engineering. There is a lot of information about Nick North in the Sebastian family archives. I worked downstream from the past to the present, piecing together the evidence. You were at a disadvantage because you were trying to work upstream toward your past but you had no solid starting point."

Alice nodded. "Yes, that's how Fulton figured it out. He traced Nick North's ancestry and eventually got to me. I had no clue that what he really wanted were the crystals. It was a setup from the start. By the time I figured it out, it was too late."

Drake nodded. "In addition to the diary, Whitcomb had North's psi-code map, didn't he?"

"Yes."

"He had a map that would lead him to the crystals, but there was one really big catch. A psi-code map can only be deciphered by someone from the same bloodline as the person who created it — specifically someone with a similar kind of talent. That was another advantage that Whitcomb and I

51

both had when we set out to find you, by the way. We knew we were looking for a North descendant who possessed his brand of talent — light-talent. That limited the search pool because, as you said earlier, there aren't a lot of strong light-talents around."

"There you have it," Alice said. "The reason I agreed to an MC with Fulton Whitcomb. I was an idiot."

He winced. "Been there, done that."

Alice looked at him, startled. "You were an idiot in the romance department?"

"Oh, yeah. Someday maybe I'll tell you the whole story. But right now we need to stick to your tale."

"There's not much more to tell. I was thrilled when I realized I could read my great-grandfather's psi-code map. It gave me such a strong connection to my family history. I can't explain it, but somehow it made me feel less alone in the world."

"I understand."

"I got even more excited when Fulton suggested that we go straight to Rainshadow and search for the North treasure."

Drake smiled faintly. "In my family we refer to it as the Sebastian treasure."

"Yes, well, at the time all I had was a treasure map created by my great-grandfather. As far as I was concerned, it was the North treasure."

"What happened on Rainshadow?"

"We went to the island and immediately started treasure-hunting. It didn't take long to find the cave where the strongbox was hidden. It was just inside the psi-fence."

"You were able to go through the fence into the Preserve?"

"Yes. Fulton and I both got through it fairly easily."

"You were both talents," Drake said. "That explains why you could get past the paranormal forces of the fence. It's a wonder you both didn't get lost, though."

"We had the map and we were careful to maintain visual contact with a landmark outside the fence at all times so we weren't in danger of getting disoriented."

"You found the strongbox that contained the three crystals. What happened next?"

"I got a bad feeling when I realized that Fulton was way too excited about the crystals. I mean, they were just three murky-looking stones. But he acted like we'd found a box of rare, hot amber. Then I saw the document inside the strongbox. It made it clear that the crystals were the property of the Rainshadow Preserve Foundation. In other words, they belonged to the Sebastian family. And suddenly I understood that Fulton had used me."

"What did you say?"

"I told him that I was going to contact the Sebastian family to find out more about my history and my rights to the treasure. Fulton was furious. Then he showed me another document, one he had concealed from me. It was signed by both my great-grandfather and yours. It guaranteed that any North descendant would receive half of all profits made on anything of value that was ever discovered inside the Preserve."

"Son of a ghost," Drake said very softly. "Fulton planned to seduce you into a full Covenant Marriage so that afterward he would be able to claim half of whatever came out of the Preserve."

"Yep." Alice ate the last of her breakfast and put down the fork. "Between you and me, I got the distinct impression that I wasn't expected to live long after Fulton finally got me into a CM. In fact, I have reason to think that he intended to force the issue by getting me pregnant."

"But you said you got the shots."

Alice smiled grimly. "I learned later that Fulton had gotten a prescription for the antidote. He intended to sneak it into my food after he had seduced me. After a baby was born, the MC would automatically convert to a CM. I think both the baby and I would have suffered a fatal accident.

"And after you conveniently died, he would inherit whatever there was of value inside the Preserve." Drake stopped, mentally fitting the pieces of the puzzle together. "That implies that he thought there was something very important inside the fence, something worth marrying and murdering you for. Did he think the crystals were of such great value?"

"Not exactly," Alice said. "He called the crystals the Keys. He said they would unlock the real treasure inside the Preserve."

"Did he say anything else?"

"Not much because about that time I told him that I intended to get a divorce. He reacted by trying to kill me. I pulled my invisibility trick and escaped from the cave. I was running for my life. I blundered through some kind of dark energy field and became thoroughly disoriented. It took me a couple of days to find my way back out of the Preserve. When I returned to Resonance City, the news of Fulton's death was the headline story in the media and I discovered that I was the chief suspect."

"What about the crystals?"

Alice shook her head. "I have no idea what

happened to them. I assumed that Fulton got out of the Preserve with them and that he was killed by a partner in crime who didn't like the way things had gone down on Rainshadow. After all, Fulton had really screwed up by failing to sucker me into a CM. What makes you think the crystals are on the island?"

"Because Rainshadow is getting dangerously hot."

She raised her brows. "I assume you're talking about heat in the paranormal sense?"

"Right. The crystals are mostly a mystery, but one thing we do know about them is that under certain circumstances they resonate with the natural paranormal forces of the planet. That effect is enhanced in hot zones like Rainshadow. We're certain the two missing crystals are on the island and that they are overheating the place."

"Define overheating," Alice said.

"They are having a dangerously destabilizing effect on the local geothermal and atmospheric forces. The ocean currents and tides were always strong and treacherous in the area, but now they've become bizarre and unpredictable. The last time I was able to get through to my brother, Harry, was three days ago. He said the weather is following an equally unstable pattern. A heavy fog that seems to be infused with a lot of paranormal energy has been rolling in over the town every night. He said the island had just lost power and that he was organizing an evacuation. The problem is that a lot of folks on the island won't leave."

"You haven't talked to Harry in the past three days?"

"Communications are down. I can't get through on the phone or computer. No one is sure what's happening in the Preserve, but Harry said there is growing concern that the unstable forces may be affecting plant and animal life as well as the weather."

"And all because of those two crystals," Alice said. "Damn. I knew they were going to be trouble."

"You're sure you don't know where they are?"

"I'm positive. Trust me, if I had two really powerful crystals like that I would be trying to sell them to some outfit like Sebastian, Inc."

He smiled. "And we would pay any price you asked."

She sighed. "Well, I don't have them to sell or give to you. What happens now?"

"We need to find the two missing crystals."

"Be my guest. I'm not stopping you."

"I'm going to need your help and I'm willing to pay for it."

She went still again. "How much?"

"Name your price."

"That offer is never a good sign. It means you're desperate."

"I am desperate."

She looked skeptical. "I can't see you as desperate, but it's obvious those crystals are important to you. What I don't understand is how you think I can help you locate them."

"I'm not sure, either. But from what I can tell, you're the last person who saw them before they disappeared."

"No," Alice said. "Whoever killed Fulton Whitcomb is the last person who saw those crystals."

"Then there's a very good chance that person is the one who took them back to Rainshadow. You're the key to this thing, Alice."

"I was afraid you were going to say something like that."

CHAPTER 4

Drake de-rezzed the flash-rock engine of the rental car he had picked up at the airport. He sat quietly for a moment, his hands resting on the steering wheel, and studied the four-story apartment building. The sign at the entrance read: DEAD CITY SUITES — YOUR HOME AWAY FROM HOME. RENT BY THE WEEK. CASH ONLY.

"I know what you're thinking," Alice said. She freed herself from the seat belt. "Not exactly what a Sebastian would consider a suitable home away from home. But it's clean and for the most part the plumbing works."

She opened the door, got out, and reached back for her tote. She slung the tote over one shoulder and held out an arm to Houdini, who was perched on the back of her seat.

"Cleanliness and good plumbing are important considerations when choosing an apartment," Drake said as he climbed out of the car.

It wasn't the amenities of the Dead City Suites that concerned him. It was the location. The Colonial-era apartment building didn't look as run-down as some by-the-week flophouses he'd seen, but he did not like the idea that Alice had been walking home late at night through the scruffy neighborhood.

"Relax." Alice looked at him over the top of the car. "There hasn't been a mugging around here in days. We've got a very active neighborhood crime watch program."

"Is that right?"

"A few retired ghost hunters live in this part of town. Some of them were at the Green Gate tonight. They've organized themselves into a regular night patrol. It's a lot safer here than it is in the area near the theater."

"If you say so."

He got Alice's wheeled suitcase out of the trunk of the car and started toward the entrance of the Dead City Suites. Alice did not move. When he realized she was not coming with him, he stopped and looked back.

"Something wrong?" he asked politely.

"Look, you really don't have to walk me

to my front door," she said. "I appreciate the gesture but I'll be fine."

"I'll see you to the door," he said.

He resisted the urge to take her arm. He wanted to touch her, he realized. *But she probably wouldn't appreciate the familiarity.* She was on edge now, ready to run. So he waited, not pushing it.

She hesitated and then reluctantly started walking with him toward the entrance.

"I'm making you nervous," Drake said halfway across the parking lot.

"Members of powerful, reclusive families that operate large business empires definitely make me nervous." Alice gave him a breezy smile. "After my little brush with the Whitcomb clan, I learned a really expensive lesson."

"For the record, the Sebastians are not close with the Whitcombs."

"Give me a break." Alice stopped in front of the lobby door and de-rezzed the lock. "It's a small world at the top of the social and business ladder. I'm sure you're well acquainted with the Whitcombs."

"They live in Resonance City." He kept his tone flat and cool with an effort. "The Sebastians have always maintained their headquarters in Cadence City. I'm not saying we don't know one another. Occasionally we end up at the same events."

"Same clubs, same charity balls, same golf courses, same art museums and hospital boards, et cetera, et cetera. Yep, I know how it works."

"I'm saying that the Whitcombs and the Sebastians are not close," Drake repeated. "I'd appreciate it if you did not twist my words."

"Sorry." She made a face and went through the door. "It's not your fault that you associate with the family of my ex. I realize that in your world you can't avoid that kind of contact. But you can see why that fact complicates things a tad for me."

Drake kept his mouth shut. Sometimes that was the safest course of action.

Alice looked around the dingy lobby with obvious relief. "Well, at least my landlord hasn't locked us out yet, Houdini. The night is looking up."

Houdini made cheerful noises.

"Easy for you to say," Alice grumbled. "You don't care if we have to sleep in a doorway."

There was no elevator, Drake noticed. Alice took Houdini off her shoulder and set him on the first step of the staircase.

"You can walk," she told him. "I'm not

carrying you up four flights of stairs to-night."

Houdini chortled again, as if going up the stairs was a game. He bounced up each step, keeping pace with Alice. And then, because she evidently moved too slowly, he bounced down a couple of steps, turned around, and scampered back to meet her.

Drake followed, allowing himself to enjoy the rear view of Alice in her snug black jeans.

"What is it with Rainshadow?" Alice paused at the second-floor landing, gripped the railing, and looked down at Drake. "That island has always had a weird psi-vibe from what I've been able to find out."

"Based on what we learned recently, it looks like Rainshadow was at one time a gi-ant bioengineering lab for the Aliens."

Alice's eyes widened. "Okay, that's a chill-ing thought."

"My brother and his fiancée recently found the ruins of an ancient aquarium filled with the results of some of the Aliens' genetic experiments on marine animals."

Alice started up the next flight of stairs. "Fossils, you mean?"

"Not fossils," Drake said. He rounded the landing. "Living fish. Really, really bizarre fish. Sea monsters."

"In an *aquarium*?"

"A giant, crystal-walled aquarium in a huge cavern. The aquarium was still operational and so were the creatures inside. They were bioengineered to survive in high-psi environments like Rainshadow. There was an explosion inside the cavern triggered by one of the three crystals. A lot of the creatures escaped into the flooded caves on the island."

Alice paused on the third-floor landing to catch her breath. "Are we talking the kind of marine animals that snack on seaweed?"

"No. We're talking the kind of monsters that would eat any human unlucky enough to fall into one of the cave pools."

Alice started up the last flight of stairs. "That doesn't sound good."

"No, it's not good."

"But I still don't see what I can do to help."

"Neither do I, but my brother is convinced that we need you, and Harry is never wrong when it comes to this kind of stuff."

"What kind of stuff, exactly, is he never wrong about?"

"Harry is in the security business. Specifically, he's the head of Sebastian, Inc. security, which has responsibility for Rainshadow Foundation Security. When he's working a case his intuition is off the charts."

"Your brother has never even met me."

"No, but now I have met you and I think he's right," Drake said. "We need you on the island. My intuition is pretty good, too."

She glanced back over her shoulder. "You said your brother handles security for Sebastian, Inc. and the Foundation. But according to the business press, you're in line to take over as CEO of the family empire."

"You read the business press?"

"I became somewhat obsessed with it after Ethel Whitcomb started hounding me. It's the only way I can keep track of her. As the head of Whitcomb Industries, she appears in the papers a lot."

"Smart," he said, appreciative of the tactic. "In answer to your question, my grandfather runs Sebastian, Inc. now. He intends to retire soon. No one else in the family, except me, wants to take over the job."

She paused again and looked back, studying him. "But you want the job?"

"Oh, yeah," he said. "I've wanted that job from the cradle."

"Must be nice to know what you're supposed to be doing in life," she said. There was a wistful note in her words.

She arrived on the fourth floor and started toward the end of the hall, Houdini scampering along at her heels. Drake followed with the suitcase and pondered his strategy. He was pretty sure that Alice would go to Rainshadow with him, but it was by no means a done deal. She was still leery. He could not blame her. It was starting to look like he would be spending the night in the car, keeping watch on the Dead City Suites to make sure Alice did not pull another vanishing act.

He had told her nothing less than the truth. They needed all the help they could get on Rainshadow. The fact that Alice had been able to decipher Nick North's psi-code map was important, so was her high-rez light-talent. But he was also increasingly certain that whatever had gone down before, during, and after the disastrous honeymoon on Rainshadow with Whitcomb was the real key to unlocking the mystery.

Someone was convinced that there was something worth killing for on the island.

Alice stopped in front of Number Three and took out a key. When she got the door open, a draft of fresh night air flowed out. Drake knew from her startled reaction that she had not left a window open inside the apartment.

In that instant Houdini growled and sleeked out, showing a lot of eyes and teeth.

"Oh, crap," Alice whispered. "Not again."

She stepped swiftly back into the hallway and promptly vanished, taking Houdini with her. Evidently she did not have enough energy left to shield the cobalt-blue tote bag because it was left hanging in midair.

Drake jacked up his senses so that he could see Alice. She reappeared a short distance away, Houdini crouched tensely on her shoulder.

"Stay clear of the door," Drake said.

He had already let go of the suitcase and was on his way into the apartment, the light spear in his hand.

There was a lot of frantic movement somewhere inside. A hard object crashed to the floor.

The interior of the apartment was illuminated by the green psi-light streaming in through the windows. A man in a stocking mask rushed across the room, heading toward the sliding glass door that opened onto a minuscule balcony.

The intruder was fast, but Drake aimed the spear, got a fix, and rezzed the weapon. He used considerably less energy for the shot than he had used on the thugs in the alley. This time he wanted to have a conversation with the target.

Dark lightning flashed, striking the intruder.

The fleeing man gave a hoarse, panic-stricken cry. He staggered, flailing wildly as he lost his sense of balance. He went to his knees, tried to scramble back to his feet, and finally collapsed on the floor.

"Don't move," Drake said, "or I'll use a higher setting."

The intruder lay still, breathing hard. He stared at Drake through the holes in the stocking mask.

"Who the freaking hell are you?" he gasped.

"Enough about me," Drake said. "Let's talk about you."

"Shit. I'm a private investigator. Jerry McCarson. License is in my wallet. What did you do to me?"

Drake ignored the question while he conducted a quick search for a weapon. He did not find one, but he did find a wallet.

The room lights came on just as he took out the license.

"I heard him say he's a PI." Alice sounded grimly resigned. She pulled the suitcase into the apartment and closed the door. "That means he's working for Ethel Whitcomb. Looks like this is just not my night."

Houdini was fully fluffed again. But he still had all four eyes open. He growled at McCarson.

Drake glanced at Alice. "You know this guy?"

"No, but he's not the first snoop Ethel has sent after me," Alice said. "She uses them to find out where I'm living, what name I'm using, and where I'm working. Then she systematically goes about getting me evicted and fired. It's her idea of revenge."

McCarson sat up nervously. "I was told you were blackmailing the Whitcomb family. They sent me to find out whatever I could so that they could send the cops after you."

"Is that the story Ethel used this time?" Alice dropped her tote on a small table. "The last PI they hired to track me down thought he was looking for a long-lost daughter of the Whitcomb clan."

"Look, I can explain this," McCarson said. "It was just a job."

Drake got to his feet. "No need to explain yourself to us. I'm going to call the cops. You can talk yourself hoarse to them."

McCarson snorted. "Fine. But I can guarantee you that I won't spend more than five minutes in jail, assuming the cops arrest me in the first place."

Alice folded her arms and eyed McCarson with an air of acute disdain. "He's right. It would be a waste of time to call the cops. And not in my best interests. You can bet that one way or the other, I'll end up being questioned as a possible blackmailer. I know Ethel Whitcomb. I've been on the wrong end of this scenario often enough in the past year to know how it's going to end. Ethel is engaged in a sophisticated form of stalking. She uses people like Mr. McCarson to do her dirty work for her."

McCarson looked alarmed and somewhat offended. "Are you crazy? I'm a professional."

Alice smiled her stage smile. "A professional stalker?"

"I'm not stalking you," McCarson growled. "Like I said, I was told that you were blackmailing my client. Now, if you can prove otherwise —"

"She doesn't have to prove anything," Drake said. "You're the one who broke in here tonight. Turns out I'm a witness. Convincing the police you're not a stalker or a burglar will be your problem."

"Go ahead, have it your way," McCarson said. He shook his head. "But I'm telling you, you're wasting your time. Ms. North is right in saying that the Whitcombs are powerful. They could buy and sell half of Resonance City. Who do you think the cops will believe?"

"I'm pretty sure they'll take my word for what happened here tonight," Drake said.

"Yeah?" McCarson looked amused. "Who do you think you are?"

"Drake Sebastian. My family owns Sebastian, Inc. Maybe you've heard of the firm. It could buy and sell Whitcomb Industries."

McCarson groaned. "Ah, shit."

"It gets better," Drake said. "Among other things, we design and manufacture most of the high-tech security equipment and the psi-tronics that the local cops use. Sebastian, Inc. has a lot of connections with the Crystal City PD."

McCarson grimaced. "Shit."

"We've also got an excellent relationship with the local Ghost Hunters Guild. I could call in a favor from the Crystal City boss. Trust me when I tell you that the Whitcombs don't have any influence over him. The Guilds have always been good at making problems disappear into the tunnels."

McCarson exhaled heavily. "I believe you. You've made your point. I knew this job sounded a little too good to be true."

"Unfortunately, pressing charges against

you and making them stick would be more trouble than it's worth," Drake said. "I don't have the time to spare. I think we might be able to resolve this situation to everyone's satisfaction, however."

McCarson eyed him with deep suspicion. "What's it going to cost me?"

Drake smiled. "Your specialty: information."

McCarson looked even more wary. "Information about who or what?"

"Your client must have given you a file on Ms. North."

"What of it?"

"I want everything that's in it."

McCarson managed a fairly good imitation of appearing deeply offended. "Haven't you ever heard of client confidentiality?"

"Sure, but your little act of breaking and entering tonight indicates to me that your ethics are somewhat flexible."

McCarson's mouth twisted. "Just trying to make a living." He shot a veiled look at Alice. "Besides, as far as I knew, Ms. North is a blackmailer. That ranks pretty damn low on the ethics scale."

"It would if it were true," Drake said. "But it's not."

"How do you know that?"

Drake started to respond but there was

no need.

"Get real, McCarson," Alice snapped. She threw out her arms to indicate the shabby little studio apartment. "Do you think I'd be living in a dump like this if I was making big bucks blackmailing the Whitcombs?"

McCarson blinked. It was clear he had not considered that angle.

"Huh," he said. His brow furrowed. "Well, maybe you haven't been able to spend the money yet."

Alice raised her eyes to the ceiling. "Oh, for pity's sake. Face the truth, Mr. McCarson. You're working for a woman who is obsessed with revenge. I get that. But she's wasting time and money looking in all the wrong places. She should be looking for whoever murdered her son."

"That's enough," Drake said. He studied McCarson. "I want the file. I assume it's on your computer."

"No, Mrs. Whitcomb's assistant gave me a hardcopy file when I agreed to take the job," McCarson said. "For some reason the client doesn't want a computer file created."

"Sure, because it would be evidence that she's been stalking me," Alice said.

McCarson ignored that. "The file that I was given is locked in the trunk of my car.

But I'll tell you right now, there's not much in it."

"Let's take a look," Drake said.

They all trooped down the hall and back downstairs to the lobby. Outside McCarson led them to an inexpensive rental parked at the curb. He opened the trunk, reached into a briefcase, and removed a file folder. He handed it to Drake.

"Knock yourself out," McCarson said. "Can I go now?"

"Sure," Drake said. "One more thing, though."

"Now what?"

"When you tell Ethel Whitcomb that you're off the case, you can tell her something else."

"What's that?" McCarson asked.

Drake looked at him. "Let her know that Ms. North has moved on with her life. Tomorrow she will be entering into a Marriage of Convenience with me."

Alice opened her mouth on what he knew was going to be a shocked — make that horrified — protest. He moved his head ever so slightly, willing her to keep silent. Somewhat to his amazement, she closed her mouth again without uttering a word.

McCarson did not appear to notice the byplay. He just snorted and slammed the trunk of the car.

"I don't know why you want to enter an MC with Ms. North, given her track record with husbands, but I assume you have your reasons. Good luck and watch your back is all I can say. Can I go now?"

"Yes," Drake said. "But make certain the news of the marriage gets to Ethel Whitcomb."

"No problem," McCarson said.

He walked around to the driver's-side door and got behind the wheel.

Alice stood beside Drake. He could tell she was seething. Together they watched McCarson's car turn the corner and drive away into the night.

"What in the world was that all about?" Alice asked.

"I need you on Rainshadow. I do not need an endless series of investigators following you to the island and getting in my way."

"I see." She gave that a moment's consideration. "You think that if Ethel believes that I'm in an MC with you she will back off on the stalking?"

"Ethel Whitcomb might be determined to carry on with her campaign of harassment, but she's going to have a big problem finding private investigators who will agree to work for her once they find out that you're married to me."

"Oh. Yeah." Alice blew out a long sigh. "I see where you're going with this."

"I'm fairly certain that common sense and a healthy survival instinct will convince ninety-nine out of a hundred PIs to decline her offer of a job. They'll know what they're going up against."

"And the one who isn't convinced?"

"We'll know something important about him, whoever he is."

"Which is?"

"That he's not the sharpest tool in the shed." Drake hesitated. "But this plan will only work if the marriage is for real."

Alice's brows shot up. "You're suggesting we actually go through with an MC?"

"Ethel Whitcomb is bound to check, don't you think?"

Alice groaned. "Probably. What happens if I accept your job offer and agree to an MC and we actually find those missing crystals?"

"After the business on Rainshadow is finished, I'll take care of Ethel Whitcomb for you."

Alice gave him a searching look. "Geez, you're serious, aren't you?"

"Consider it a bonus payment for helping us find the crystals."

"Do you really think you can get Ethel

out of my life for good?"

He smiled slowly. "Making problems like Ethel Whitcomb go away is what I do, Alice. You might say I've got a talent for it."

She watched him with a thoughtful expression. "A paranormal talent?"

He shrugged.

"I think I believe you," she said slowly. "But to be clear, there's something I would rather you did for me in exchange for my help on Rainshadow."

"Find out who really killed Fulton Whitcomb?"

"Yes."

"Deal."

She blinked. "You're that sure you can do it?"

"Whitcomb's death is tied to everything else that is happening on Rainshadow," Drake said. "When we find those two missing crystals, we'll find the killer."

"Suddenly you've got my full attention."

"You'll come to Rainshadow with me?"

"You couldn't keep me away, not now."

"Good," he said. "That leaves us with just one more issue to settle this evening."

"What's that?"

"Do I spend the night in my car or on your couch?"

She thought about that for a moment

longer than he would have liked.

"I've accepted your offer of a job and an MC, so the least I can do is let you sleep on the couch," she said.

"Thanks."

"Don't thank me yet. The couch came with the apartment. It's really old and lumpy. The springs are shot. Houdini likes to bounce on it."

CHAPTER 5

The lights in the apartment were off when Alice emerged from the bathroom. The balcony slider was open. Drake was outside, lounging against the railing. His broad shoulders were silhouetted in the ambient green glow that illuminated the Quarter. Houdini was perched on the railing beside him. Both males appeared to be savoring the energy of the night.

She was quite certain that Drake had stepped out of the tiny apartment in an act of gentlemanly discretion to give her some privacy while she got ready for bed.

What had she done by agreeing to go back to Rainshadow? This was not the first time she had made life-changing decisions on the fly. The one thing she had learned early on was how to rez with the currents, as the kids said. She was good at analyzing her options and making decisions quickly. She was nothing if not adaptable. She was also very good at cutting her losses.

It was not the decision to accept the job offer that she questioned. That was easy to understand. She needed the money and she had been told that she could name her price. Drake Sebastian was a powerful man with resources far beyond anything she could muster. If anyone could find the man who had murdered Fulton, it was Drake.

It was the second part of the deal — the Marriage of Convenience to a man she had only just met — that had her second-guessing herself. The last time she had been talked into an MC followed by a honeymoon on Rainshadow, things had not gone well.

She tightened the sash of her robe and crossed the room to the open door. She knew that Drake was aware of her presence, but he did not turn around until she spoke.

"The bathroom is all yours." Hesitating, she added, "I lowered all the lights for you."

"Thanks. That was very thoughtful of you."

He turned toward her then, and she realized that he had removed his mirrored sunglasses. She saw his eyes for the first time. It was impossible to be certain of the color because he was etched in the eerie green chiaroscuro created by the glow of the ruins. But they burned with a silvery paranormal energy that both startled and fascinated her.

A shiver of excitement kicked up her pulse.

This is the real reason why the MC is a huge risk, she thought. *There is something between us, something hot and potentially dangerous.*

"Your vision is okay in this kind of light?" she ventured.

"Yes," he said. "But warn me if you decide to turn on a lamp, okay?"

"Okay."

She could not think of anything else to say, so she started to retreat back into the darkened apartment. She paused when Houdini chortled a cheerful farewell and bounded down to one of the lower balconies. He quickly vanished into the night.

"Where's the dust bunny going?" Drake asked.

"I have no idea," Alice said. "Maybe down into the rain forest. Dust bunnies are night hunters, I think. Or maybe he just went out to meet a girlfriend. He'll be back before dawn."

"He seems to have bonded with you," Drake said.

"We've been a team ever since he rescued

81

me on Rainshadow."

"That's how you found your way out of the Preserve?"

"Yes. I told you, after I ran from Fulton I got lost almost immediately."

"Most people do inside the Preserve. Houdini found you?"

"I was in a panic," Alice said. "You know how it is inside the fence."

"Beautiful but treacherous."

"I wandered around for hours. Spent a night in a cave. The next morning I was sitting on a rock near a grotto pool, trying to come up with a strategy for finding my way back to the fence. Houdini showed up. He started dashing back and forth. Eventually I realized he was trying to get me to follow him. He seemed to sense that I was in trouble. I decided I had nothing to lose, so I followed him."

"He led you back through the fence?"

"Yes. And then he seemed inclined to stick around. We became partners. He loves the magic biz." Once again she started to step back into the shadows. "It's getting late."

"Were you the only suspect in Fulton Whitcomb's murder?"

The question jolted her to a stop. "As far as I know. But remember, officially, Fulton's death was ruled as from natural cause, so

I'm not sure how hard the police looked for other suspects."

"Do you have any theories?"

"No. I hired a private investigator of my own, Samson Crisp of Samson Crisp and Associates. Turned out there were no associates, just Samson. He took my money and made a lot of promises but he never came up with any leads. I got regular updates at the beginning. And regular bills."

"He assured you that he was making progress," Drake said. "All he needed was a little more time and a little more money."

She winced. "Sounds like you've done business with Mr. Crisp."

"No, but I had a feeling your business association with him didn't end well."

"You're right. Eventually he stopped calling. The bills stopped, too. I went to his office a couple of times but he was never there. By then, Ethel was after me in full force and I didn't have any money left to hire another investigator. I had to disappear."

Drake smiled. "Something you happen to be very good at."

"Like I said, the talent has its uses. It was how I got away from Fulton that day in the cave. He flew into a rage and came at me with the nearest blunt object, which happened to be one of the crystals. I pulled my vanishing act and ran. It caught him off guard."

"He knew you were a light-talent but he didn't know about the invisibility thing?"

"No. I never told him or anyone else at the museum, for that matter. For the most part, I've kept my ability a secret all of my life. It's not what you'd call a socially acceptable talent. Tends to make people nervous. Men, in particular, always freak out if they think a woman can actually become invisible."

Drake seemed amused. "I can see where it would add an element of unpredictability to a relationship."

"That's one way to describe it." She thought about the folder on the kitchen table. "Find anything interesting in the file that you took from McCarson?"

"I haven't had a chance to study it yet, but it looks like a lot of detailed reports about your previous addresses, phone numbers, that sort of thing." Drake paused. "Which reminds me, I've been meaning to ask, have you kept in contact with anyone?"

"No. I told my closest friends, the few who believed I didn't murder Fulton, that I was going to disappear for a while until the scandal died down. They understood. I was afraid that if I stayed in touch with them, Ethel's thugs would go after them and try to use them to find me."

"Cutting yourself off from your friends was good strategy, but it must have made for a lonely life this past year," Drake said.

"Luckily I had Houdini. I'm not sure I would have been able to keep going without him."

"You would have kept going, with or without Houdini," Drake said.

"Think so?"

"It's how you're built."

She folded her arms. "You know this . . . how?"

He shrugged. "I just know it."

"An aspect of your talent?"

"Beats me. I've always been fairly good at analyzing a person's strengths and weaknesses. It's what makes me good in the business world and is one of the reasons why my family decided to put me in charge of Sebastian, Inc."

"You say that like it's no big deal, that it's just a gift."

His mouth curved in a grim smile. "Doesn't mean I don't make mistakes. And when I do, they tend to be memorable."

"Is that so? When did you make your last really serious mistake?"

He was silent for so long she started to think that he was not going to answer.

"Three years ago," he said finally.

She caught her breath. "The lab accident that ruined your day vision?"

"Uh-huh."

"I'm sorry. I didn't mean to go there."

"I know. Don't worry about it. Not like it's a secret."

And suddenly she knew.

"But it is a secret," she blurted before she could stop herself.

He stilled. "What?"

"Never mind." She realized she was turning warm. "It's not any of my business."

"What are you talking about?"

She uncrossed her arms and held up both hands, warding him off. "It's nothing. I just got the impression that there was a lot more to the lab accident than you want outsiders to know. It's okay. A proprietary business secret, right? Wouldn't be good if your competition found out about it. I'm okay with that, really."

"Are you?"

He watched her with his molten eyes, and she knew that he was assessing her, probably trying to decide if she was a threat to the family empire.

"Hey, I'm in the magic business, remember?" she said brightly. "Secrets are my stock in trade. Besides, I don't even know what your secret is, so there's no problem here. Well, it's late. We should both get some sleep."

"Yes," he said. "Long day ahead. We'll get married first thing in the morning and head for Rainshadow. If the weather in the Amber Sea holds, we'll be on the island by late afternoon."

"Right."

She turned away and started toward the small alcove. *Not like I'm going to get much sleep tonight,* she thought.

She hauled a spare blanket out of the cupboard and, in a burst of what she considered stunning generosity, gave up one of the two pillows from her bed. When Drake disappeared into the bathroom, she put the blanket and the pillow on the sofa.

She hurried back into the alcove, pulled the curtain closed around the bed, and crawled under the covers.

For a time she listened to the muted sounds that Drake made as he moved around in the small space. After a while she heard the ancient springs of the sofa groan under his weight. Then all was silent.

She was right about one thing: She did not sleep well. She lay very still, intensely aware of the stranger with the silver eyes on the other side of the curtain.

Sometime before dawn she heard the balcony door open and close. Drake said something in soft, low tones. Houdini chortled a response and fluttered under the curtain. He vaulted up onto the foot of the bed and murmured a greeting.

"It's about time you got home," Alice whispered. "I hope you had fun."

Houdini settled down and closed his baby blue eyes.

Alice slept better after that.

CHAPTER 6

The sound of someone banging loudly on the front door brought her out of a groggy twilight sleep. Houdini growled. Alice opened her eyes just in time to see him sleek out and hop down from the foot of the bed. He dashed under the curtain, his small claws clicking on the wooden floor.

Alice glanced at the clock and winced. There was only one person who would be pounding on her door at six thirty in the morning. She pushed the covers aside, got to her feet, and reached for her robe. She was tying the sash when she heard Drake speak to Houdini.

"I'll take care of this," Drake said. "No need to risk a lawsuit."

The front door opened.

"Where is she?" Fred Malloy roared. "She owes me a week's rent. And I swear, if that little rat of hers bites me, I'll sue."

Alarmed, Alice whisked the curtain aside.

Drake was at the door. He was barefooted and dressed in trousers and a black T-shirt. He had put on his wraparound sunglasses, and Houdini was crouched on his shoulder, all four eyes open. Malloy was backing out into the hall, watching Houdini as if the dust bunny were a snake.

Malloy was a big, burly man who had no doubt been hired because of his intimidating size and junkyard-dog demeanor. He was very good at collecting rent from a clientele that was equally skilled at explaining why they needed one more day to get the money together.

"Houdini, no," Alice said. She rushed across the room, whisked him off Drake's shoulder, and tucked him into the crook of her arm. "Please. We don't need any more trouble."

Malloy stopped retreating. He glowered at Alice and jerked a beefy thumb at Drake. "I told you, no sneaking in overnight guests. There's an extra charge if a second person spends the night in the apartment."

"It wasn't a whole night," Alice said. "We didn't even get here until after midnight."

"Doesn't matter," Malloy announced. "Rules are rules. I already bent one of 'em when I said you could keep the rat here in the apartment."

"Yes, I know," Alice said. "It was very kind of you. I realize you're not going to believe this, but the show closed last night."

"You're right, I don't believe it," Malloy rasped.

"But I've got a new job," Alice said quickly.

"Is that right?" Malloy did not look impressed.

Drake held up a hand. "How much does she owe you?"

Malloy slitted his eyes. "One fifty."

Drake looked at Alice, his brows slightly elevated in a silent question.

She sighed. "I'm afraid that's the correct amount. I had to pay extra for Houdini." She cleared her throat. "Would you consider advancing me the money and deducting it out of whatever you're going to pay me for the work on the island?"

"No problem," Drake said. He went to the small end table next to the couch and picked up his wallet. He took out some cash, came back to the door, and handed the money to Malloy. "You can leave now. And by the way, Ms. North is checking out today."

"Huh." Malloy took the bills and glared at Alice. "If you're not out by noon, you'll owe me for another full week."

91

"We'll be out by noon," Alice said.

"Also, there's a cleaning fee," Malloy added. "Another one fifty."

"You got that up front," Alice shot back.

"We have a policy here at the Dead City Suites. Policy says you pay a move-out cleaning fee as well as a move-in cleaning fee."

"There was nothing about a second cleaning fee on the rental agreement," Alice said.

"Policy is policy," Malloy said.

"You're right," Drake said. "Policy is policy, and it had better be in writing because if you really want to collect that cleaning fee, you will have to contact the legal department at Sebastian, Inc. I can guarantee you that the lawyers there will want to see a written agreement detailing cleaning fees."

Malloy squinted. "Legal department? What the hell are you talking about?"

"Policies," Drake said. "My company, Sebastian, Inc., has them, too. One of our policies is to make sure our employees don't get scammed. Ms. North is an employee of the firm so she is entitled to full legal representation in this dispute."

"Look, I don't want any trouble with a big-time legal department," Malloy said uneasily.

"Then get lost."

Malloy took off, and Drake closed the door.

Alice sighed. "Welcome to my life. It's a little embarrassing at times."

"You'd better start packing."

"That won't take long," she said. "I've been living out of a couple of suitcases for nearly a year. It's amazing how much you can do without."

Drake looked around the sparse space and shook his head. "You've been living like this all these months because of Ethel Whitcomb?"

"I told you, the woman thinks I got away with murdering her son. She's obsessed with punishing me."

"No question about it," Drake said. "We need to find out who really did kill Fulton Whitcomb."

She paused in the bathroom doorway. "Thanks for the cash advance."

"Money can't fix everything, but it can make a lot of problems go away."

The marriage of convenience took place in the Crystal City Courthouse. Alice estimated that the short business-like process required about the same amount of time as paying a parking fine and involved possibly even fewer ceremonial trappings. The clerk, a plump, gray-haired woman with a kindly face, tried to put a romantic gloss on it all, but when you got right down to it, there was nothing heartwarming or romantic about an MC.

Alice was pretty sure she knew what the sweet-faced woman on the other side of the counter was thinking. Men of wealthy families — families such as the Sebastians — were notorious for using Marriages of Convenience to placate lovers and mistresses who demanded something more in the way of a commitment. The MCs were always terminated when the next woman came along or when the man finally did his duty by the family and entered into a formal Covenant Marriage. He might continue to have women on the side after contracting a CM, of course, but he could no longer offer his lovers the sop of a quasi-legal relationship. They, in turn, had no claim on him.

Although the clerk's assumptions were obvious enough, Alice was amused to see that Drake was evidently oblivious to them. He focused on the expeditious handling of the business at hand, working swiftly through the paperwork. It was becoming clear that he approached every task with the same single-minded focus.

The only one who appeared to enjoy the short ceremony was Houdini. He went into full-on cute mode and blinked his baby blue eyes at the clerk.

"Aren't you adorable," the clerk cooed.

Houdini stared at a jar of wrapped candies and made encouraging noises. The clerk looked at Alice.

"Is it okay to give him one?" the clerk asked.

"I think so," Alice said. "He seems to be omnivorous."

The clerk whipped the glass lid off the jar and plucked a candy wrapped in gold foil from the bouquet inside.

Houdini ignored the offering. He sidled up to the jar and selected a different piece of candy — one wrapped in red foil — instead. Chortling with glee, he scurried back to Alice's shoulder and went to work tearing off the wrapper.

"He likes red," Alice explained. "It goes with his bow tie."

The clerk smiled. "I can see that."

Ignoring them all, Drake signed the last piece of paper registering the MC and handed it to the clerk.

"How long before the record gets into the system?" he asked, indicating a nearby computer.

"Right away," she assured him. "I'll enter it as soon as you leave."

"We'll wait," Drake said. "I want to be sure the MC comes up immediately if anyone does a search."

The clerk raised her brows but merely nodded and moved to the computer. Alice got the impression that people rarely said no to Drake.

It took the clerk only a few minutes to enter the record of the MC.

"There you go, Mr. Sebastian," she announced. "Congratulations to you both." She winked at Drake. "You may kiss the bride."

"Thanks," Drake said. There was a distinct chill in his voice now. He clamped a hand around Alice's elbow and steered her toward the door. "Let's get out of here. We have a plane to catch."

So much for kissing the bride, Alice thought, torn between chagrin and amusement. A phony embrace in front of the clerk would have been very awkward under the circumstances, but being hustled out of the building by her new groom was embarrassing, too.

They started down the stairs to the first floor of the courthouse. It finally dawned on her that Drake was not merely in a hurry.

He was quietly furious.

"Why were you so concerned about getting the MC registered immediately?" she asked.

"Ethel Whitcomb is obsessed with you," Drake said. "Trust me, when she hears you're married to me, she'll verify the facts."

Alice glanced at him, fascinated by his certainty. "You're probably right."

"If I sent an investigator to find you and he came back with a story about an MC, I'd sure as hell double-check."

She was not sure how to take that. He sounded as if he would be seriously annoyed if he discovered that she was in an MC with another man. It was hypothetical, but why was he simmering?

Drake whisked her outside and across the street to the parking garage. They walked through the shadowy space to the slot where the rental car waited. Drake opened the door on the passenger side.

Delighted at the prospect of another car ride, Houdini fluttered down from Alice's shoulder, scurried into the front of the vehicle, and hopped up onto the back of the seat.

"He's a little speed junkie," Alice explained.

"He's going to love the company jet."

"Probably."

Alice made to slip into the front seat, but Drake touched her shoulder. She stilled, intensely aware of the energy flaring in the atmosphere around them. Her heart rate kicked up and her intuition went into the hot zone.

"What is it?" she whispered, searching the nearby shadows. "Something wrong?"

His hand tightened gently on her shoulder. "It's okay," he said. "You're safe. No need to disappear again."

"Sorry." She tried for a smile. "I have a tendency to overreact these days. Parking garages always make me nervous. So many shadows. So many hiding places. I sometimes wonder if one day Ethel will go over the edge and escalate her campaign of harassment to physical assault or . . . worse."

Drake searched her face. "Do you really think she might send someone to kill you?"

"That's just it. I have no idea what she'll do next. I don't know the woman. I just know she wants revenge."

"I can't even imagine the toll that kind of stress has taken on you this past year."

"Yeah, well, you get used to it," Alice said, going for tough and breezy.

"I doubt it."

"Is there something bothering you?" she

asked. "I mean, aside from the situation on Rainshadow? You've been acting a little weird ever since we signed those papers a few minutes ago."

"The clerk back there in the courthouse," Drake said.

"What about her? I thought she seemed pleasant and efficient."

"She thinks I'm marrying you in an MC because it's a socially acceptable way for a man to keep a mistress happy for a while."

"Oh, that," Alice said, relaxing. "Well, naturally. What else would she think under the circumstances? I didn't realize that you had noticed."

"You didn't think I was aware of how she was looking at me?"

"It doesn't matter. It's not important. She has no way of knowing that you married me to protect me from my ex-mother-in-law."

Drake flattened one hand on the roof of the car and looked off into the shadows of the garage.

"There's something you should know before we drive out of here," he said.

"You're starting to make me nervous. We've already discussed sea monsters, paranormal weather disturbances, danger-ous ocean currents, and an overheating island. What else is it that you want me to know?"

He turned to look at her. Light from the overhead fixture glinted on his mirrored shades. "When the clerk said that I could kiss the bride, I wanted to."

Once again everything within her seemed to still. Her intuition spiked but not the way it had a moment ago. There was danger here but not the kind that she had been running from for the past year.

"Oh," she said. It took everything she had to squelch the thrill that feathered her senses. She managed another stage smile. "Well, why didn't you?"

"Why didn't I?" he said a little too evenly.

"I would have understood." She waved one hand in a dismissing motion. "A kiss would have made the scene look more natural to her."

Drake did a single staccato drumroll on the car roof with his fingers. His jaw tightened.

"I didn't kiss you because I knew what the clerk was thinking. Also, I was pretty sure I knew what you were thinking and I didn't want to embarrass you."

"Well, that was very thoughtful of you, but I can assure you that after what I've been through this past year, it would take a lot more than a fake kiss in front of a courthouse clerk to embarrass me."

"That's what I'm trying to explain," Drake said. "The kiss would not have been fake."

She caught her breath. "Oh."

She did not dare to move for fear of shattering the crystalline moment.

"It would have been this kind of kiss," Drake said.

He wrapped a hand around the back of her neck, drew her close, and covered her mouth with his own.

CHAPTER 7

The kiss was real, all right. She had been out of practice for a year, but she had no problem recognizing the genuine article when it sent shock waves across all her senses.

Behind the shock waves of that first intimate connection came the slow burn of an exquisitely controlled but breathtakingly masculine passion.

Fire and ice splashed through her veins. The kiss was beyond real. At least it was beyond the reality of any kiss she had ever before experienced. It dazzled and astonished her. A strange confusion and a sparkling chaos made her head spin. *It was just a kiss*, she thought. *Just a kiss. Get a grip.*

But the energy of the embrace was having a bizarre effect on her. She was breathless, overwrought, and overwhelmed. It was too much. She had been walking an invisible tightrope for so long, lurching from crisis to crisis. She ricocheted between bursts of adrenaline and fury at her own inability to escape Ethel Whitcomb's net. There had been too many nights when she had slammed her fist into her pillow, which were nights of bad dreams and cold sweats. Too many useless crying jags in the shower. Too many times when she had been forced to vanish at a moment's notice. Too many times when she walked the floor until dawn with Houdini in her arms, searching for a way out.

Everything within her had been precariously balanced on high-alert status ever since she had run from the man who had tried to kill her. The edgy fire of Drake's kiss sent her over the edge.

She clutched at his shoulders and threw herself into the embrace with ferocious abandon. She was frantic for release, any kind of release. She needed something, and in that moment she did not care if it came in the form of an act of violence or an act of passion. She just wanted to be free of her invisible prison, if only for a short time.

If Drake was startled or taken aback by her fierce response, he did not show it. There were a few seconds — the span of a couple of fast heartbeats — during which he seemed to be adjusting to the unexpected development in their short acquaintance. And then, like a driver who thought he was going to be getting behind the wheel of a compact car but discovers that he is piloting a turbo-rezzed sports car instead, he took back control of the kiss and floored the accelerator.

With a low, husky groan, he whipped her around and pushed her up against the nearest concrete pillar, caging her in. He deepened the kiss, giving her the kind of wild, over-the-top intensity that she wanted and needed. She fought him for the embrace with a passion that bordered on violence.

Until that moment she would not have believed that she was capable of such a response to a man. She could feel the hard shape of Drake's heavy arousal and knew that she was not going into the wildfire alone.

Drake finally broke free of her mouth to kiss her throat. He flattened one hand against the pillar, leaning into her, and started to unfasten the front of her jacket. She found his belt buckle with her fingertips and fumbled with it until she got it undone.

The sound of an approaching car shattered the overcharged atmosphere.

Drake surfaced first. His fingers stilled on her jacket. He wrenched his mouth free and rested his damp forehead against hers.

"Damn," he said. He was breathing hard. He used his hand on the pillar to push himself away from her. Quickly he refastened his belt. "Wrong place, wrong time."

"Good grief," Alice whispered.

She was stunned. Her legs were shaky. She was breathing too fast, and her senses were sparking and flashing, leaving her thoroughly disoriented.

A car turned the corner and entered the aisle in which the rental was parked, the driver cruising for a free space. Drake bundled Alice into the front seat, closed the door, and went quickly around to the driver's side. He got behind the wheel.

Together they both sat silently, staring straight ahead through the windshield, as the innocent sedan moved slowly past the rear of the rental.

When the sedan disappeared around the corner, Drake made no move to start the car. Instead he continued to focus on the view of the shadowed garage. Alice did the same. Her brain seemed to have gone blank.

"Are we going to talk about this?" Drake asked evenly.

Alice took a deep breath. "Probably better if we don't."

"Maybe, but sooner or later we're going

to have to talk about it."

"Stress," she said. "It's been a tough year."

"That's your excuse," he said. "What's mine? I was about to have sex with you in a parking garage."

"I take it you don't do that on a regular basis?"

"No," he said. He gave that some thought. "Not that I'm against sex in a garage, or anywhere else, for that matter."

The laughter welled up from out of nowhere. It swept through Alice in a cathartic kind of hysteria. She laughed until she cried. Houdini jumped down onto her lap and made soft little sounds. She clutched him close and sobbed into his fur.

Drake sat quietly until the tears stopped flowing. When it was over he handed her a tissue without saying a word.

"Thank you," she mumbled.

She blotted up the last of the moisture from her eyes. An unfamiliar sensation came over her. It took her a moment to identify the feeling. She finally came up with the right words.

"This is going to sound weird," she said, "but I feel much better now."

"Good to know." Drake started the car and reversed out of the parking space. "Speaking personally, I may never recover."

She laughed again, but this time the laughter sounded right, at least to her ears. Drake flashed her a quick, wicked grin and drove out of the garage onto the street.

Houdini hopped up onto the back of Alice's seat and bounced up and down a little, unable to contain his excitement.

"You're such a little speed junkie," Alice said.

CHAPTER 8

Fifteen minutes later they drove through the gates of a private airfield. A sleek, unmarked jet stood ready and waiting. Drake's overnight bag and Alice's two suitcases were removed from the trunk of the rental and stowed aboard.

"Are we going to fly all the way to Rainshadow?" Alice asked as they walked toward the plane.

"No," Drake said. "There's no landing strip on the island. No strip long enough for the jet on any of the neighboring islands, either. We'll use the jet to get as far as Cadence and take a floatplane from there to Thursday Harbor. I've arranged to have a company boat waiting for us there."

"Why not take the floatplane all the way to Rainshadow? I remember seeing floats landing in the bay."

"The last I heard from my brother is that it's not safe to fly anywhere near the island now," Drake said. "The energy in the atmosphere is screwing up the instruments and creates mirages that are so bad a pilot can't rely on visual cues."

"Why isn't any of this information about Rainshadow in the news?"

"Because the last thing we need are a lot of curiosity seekers trying to crash through the psi-fence into the Preserve. If that happens, we'll end up wasting valuable time rescuing trespassers instead of locating the crystals."

"Okay, that makes sense," Alice said.

Drake escorted her up the steps into the cabin of the jet. He paused to speak briefly to the pilot and the copilot. Then he took the seat across from Alice. They fastened their seat belts.

Drake took the file he had confiscated from McCarson out of a briefcase and immediately became immersed in the contents.

Houdini tried to ride out the takeoff perched on the back of one of the seats so that he could see out the window. Alice grabbed him and held him in her lap until they were safely airborne. Then she released him. He bounded onto a seatback and gazed, enraptured, out the window.

"He likes to ride in anything that goes

faster than he can," Alice explained to Drake.

Drake did not look up from the file. "Who doesn't?"

She smiled. There was something oddly endearing about Drake Sebastian when he was focused the way he was now. After a time he took out a pen, made a few notes, and closed the file.

"Find anything of interest?" she asked.

"Not much." He handed her the folder. "But it's your life. Maybe you'll see something that looks wrong or weird."

She opened the file and saw several photos of herself. A few had been shot while she was on stage. Those did not bother her. But most of the pictures had been taken when she was completely unaware of the camera. They sent cold chills down her spine. There were pictures of her coming and going from the various places she had lived in the past year as well as shots of her walking out of a grocery store, boarding a city bus, and sitting on a park bench, watching Houdini climb a tree.

"Geez," she whispered, shaken. "I knew she was stalking me, but actually seeing the pictures her investigators snapped makes me feel sick to my stomach."

"Don't look at the photos," Drake said

quietly. "Read the file."

She flipped through the handful of print-outs with a wistful feeling. "Not much to my life, is there? No family. No permanent address after the orphanage. A bunch of different jobs. Several failed attempts at finding a husband through a professional matchmaking agency. One failed Marriage of Convenience. One MC husband dead under suspicious circumstances." She looked up. "It's kind of awful to see your whole life boiled down to a few pages like this."

Drake watched her steadily through his glasses. "Did the matchmakers give you any reason for their failure to come up with a good match?"

"They were all very polite about it, but the reasons were obvious. Non-standard, high-rez talent combined with a lack of family background information was a nonstarter for most of the agencies. Boy, I sure wasted a lot of money on marriage brokers in the past few years. The few matches they did come up with didn't work. I've had a lot of first dates that never got as far as a second date."

"Count yourself lucky."

She raised her brows. "Why is that?"

"I met someone about three years ago. We hit it off right from the start. Had a lot in common. She was also a light-talent. We registered with an agency. Lo and behold, we found out we were a near-perfect match."

"What happened?"

"Her name was Zara Tucker, Dr. Zara Tucker. She was beautiful, brilliant, and charming, and she worked in one of the Sebastian, Inc. labs. She was the cause of the accident that made me day-blind."

"How awful," Alice whispered. "She must have been devastated by what happened. Is that why the two of you didn't marry? She just couldn't deal with the guilt of what she had done to you."

A cold amusement edged Drake's mouth. "Not exactly. More like she couldn't deal with the fact that, in spite of what the matchmaking agency claimed, I decided that we were not a good match. She was furious. She grabbed an Alien artifact from the lab vault — a kind of psi-laser — and managed to fire a blast at my eyes."

Alice caught her breath, horrified. "She was a psycho."

"Oh, yeah. But to her credit, she hid it well."

Alice shuddered. "Well enough to pass the matchmaking agency's test? That's surprising and more than a little unnerving. I've heard those tests are extremely accurate."

"Harry and I conducted an investigation later. We found out that she bribed the agency consultant to rig the results of the tests. Zara was obsessed with marrying me."

"Sounds like your perfect match and my ex had a few things in common."

Drake surprised her by going suddenly thoughtful, as if she had made a significant observation.

"Yes, it does, doesn't it?" he said. "And three of the four of us are light-talents." He paused. "I'm assuming Fulton Whitcomb was not a light?"

"No." Alice frowned. "You think the fact that three of the four people we're talking about are lights means something?"

"Probably not, but coincidences always interest me."

"What happened to Dr. Tucker?"

"When she realized that we were never going to get married, she took her own life."

"Suicide." Alice closed her eyes briefly and then opened them to look at Drake. "Her death was supposed to be your punishment. She wanted you to feel guilty."

"I believe that was part of it, yes. But who knows how a mentally ill person thinks?"

"How did she kill herself?"

"One day she simply went down into the

catacombs without tuned amber and started walking."

"They say that suicide-by-catacomb happens more often than most people realize. Did she leave a note?"

"Yes."

"Blaming you?"

"Sure."

"Did they ever find the body?" Alice asked.

"No. But they rarely do with catacomb suicides. Pretty sure that was deliberate, too. She wanted me to spend the rest of my life wondering if she was really dead."

"Her final revenge."

Drake's smile could have been chipped out of glacial ice. "Yes."

"Oh, man, you think she might still be alive, don't you?"

"I don't know." Drake shoved his fingers through his hair. "That's the hell of it. I just don't know. In the course of our investigation, Harry and I pulled out all of the Sebastian, Inc. resources. Called in favors from the Federal Bureau of Psi Investigation and the local Guild boss. We found nothing that indicated that Zara Tucker might have faked her own death."

"But nothing that proved she didn't, either?"

"Right."

"When did she disappear?"

"Nearly three years ago."

"I dunno, Drake, that's a long time for someone to stay lost while consumed with revenge. You'd think that if she was truly obsessed with you, she would have made some obvious move by now."

"That's what I keep telling myself."

She watched him closely. "But in the meantime you haven't registered with any more matchmaking agencies, have you? You're afraid that if you do go into a Covenant Marriage and if Zara is still alive, she might reappear. You think she would be a threat to your wife."

Drake gave her a long, considering look. "You're right. That's a very perceptive observation. The only other people who have figured that out are the members of my family."

"Probably because they are the only other people who know the whole story."

"Harry and the others in my family tell me I'm wrong to put my life on hold because of a threat that may or may not exist. They think that I'm the one who has become obsessed. They point out that if Zara is still alive somewhere, she's probably in an institution by now. And if she did come out of the woodwork, my family has the resources to make her disappear again. For good this time."

"But still you're having a hard time moving on with that part of your life."

Drake shifted in his seat, stretching out his legs. "Zara is my past. Let's talk about yours."

"What about it?"

He angled his head to indicate the folder on her lap. "Notice what is not in that file?"

She glanced down at the folder. "There's not much here. What am I missing?"

"There is no information at all about Fulton Whitcomb beyond the fact that his body was found in his apartment. There's no mention of your honeymoon from hell on Rainshadow."

"Well, there's no reason why Ethel would have gone into those details. She's out to make my life miserable, not solve her son's murder. As far as she's concerned, I'm the killer. She wouldn't waste time pointing an investigator in other directions."

"True," Drake said. "But everything in the case is linked to Rainshadow. You'd think that there would be something about that last trip in the file. If I were Ethel, I'd want to know exactly what happened on the island. And I'd also be asking questions about how Fulton was killed. Most of all, I'd want to know what was discovered that was worth murder."

"You think like that because you are a logical, reasonable person. Trust me, Ethel is not logical or reasonable when it comes to her son's death. Where are you going with this, Drake?"

"I'm not sure yet. But the focus on you makes me wonder if someone else is involved, someone who doesn't want Ethel to look in another direction."

A small shiver zapped through Alice. "The real killer?"

"It's a possibility," Drake said. "We need more information. And we'll get it."

"Okay," Alice said. "Thanks."

Drake studied her for a long moment.

"Do you know what I see when I look at that file?" he asked.

She smiled ruefully. "A misspent life? A person who can't seem to focus on a career path? A woman who has been questioned in a possible homicide and declared unmatchable by a string of matchmaking agencies?"

"No," he said. "I see a strong, intelligent woman who has managed to keep going in the face of some bad odds. I see a survivor."

She thought about that. "Well, it's not like a person has much choice."

"There is always a choice," Drake said. "And you keep making the choice to go forward. In my family we admire that kind of spirit."

CHAPTER 9

Rainshadow materialized out of the strange mist like a ghostly afterimage appearing after the real image has ceased to exist. A ring of dark fog encircled the island. The mist was crouched just offshore.

The island was always a forbidding sight with its sheer granite cliffs, darkly wooded interior, and craggy volcanic peak. To Drake it resembled some artist's vision of an Alien fortress. But in the early and unnatural twilight that had swept over the island and the surrounding sea, it looked more surreal than ever, a landscape that could only exist in a dream.

"We've got a problem," Drake said. He raised his voice to be heard above the roar of the cruiser's engines and the mounting fury of a storm that had not existed until five minutes ago when it had erupted out of nowhere.

He was at the helm of the small, fast boat

that they had picked up in Thursday Harbor a couple of hours earlier. He and Alice were both wearing life jackets. Alice stood beside him, holding her wind-whipped hair away from her face. Her expressive eyes were shielded by a pair of standard-issue sunglasses. She had put them on in Thursday Harbor to deal with the glare off the sea.

Houdini was perched on the ledge above the instrument panel, chortling gleefully as the craft rode up and over the crest of the raging waves.

"What's going on?" Alice asked. She watched the island through the windshield. "Why does Rainshadow look so unreal? It's like it's in another dimension or something."

Drake studied the bank of high-tech electronic navigation equipment in front of him. All of the displays were flat-lined.

"Or something," he said. "Remember the mirage effect that I told you about? The optical illusions that make it impossible to get to the island by floatplane these days?"

"Yes, what about them?"

"Looks like the distortion has gotten worse since I last talked to Harry. There's a lot of paranormal energy in the atmosphere. It's knocked out my instruments. That fog must be the mist that Harry mentioned. It's darker and thicker than he described it."

Alice gave him an uneasy look. "The boat feels like it's going faster."

"It is. We're caught in a current that is carrying us toward the island."

"I understand now what you meant when you said there was some force stirring up the weather. I didn't have a real fun time on Rainshadow the last time I was here, but it wasn't this scary, at least not outside the Preserve."

"The situation has obviously deteriorated significantly since I spoke with Harry four days ago. No wonder they told us in Thursday Harbor that the ferry service had been cancelled."

He tried to ease the cruiser out of the surging current. The boat responded only minimally, making it clear they were not going to escape. He could feel the powerful energy of the water beneath the hull, forcing them toward the rocky cliffs. His job now was to keep the boat from capsizing before he could get close to a safe place to beach it.

"There's no way we're going to make it around the island to Shadow Bay," he said. He kept one hand on the helm and used the other to open a leather-bound volume he had brought with him.

Alice peered at the book. "What's that?"

"Nav charts of this area. Harry and I have both spent a lot of time exploring the shoreline around the island. In addition, the Foundation has a big collection of the old seafarers' charts in the archives." He flipped through the pages until he found the one he wanted. "Here we go. There's a small natural harbor not far from here. Deception Cove. I'm going to try to get into it."

"Then what?" Alice asked.

"We'll go ashore. Can't risk taking the boat back out into the open sea until things settle down. We'll spend the night on the beach. Tomorrow morning, if conditions are still this unpredictable, we'll have to walk around the shoreline to Shadow Bay."

"That's going to be a very long walk," Alice observed.

"Given the rough terrain it will probably take a full day. The energy fence that protects the Preserve is set back several yards from the shore around this sector of the island though, so we won't have to deal with the force field."

He did not take his attention off the wild sea, but out of the corner of his eyes he could see the determined expression on Alice's face. She was scared but he knew she would not panic. That was good to know. He did not have time to deal with panic.

Houdini was no longer chortling with glee. He seemed to sense that the situation had shifted from being a dust bunny thrill ride to something far more treacherous. When Alice reached out to scoop him up, he did not try to evade her grasp. He found his favorite perch on her shoulder and opened all four eyes.

Drake glanced at Alice. "Tell me that you can swim."

"I know the basics but I'm no expert," Alice admitted. "All of my swimming has been done in pools."

"What about Houdini?"

"I've seen him swim in a bathtub but I doubt that he's ever been in the ocean."

"Get one of the life preservers ready for him," Drake said. "Attach it to my vest with that cord. Maybe he'll figure out what to do if we end up in the water."

Alice took the round preserver down from a nearby hook and connected it to Drake's vest.

"Are we going into the water?" she asked quietly.

"Not if I can help it."

The fierce current was growing stronger. The boat was hurtling toward the wall of fog that ringed the island. He searched for the major landmarks that indicated the entrance to Deception Cove, twin pillars of stone that formed a natural gate to the cove. He spotted them at last, rising out of the fog bank, but the narrow entrance was hidden by the thick, dark mist.

He knew he would have only one chance to break free of the underwater river that was sweeping them toward the island. If he miscalculated they would either go under or slam into the rocks.

He powered up the big flash-rock engines and leaned into the wheel, turning to port, searching for the very edge of the fierce current.

The water fought back but he was able to slip the cruiser to the side.

"Hang on," he said.

"Already doing that," Alice said. She clutched Houdini and the life preserver in one arm and gripped the nearest handhold.

He could feel the slight disruption caused by the cove current. He took advantage of it, pushing for one last burst of power from the laboring engines.

He hauled hard over on the wheel. The cruiser responded by popping out of the rip and into the cove current. The momentum took the boat straight into the fog bank.

A sudden darkness descended. The dark fog seethed with energy. An eerie calm enveloped the cruiser. The current slackened. A strange, muffled silence fell.

"It's like we stepped into another dimension," Alice whispered.

Drake throttled back until the boat was gliding slowly through the fog, skimming over the glassy, smooth surface of the water.

"I can't see a thing," Alice said, her voice tight with tension.

Cautiously, Drake took off his glasses and looked at the darkly illuminated world around them.

"I can," he said quietly.

It was a realm lit by all the colors of midnight. The mist still enveloped them, but when viewed through his other vision it was no longer impenetrable. Instead the stuff was thin and wispy. If it weren't for the currents of hot energy, it would have been like any other light fog. He could make out the rocky pillars that guarded the entrance to the cove.

Alice turned her head very quickly, searching his face. "It's dark light energy, isn't it? I can sense it."

"Yes. I've never seen it manifest like this, though."

Alice reached up to touch Houdini. "It

feels ominous, as if a storm is coming in."

He could sense it, too, Drake thought. The rising chaos of a greater darkness that would coalesce into something more dangerous when the last of the daylight vanished.

"We need to get settled on shore before night falls," he said. "Got a feeling this fog will get worse in an hour or so."

"I think you're right. Can you actually see through this stuff?"

"Partially. I can see where I'm going now but that might not be possible later. What do you see?" he asked.

"I can't see anything beyond the bow of the boat."

He reduced the power further and motored slowly through the entrance to the Cove. Once they passed the stone columns, they emerged from the fog. The water remained calm.

"That's a relief," Alice said. "I can see the beach now."

Drake cruised toward the crescent of sand that edged the quiet cove. When he could not go any further without running aground, he cut the engines and lowered the anchor.

He studied the half moon of a beach and the dark, heavy woods beyond. The twilight drenched the scene in thick shadows.

He looked at Alice.

"Welcome back to Rainshadow," he said.

"A second honeymoon on this damned island," Alice said. "What could possibly go wrong?"

CHAPTER 10

They used the dinghy to take some emergency equipment and camping supplies ashore. The fog was still hovering out over the water but it was moving in slowly, swallowing the cove as it approached.

Houdini, evidently oblivious to the ominous mist, quickly discovered the pleasure of surfing with a life preserver. He frolicked in the shallow water, clinging to the device with his two front paws while he paddled with his hind legs. Every so often he caught a small lapping wave that carried him up onto the sand. He chortled madly and immediately set out to catch another wave.

Alice took one last look at the dark fog offshore and turned to watch Drake establish camp for the night. She liked watching him, she realized. He went about the business of setting up the tent, bedrolls, and small amber lantern in the efficient, competent way that characterized everything he did. He had put his sunglasses back on, she noticed. Evidently what little daylight was left was too much for his sensitive eyes.

"I'm sorry I'm not much help here," she said. "I've never gone camping in my entire life."

"Don't worry about it." Drake rezzed the amber lantern. "Harry and I used to camp out a lot here on Rainshadow. Got it down to a fine art."

"I can see that." She walked toward him across the sand. "I assume the amber lantern is for my sake. I appreciate it. Will it bother your eyes?"

"Not as long as I keep my glasses on."

She watched him take a small gadget out of a pack. He aimed it at the pile of kindling and driftwood he had made. A flame shot out from the device. The kindling caught immediately.

"What is that thing?" Alice asked.

"Basically it's just a fire-starter, an ignition device. But it's been modified in a Sebastian lab to function as a small blowtorch, if necessary. I've got two of them. You can have one."

"Good grief, why would I want a blowtorch?"

"Makes a handy weapon."

She winced. "I see."

129

Drake crouched in front of the fire, watching the flames through his sunglasses. "Fire is one of the few forms of normal energy that can be used inside the Preserve."

"Are there a lot of dangerous animals on the other side of the fence?"

"Until recently, the only dangerous critters we had to worry about were the human variety. But that's not true any longer."

"Right, those mutated sea creatures who are living in the cave pools."

"And maybe other things as well." Drake glanced back over his shoulder at the dark woods that bordered the cove. "There's so much psi in the ecosystem inside the Preserve now that it's bound to have an effect on the plant and animal life."

Houdini splashed out of the cove, dragging his life preserver by the cord. He paused to shake the water from his fur and then trotted over to the fire. He stared at the emergency rations.

"I think he's hungry," Alice said.

"I know I am." Drake got to his feet. "Time to open up some of those tasty instant meals. Sorry I forgot to bring the wine."

Alice smiled. "So am I." She glanced toward the cove. The cruiser was slowly disappearing into the fog. "Why do I have the feeling that I'm never going to see my suitcases and my costumes and props again?"

Drake ripped open one of the containers. "Don't worry, we'll come back for the boat and your stuff after we take care of business on the island."

There was nothing in the suitcases that could not be replaced, she reminded herself. Nevertheless, her whole life — or what was left of it — was in the two suitcases she had been forced to leave on board the boat.

Get a grip, woman. You're alive and so is Houdini. That's all that matters. She did not doubt for a moment that they had all been in serious danger a short time ago.

"You saved us, Drake," she said quietly.

"What?"

He opened another container and then a third.

She watched him break a seal on each package. The scent of heating food wafted toward her.

"Piloting the boat through those awful currents and that fog was brilliant work," she said. "You saved all of us."

He glanced at her, amber light flashing on his glasses. "You and Houdini wouldn't be here in the first place if I hadn't brought you here."

"Yes, well, we are here and you saved us. That's all that matters tonight."

He looked amused. "You're a real live-in-the-moment kind of woman. A lot of folks would be pissed as hell at me if I'd brought them into a situation like this."

"It wasn't like my life was going so great in Crystal City. At least now I've got a shot at getting Ethel Whitcomb out of my life and making a few bucks to boot. I can contemplate a whole different future, thanks to you."

"We're not there yet." He glanced toward the fogbound cove. "You were serious when you said that just about everything you own is in those suitcases, weren't you?" he said.

"Yes." She settled down on a large chunk of driftwood. "Ethel Whitcomb has done a pretty good job of destroying my life this past year. It's amazing what you can do to another person when you've got a lot of money and power."

"You've been living out of a couple of suitcases for damn near a year?" Drake asked. He sat down beside her and handed her one of the emergency meals. He gave another one to Houdini and took the third for himself. "That's all? Nothing in storage? No property?"

She watched Houdini explore his emergency meal. He seemed enthralled with the little compartments in the plate, each of which was filled with different food. He dithered between the pear crisp and the stew.

"It wasn't like I owned a lot of stuff before Ethel set out to ruin me," Alice admitted. "Nevertheless, I had a job, a car that was almost paid off, some savings in the bank, and a couple of credit cards."

"All gone?"

"My job in the museum gift shop vanished first because Ethel Whitcomb owns the Whitcomb Museum. The director, Aldwin Hampstead, had no choice but to let me go after Ethel put some pressure on him. The car was mysteriously repossessed soon after that. The credit cards got cancelled. When I realized what was going on, I managed to get my money out of the bank before Ethel could find a way to put a lien on it, but it was a near thing. I've used up all of my savings just trying to stay one step ahead of the Whitcomb thugs. You'd be surprised how much it costs to buy new IDs every few months."

Drake whistled softly. "You really have been on the run."

She ate some stew. There wasn't much flavor but it wasn't terrible, and best of all it was pleasantly warm. Houdini made his decision. He went for the pear crisp.

"Good choice," she said. "Always eat dessert first. You never know when one of Ethel's creeps will show up." She paused and then smiled a little as a thought struck her. "I have to say that is definitely one bright spot about returning to Rainshadow. It's highly unlikely that Ethel Whitcomb's people will come after me here, not now with this fog and all communications down."

Drake ate some of the stew. "If they do manage to follow you, they'll have to go through me to get to you. That's not going to happen."

The mag-steel edge on the words was so lethally honed she was pretty sure that it could have drawn blood.

She managed a breezy, flippant smile. "Oh, wow, I've got a bodyguard now as part of our deal?"

"Yes," he said, very seriously.

Some of the survival-mode tension that had been churning inside her for the past year eased a little.

"I believe you," she said.

CHAPTER 11

Drake knew the exact instant when Alice came awake on a rush of nightmare-fueled adrenaline. He crouched in front of the tent.

"Take it easy," he said. "Everything's okay."

She sat up so quickly she bumped her head against the roof of the small tent. Her eyes widened in horror as she looked past him into the fog.

"What?" she whispered.

He knew what she was seeing. The hallucinations had been growing stronger for the past hour. Like primal monsters of the night, they hovered just beyond the glow cast by the fire.

"They're not real," Drake said.

She ignored him, still caught between the dream world and the waking state.

"Houdini," she gasped. *"Houdini."*

The dust bunny hopped off the driftwood log where he had been sitting earlier, keeping Drake company, and raced into the tent. Alice clutched him close and took several deep breaths.

"What in the world is going on?" she finally asked.

Her voice was remarkably steady given the disorienting and disturbing circumstances, he thought.

"The energy in the fog is creating hallucinations," he said. "It's similar to the kind of thing that happens when you go through the psi-fence."

She pulled herself together with visible effort. "You took off your glasses."

"Yes."

"What happened to the amber lantern?"

"The firelight seemed to be more effective against the fog, so I decided to conserve the lantern energy," he said. He did not add that he thought it best to save the lantern in the event that they wound up spending another night out in the open.

"Is everything okay?" she asked.

"So far," he said. "I wondered how long you were going to be able to sleep through the effects of this fog. An hour ago the energy levels started to get really hot. It's turning into a paranormal storm that affects the senses, generating audio and visual hallucinations."

"Oh, that's just great." Alice groaned. "And here I thought we weren't going to have to worry about that kind of stuff until we went into the Preserve."

"Whatever is going on inside has spilled out through the fence, at least in this sector. It's nearly midnight now. It's a good bet that things are going to become more unstable and more intense for the next few hours. You know how it is with paranormal energy."

"Always stronger after dark."

"And especially after midnight," he said. "The psi-heat will probably ease up as we get closer to dawn."

"Well, one thing's for sure: I certainly won't be getting any more sleep tonight," she said.

"Come out and sit by the fire," he said.

"Sounds like a plan."

He straightened and backed away from the front of the tent. She released Houdini and scrambled out of the confined space. She stretched and dropped down onto the driftwood log.

Drake lowered himself beside her. Their shoulders brushed. Drake felt something spark between them. *Talk about your imagination, Sebastian. Now you really are dreaming.*

"Huh," Alice said. "That's interesting."

"What?"

She leaned closer so that their shoulders touched again. Drake got another deep jolt of awareness when they made contact. This time Alice did not pull away. The flash of connection steadied and seemed to grow stronger and more intimate.

"When we have physical contact, I can see deeper into the fog," Alice said.

"Yeah?"

"I think I'm picking up some of the currents of your aura," she said. "It's like I'm tapping into your talent a little."

"I can feel your energy field, too."

There was a subtle shift in the atmosphere, and he knew that she had jacked up her talent. After a moment some of the tension seeped out of her shoulders.

They sat quietly, shoulders pressed together. Houdini perched on the end of the log and gazed fixedly toward the dark woods.

"What if we go looking for those two missing crystals and come across something a lot more dangerous than those sea monsters your brother and his fiancée discovered," Alice asked after a while. "Maybe something humans can't handle."

"It's possible," Drake said. "But it's not

like we've got a choice. We need answers."

"And if you don't like the answers?"

He never got around to responding because at that moment a cold frisson of alarm crackled across his senses. On the end of the log, Houdini sleeked out and uttered a low, warning growl.

Drake looked toward the fence line. A pair of faceted eyes the size of basketballs stared back at him from the darkness. They glowed with icy-cold ultraviolet psi-light. The creature's mouth was festooned with two pincer-like mandibles. Its body was swollen and bulbous in shape and was supported by six spindly, jointed legs. The damned thing was as large as a dog.

"We've got a visitor," Drake said quietly. He reached for the fire-starter, moving very slowly. "Behind you, near the psi-fence boundary."

Alice turned, keeping her shoulder pressed against his. She gave a sharp, horrified gasp.

"Good grief," she whispered. "Is that what I think it is?"

"Some kind of insect," Drake said. His hand closed around the fire-starter. "But not like anything I've ever seen inside the Preserve."

"Looks like your brother was right. Whatever is going on in there is starting to affect the wildlife."

"Insects evolve rapidly. It makes sense that they would be among the first creatures to respond to the changes in the environment."

"But that monster is outside the fence," Alice said. "I thought nothing inside the Preserve could get out."

"Humans and dust bunnies come and go through the fence all the time."

"Yes, but we're different. That . . . That thing evolved inside the Preserve in a very hot environment. How can it live out here on the beach?"

"Just taking a wild guess here — I'm no biologist — but I think it's safe to say that the energy of the fog provides enough psi for it to come outside the fence at night to hunt."

The glowing ultraviolet eyes moved toward them with the quick, sharp movements typical of a creature with a jointed exoskeleton. It hesitated, probably because it didn't like the fire, Drake thought. Then, as if it had come to some decision regarding prey, the monster skittered forward swiftly.

Houdini hissed.

Drake waited until the giant insect was within range. He aimed the fire-starter at one of the compound eyes and released the device at full power. The narrow blowtorch beam struck one of the insect's eyes. There was a loud crackling noise and then a pop when the creature's exoskeleton exploded under the fiery impact.

The smell of torched insect drifted through the fog.

Houdini chortled exultantly.

There was a short silence. Drake could feel Alice's tension.

"You know," Alice said, "in my experience, whenever you come across one insect, you can usually expect to find more in the vicinity."

"I was just thinking the same thing."

The second set of glittering eyes appeared from the far end of the cove. Drake waited until it got within range and ignited the fire-starter again. The big insect exploded in a flash of black smoke that quickly faded. Houdini chortled again, getting into the game now.

"Did you say you had a second fire-starter?" Alice asked.

"I did say that." He pulled it out of the pack and gave it to her. "Just press this button. Maximum range is only about twenty feet, so you have to wait until the target gets as close as that pile of rocks over there."

She examined the fire-starter in her hand. "Got it."

"We'll sit back-to-back on this log," Drake said. "That way we'll still have physical contact, but I'll be able to keep watch in one direction while you keep an eye out for anything coming up from the opposite end of the beach."

"Works for me."

She put one jean-clad leg over the log, sitting astride. He did the same. They pressed their backs together, and energy shivered around them as they both jacked up their talents.

For a time the strange night was silent except for the muffled lapping of the waves in the cove. Drake savored the feel of Alice's sleek back. She was warm and smelled good. It was ridiculous under the circumstances but it felt right to be here like this together.

Houdini made an eager, chittering sound.

Alice stiffened. "My three-o'clock position. Here goes."

Drake turned his head and saw a monstrous beetle. "Aim for the biggest part of the thing."

Alice rezzed the fire-starter. The beetle disintegrated into a smoky ruin.

Houdini went wild and did a victory lap around the fire.

Alice sighed. "Maybe he thinks we're in

the middle of some kind of game."

Drake zapped another insect.

"I do realize that, as honeymoons go, this one is probably not going to make any woman's top-ten list," he said.

"Now, see, there's where you're wrong," Alice said. "It's all a matter of perspective. I can promise you that this honeymoon is a lot more fun than my last one."

"Yeah?"

"Hey, this time my husband isn't trying to murder me. He's saving me from giant cockroaches."

"I like your glass-half-full attitude."

CHAPTER 12

The terrible fog began to retreat a couple of hours later. Alice could not be sure of the time because her watch and Drake's had both stopped, victims of the heavy psi in the area.

The war with the oversized insects ended shortly thereafter as the surviving monsters retreated back through the fence into the Preserve. The first faint light of dawn appeared.

Drake swung one leg back over the log so that he was no longer sitting astride and took his mirrored sunglasses out of his jacket.

"They're gone," he said as he put on his glasses. "I was right, they can't live outside the Preserve during the day. They need the fog to survive."

"Thank goodness," Alice said. "The thought of hiking to Shadow Bay and zapping mutant insects along the way was a little daunting."

Houdini chortled a cheerful greeting and looked hopefully at the remaining camp meals.

"Hungry?" Drake asked. He got to his feet, reached down, and opened the pack. "So am I. Let's see what we've got for breakfast."

Alice rose slowly from the driftwood log, stretching to work out some stiff muscles. She watched Drake open the pack, intensely aware that, in spite of everything, she missed the feel of his warm, strong back pressed up against her. She missed the psychic connection that had bound them so intimately through the long, dangerous night. *Nothing like surviving an attack of monster insects together to forge a bond between two people,* she thought. *Don't read too much into this.*

She studied the scene on the beach in the low light of a sullen gray dawn. There were a handful of charred insect carcasses scattered about on the sand. One of them was way too close for comfort.

"Yuck," Alice said. She turned away from the sight of the dead monster, shuddering.

Drake held up three meal packets. "Looks like stew and pear crisp for breakfast or stew and pear crisp."

"Choices, choices," Alice said. "I think I'll

have stew and pear crisp."

"Excellent decision."

Drake rezzed three meals. Alice dropped down on the log again to eat her breakfast. Drake sat beside her. They watched Houdini go through the same dithering process that he had gone through the night before, eventually choosing to eat the pear crisp first.

Alice realized that Drake was smiling a little, not so much in amusement but more like satisfaction, she decided.

"What?" she asked around a mouthful of stew.

"Just thinking that we made a good team last night, you, me, and the dust bunny."

She thought about that. "Yes, we did, didn't we?"

"That said, we need to get to Shadow Bay today. I don't think we want to spend another night out in the open."

Alice froze as a horrible thought struck her. "You said you hadn't heard from your brother in several days. What if — ?"

"Shadow Bay has been overrun by giant insects?" Drake shook his head. "I don't think that's very likely, not on that sector of the island."

"Why not?"

"The town is located a few miles from the

fence in a region of Rainshadow that has historically experienced a much lower level of paranormal activity." Drake angled his head toward the nearby woods. "This sector around Deception Cove, on the other hand, has always been a real hot spot, even before the recent problems. It's noted on all the old charts. That's why the fence comes so close to the shoreline around here."

"You're assuming that the mutations would start first in a place like Deception Cove?" Alice thought about it. "Makes sense."

"That's my best guess." Drake finished his meal and got to his feet. "Let's move out."

It did not take long to pack up the camp, mostly because Drake did all the work, Alice thought. She didn't even know how to fold the tent.

"I feel more than a little useless," she said. "Please don't hesitate to give instructions."

"I won't." Drake gave her a coolly approving smile. "And you sure as hell weren't useless last night."

She decided that comment made her feel a lot better.

Drake handed her the smaller of the two packs. "Here you go."

She struggled into the pack and followed

him down the beach. Houdini scampered along at their feet, pausing here and there to investigate an interesting rock or log.

"Everything's a game to you, isn't it?" Alice asked him, smiling.

Drake glanced at Houdini. "Life is simple for a dust bunny. Deciding whether to eat the pear crisp before the stew is probably about as difficult as decision-making gets."

The beach ended in a tumble of rocks. Drake wove a path through them and started into the tree line. Alice followed, concentrating on her footing so intently that she blundered into Drake before she realized that he had stopped and was standing very still.

She opened her mouth to ask a question, but he silenced her with a small motion of his hand. Houdini, too, had gone silent. He was still fully fluffed and was looking at the woods up ahead as intently as Drake.

Alice watched Drake take out the fire-starter.

Oh, crap, she thought. *More mutant insects.*

Drake closed his hand around her arm and drew her into the shadows cast by a pile of boulders. They hunkered down and waited.

Alice heard the crackle of dead branches and pine needles. Small pebbles skittered.

Next came the muffled thud of footsteps and the sound of heavy, labored breathing.

Not insects, she thought. She did not know if that was going to be good news or bad news.

A moment later a woman appeared, making her way awkwardly through the trees. She was young, probably not more than eighteen or nineteen, thin, and haggard looking, as if she hadn't eaten or slept well in some time. Her long brown hair straggled around her shoulders. She was dressed in dark green trousers, a matching shirt with a logo on the breast pocket, and heavy boots. A uniform, Alice realized.

As she and Drake watched, the woman trudged forward, slipping and sliding on the leaves and pebbles.

Drake straightened and moved out from behind the boulder.

"Hello," he said quietly.

The woman froze. Stark panic etched her features. She looked back over her shoulder and then, evidently deciding she could not retreat that way, took stock of the sheer granite drop into the sea. Seeing no escape via that route, she bolted for the thick woods.

"No, damn it," Drake shouted. "Stop. We won't hurt you."

Alice emerged from behind the boulder. "It's okay. Please, come back."

But the fleeing woman did not stop. She disappeared into the heavy undergrowth. Her high-pitched screams echoed in the woods for a moment and then abruptly ceased.

"Son of a ghost," Drake said. "She would have to go through the fence."

"We can't leave her there," Alice said. "We have to find her. She'll never survive the night inside this part of the Preserve."

"I know." Drake looked grimly resigned to the inevitable. "Okay, let's go. Stick close."

"Don't worry, I will."

The invisible energy of the paranormal fence line made its presence felt within a few steps. The force field was unpleasant and unnerving at first, lifting the hair on the nape of Alice's neck. She gritted her teeth against the effects and followed Drake deeper into the psi-barrier.

The hallucinations — auditory and visual — struck hard. Strange figures materialized out of the shadows, beckoning her to her doom. Specters warned her to go back before it was too late. And always, always, there were the bloodcurdling chills that wracked all of her senses. She jacked up her talent to counter some of the effects. She knew that Drake had done the same thing.

He reached back and held out his hand. She grabbed it. The shock waves of the fence diminished somewhat. *Just like last night,* she thought. Physical contact helped to ward off the worst of the psychic disturbances.

Houdini dashed along at their heels, unaffected by the forces.

And then, between one step and the next, they were through the fence and inside the Preserve. The hallucinations ceased only to be replaced by the strange atmosphere of the Preserve.

Energy stirred all around Alice — some of it from the botanical world, some from the animal and insect kingdoms. All of it felt overheated. Here and there flashes of psi-light sparked in the shadows. Patches of vegetation glowed. Mushrooms fluoresced. The thick tree canopy overhead blocked out what little daylight there was. An ominous wind stirred the leaves of the trees, causing them to shiver and glitter with malevolent light. The whole place was infused with the dark energy of a building storm front.

Drake came to a halt. Alice stopped beside him. There was no sign of the woman, but Houdini made urgent little noises and fluttered through a small forest of giant iridescent ferns.

Alice and Drake followed.

The screams started again.

CHAPTER 13

The heavy energy of the preserve distorted sound. Alice could not be sure of the direction of the screams. But she could tell that Drake and Houdini were able to track the desperate cries.

"This way," Drake said. "Whatever you do, don't get lost on me."

"I won't," Alice vowed. "I've been lost in here before, remember?"

They pushed their way through a maze of massive, phosphorescing palm fronds, Houdini in the lead. Brushing up against the hot greenery sent little sparks of energy across Alice's senses. The sensation was not painful, but the strangeness of it all made her deeply wary.

The crying was louder now. The sobbing woman was not far away, but the energy inside the Preserve was so disorienting she might as well have been a hundred miles off.

Houdini, however, had no problem navigating the strange forest. He scampered through a veil of weird blue orchids and promptly vanished.

"Wait," Alice called.

Houdini reappeared, bounced up and down a few times, and made more excited noises. When they caught up with him, he scampered forward again, heading toward a forest of giant glowing mushrooms.

It was not just the ferns and the mushrooms that seemed outsized, Alice realized. Much of the vegetation appeared unnaturally large. A waterfall of flowers — each bloom as large as a dinner plate — tumbled from a creeping vine.

It had been a year since she had last been inside the Preserve, and at that time she had been on a different part of the island. She had seen many strange and unnerving sights on that occasion, but she did not recall anything quite like the huge ferns and the towering mushrooms. A year ago the forbidden territory had been an eerie wonderland, disturbing in some ways but also enthrallingly beautiful. Today she felt as though she was walking through a demon's garden lit by garish paranormal energy.

The screams stopped. That was probably not a good sign, Alice thought. Drake was moving faster through the heavy foliage, and Alice hurried to keep up with him.

They broke out into a small clearing and saw the woman. She was no longer running. She had come to a halt between two large trees. She was still trying to scream but her cries were hoarse and breathless now. She flailed wildly but her movements were severely restricted and becoming more subdued by the second.

"Son of a ghost," Drake muttered, raising the fire-starter.

Alice finally saw what had brought the fleeing woman to a halt. She was trapped in the glistening strands of a giant spiderweb.

Houdini stopped, hissing. Dread chilled the back of Alice's neck. She looked up and saw a large, dark, bloated shape. Faceted eyes glittered like ice-cold jewels. There was something both terrifying and compelling about the unblinking gaze. Eight long limbs shifted in the shadows.

"Spider," Alice whispered, horrified.

"Here we go again," Drake said.

The spider started toward its prey. The woman was no longer shrieking. She was shivering violently and was so deeply entangled in the sticky strands of glistening silk she could not move her arms and legs.

Houdini growled. He was not treating this

encounter like a game. But Alice knew there was nothing he could do. If he tried to attack the spider, he would become enmeshed in the web.

"Houdini, no," Alice said quietly.

"Keep him out of the way," Drake ordered.

Alice scooped up Houdini and tucked him under her arm.

The spider was closing in on the almost motionless woman.

Drake rezzed the ignition button on the fire-starter. The narrow flame flashed, striking the spider. It jerked spasmodically and then its eight legs collapsed like matchsticks. The thing plummeted to the ground and didn't move.

"You're okay now," Drake told the woman. "I'll have you free in a few minutes."

He used the fire-starter like a small cutting torch and sliced through the web. Alice worried that the silk would burst into flames, but instead it shriveled and melted. The remnants flapped like the spectral cloak of a faded ghost.

The woman tumbled to the ground. She was covered with strands of spider silk but she was breathing.

Houdini was still growling, signaling that the danger was not over.

"We need to get her out of here," Drake said. "The commotion and the smell of the dead spider will probably attract other things that I'd rather we did not have to deal with. I'll keep watch while you get her free of the web."

Alice went to her knees beside the woman and started scraping off the sticky strands.

"Can you move?" she said to the blonde.

"Yes, I-I think so," the woman gasped.

She struggled to her knees, swiping at the strands of silk that clung to her face. She stared at Drake.

"Who are you?" she whispered.

"Drake Sebastian," Drake said. "This is my wife, Alice. We can talk this out later. We need to get out of here."

The woman flinched, frowned in confusion, and then pulled herself together with visible effort. "I don't understand."

"Neither do I," Drake said. "We'll deal with it later."

Alice heard something stir in the shadows. Houdini growled again.

Drake grasped one of the woman's arms. Alice took the other. They ran back toward the fence line. Houdini dashed after them.

They plunged through the psi-barrier. When they were on the far side, Alice allowed herself a small sigh of relief. Drake stopped and turned to look at the woman.

"Who are you?" he asked.

"Karen," the woman said. "Karen Rosser." She swallowed hard. "Are you going to arrest me?"

"Why would I do that?" Drake asked.

"We were told that any member of the staff who violated the terms of the contract would be subject to arrest."

Alice frowned. "What contract?"

"The one we signed with the company," Karen whispered. She pointed to the logo on her green uniform shirt. "I know that the Dream Chamber Project here on the island is supposed to be top secret. But I just couldn't take it anymore."

Drake was looking at the logo on Karen's shirt. Alice followed his gaze. Clearly embroidered was a familiar company name: *Sebastian, Inc., Rainshadow Foundation.*

"Looks like we are going to have an interesting conversation on the hike to Shadow Bay," Drake said.

CHAPTER 14

They set off in a single file, Drake and Houdini the lead. Karen fell in behind Drake. Alice brought up the rear. The walking was difficult in places but not impossible. The sky remained leaden. The dark fog crouched just offshore, waiting for the energy of the night to summon it. The ominous sensation in the atmosphere did not fade, even though they were putting distance between themselves and the cove.

"All right, Karen, let's start at the beginning," Drake said. "Tell me about the Dream Chamber Project."

"I don't know where to begin," Karen said. "It's all been such a nightmare."

"You said you were working for the Rainshadow Foundation arm of Sebastian, Inc."

"That's right. I was hired as a research assistant a few months ago. I've got the paperwork to prove it."

"And you were employed here on the

island," Drake said.

"Until I couldn't take the stress any longer. We tried to quit."

"Who is *we?*" Drake asked.

"The other research assistant, Pete Banks. Like I said, we tried to quit but she wouldn't let us. When we tried to leave she had the security people lock us up. I managed to escape this morning but —"

Drake stopped and looked back at Karen. "Who had the security people lock you up?"

"Dr. Tucker," Karen said.

"Dr. Zara Tucker," Drake said, repeating the name very precisely, making sure.

"Yes," Karen said.

"Damn," Drake said. "Well, that certainly answers a few questions." He looked at Alice. "I knew she wasn't dead."

"But what has she been doing for the past three years?" Alice asked.

"Isn't it obvious? Zara Tucker spent the last three years plotting her revenge against me and my family."

CHAPTER 15

Drake looked at Karen. "Let's start with a basic fact. Neither Sebastian, Inc. nor the Rainshadow Foundation has authorized any research projects here on the island."

"I don't understand," Karen said. "Dr. Tucker made it clear that we were signing up as research assistants at a Foundation-approved excavation project."

"Dr. Tucker is not affiliated with the Foundation," Drake said. He started walking again. "Officially she isn't even alive. She was declared dead three years ago."

"I don't know what to tell you," Karen said. "A woman named Dr. Tucker is running the project here on Rainshadow. She's got lab equipment that carries the Foundation logo. Her security people wear Foundation uniforms." She glanced down at her shirt. "Pete and I were issued Foundation gear."

"Zara Tucker is a brilliant but mentally

unstable scientist," Drake said. "She spent a full year working in the Sebastian labs. She also has a way of convincing others, usually males, to do what she wants them to do."

"You're telling me," Karen said grimly. "I've seen the way men respond to her. Even Pete thought he was in love with her for a time. He wanted to be her hero. They all do." Karen glanced at Alice. "You know how some women just seem to have a talent for making men fall all over themselves to please them?"

Alice hid a rueful smile. "Oh, yeah."

Drake's jaw hardened. "Keep talking, Karen."

"Well, the good news/bad news is that after a while Tucker's charm seems to wear off," Karen said.

Out of the corner of her eye Alice saw a pained expression come and go across Drake's face. But he said nothing.

Karen did not appear to notice.

"Personally, I knew there was something a little weird about her from the start," Karen said. "But, hey, she's some giant-brained scientific type, right? They're probably all a little weird. I figured she was really, really focused on her research project. In any event, it wasn't like I could just walk away from the excavation ruins."

Drake glanced back over his shoulder. "Why not?"

Karen waved a hand to indicate the dark woods. "It's somewhere out there in the frickin' Preserve. Ten steps outside the ruins and you're lost. The only people who can come and go on a regular basis are the security guards. Besides, Pete and I had signed those contracts and the money was really good. We planned to get married and buy a house when the project was finished. Anyhow, a few weeks ago Dr. Tucker really started losing it."

"Define losing it," Drake said.

"She was temperamental from the beginning, but when it became obvious that the Chamber was overheating, she became full-on whacko," Karen said. "That's when two of the security guys took off. That made her crazy for a time."

"What happened to the security guards?" Drake asked.

"Pete and I heard them talking just before they left. They knew the situation inside the Chamber was deteriorating. We heard them making plans to take the boat that they kept in Deception Cove. They used it to bring in supplies."

"There's no boat back there except the one we arrived in," Drake said.

"I'm assuming they got off the island."

"How many guards are left?" Drake asked.

"Only one, the boss of the security team. His name is Quinton. Pete and I are pretty sure that he and Dr. Tucker are lovers. Well, he thinks he's in love with her, at any rate. I doubt if Dr. Tucker has ever loved anyone but herself in her entire life. Quinton is definitely under Tucker's spell, though. I think he'd do anything for her. He pretty much proved it by sticking around after the other two guards took off. Now he's trapped here on the island, same as everyone else."

Drake looked back at Karen again. "How did you get away?"

"With this." Karen took a small crystal flute out of her pocket. "Pete managed to steal it. Dr. Tucker found a few of them when she excavated the underground ruins. The two guards used them to bring in supplies. They used one to get away the other day."

Alice took a closer look at the flute. "What is it?"

"Alien technology," Drake explained briefly. "Harry told me that they turned up a few of these in the aquarium. The flutes can be used to navigate the Preserve to some extent, but their usefulness is limited because they have to be tuned to specific locations."

"In other words, if you don't know where you're going, you can't get there using a flute, is that it?" Alice said.

"Something like that," Drake said.

"This one was tuned to the cove," Karen said. "This morning when I escaped I was able to follow the frequencies."

"Will it work in reverse?" Alice asked. "Can we use it to find this ruin you're talking about?"

"No," Karen said. "Not any longer." She looked at the flute, despair in her eyes. "I barely made it out of the Preserve. The psi levels are too high inside the fence now. They interfered with the tuning. I made it as far as the fence, but the flute gave out entirely when I went through the barrier. Now it's gone flat. Listen."

She blew gently on the crystal flute. There were a few faint jarringly discordant notes and then nothing at all.

Drake stopped and took the flute from her. He turned it in his hand, examining it carefully. "Chief Attridge's wife, Charlotte, might be able to retune it. There's another man on the island who has a talent for tuning, as well. Calvin Dillard. We may have some options." He put the flute in his shirt pocket and started walking again. "Tell me

165

about the research project that Tucker is running."

"All I know is that Dr. Tucker is excavating an underground Alien ruin right here on Rainshadow," Karen said. "There's this big crystal pyramid down there. Lot of energy inside, at least there is now."

Drake pushed through some low-hanging branches. "What's going on down there?"

"When Dr. Tucker found the Chamber, it was shut down. There was energy inside but it was locked in the crystals that form the walls of the pyramid. Dr. Tucker used two other crystals she called the Keys to release the power."

Alice glanced at Drake. "Sounds like the two missing crystals."

"Got to be those damn stones." Drake led the way through a tumble of boulders. "She stuck the two crystals inside the ruin to kick-start it, and now she's got a slow-rolling chain reaction going, one that is so strong it's affecting the entire island. Idiot. How do people like that get PhDs?"

Alice cleared her throat. "I suppose one might ask how people like that get past human resources departments, pass background checks, and manage to obtain security clearances at companies like Sebastian, Inc."

Drake shot her an annoyed look. At least she assumed he was annoyed. The wrap-around glasses made it impossible to read his eyes.

Karen was oblivious to the byplay. She continued with her tale.

"A chain reaction is exactly how Dr. Tucker described the situation," Karen said. "She's getting panicky, I think. She says the only way to shut down the Chamber is to remove the two crystals."

"So?" Alice said. "Why doesn't she do that?"

"She can't," Karen said. "No one can go into the Chamber for more than a minute or two at most now. She's been sending Pete and me into that light furnace every day for the past couple of weeks. She puts a rope around us and pushes us through the gate. But it's so dark in there you can't see anything, and the energy is a full-blown storm. We can only take it for about a minute and then we go unconscious. The bitch drags us out, gives us a few hours' rest, and sends us in again."

"I'm surprised she didn't leave the island while it was still possible to get off," Alice said.

"She waited too long," Drake said. He led the way through some scrubby bushes. "She was so obsessed with her revenge that she couldn't bring herself to cut her losses. Now she's trapped here on Rainshadow."

"Just like us," Alice observed.

"Don't forget Pete," Karen added anxiously. "I promised him that if I got out, I'd try to get help."

Drake automatically glanced at his watch. He appeared irritated again when he realized it was still stopped. He looked up at the sky. Alice did the same. The cloud cover was heavier and darker than ever.

"We need to move faster," Drake said. "We have to make it to Shadow Bay by sundown."

No one argued.

CHAPTER 16

Fear of being caught out in the open after dark proved to be an excellent motivator. They made good time, walking into the tiny community of Shadow Bay shortly before sunset. Relief flashed through Alice when she saw the first buildings and other trappings of civilization.

It had been an arduous trek. Drake had not allowed many rest breaks. Alice was exhausted and she knew that Karen was, also. But the realization that they would not be spending another night outdoors made the physical effort more than worthwhile.

Her initial elation faded quickly. At first glance, Shadow Bay appeared deserted.

"They all left," she whispered, her spirits plunging.

"Oh, *no*," Karen wailed.

There were no passengers waiting at the ferry dock. A small sign announced that the run to Thursday Harbor had been cancelled until further notice. The shops on the short main street were closed and, for the most part, dark. One nearby shop window was illuminated, but the glow came from the unique light of an old-fashioned amber lantern. After a moment, Alice realized that more amber lanterns lit the tavern and a couple of rooms in the small motel above the row of marina shops. Aside from the handful of lamps, however, the town looked empty. It was as if the last person to leave had forgotten to de-rez a few lights.

She reached up to touch Houdini, who was perched on her shoulder. "Does this place remind anyone of that horror movie *Ghost Cove*?"

Karen looked around with growing panic. "Yes, it does."

"Never saw that one," Drake said. He stopped in the middle of the street and surveyed the ominously quiet surroundings. "Did it end well?"

"No," Alice said. "Probably better not to go into the details. What happened here? Do you think your brother managed to evacuate the entire island and then decided to leave, as well? I have to tell you, the thought of being the only people remaining on Rainshadow besides Zara Tucker and her security guard is a little scary."

"And Pete," Karen said anxiously.

"And Pete," Alice added.

"Take it easy," Drake said. "There are people here. But the power is off. That's probably why the shops are closed and the street is empty. Well, that and the incoming fog."

"Where is everyone?" Karen whispered.

As if on cue, a man with long, unkempt hair, a scraggly beard, and fierce eyes appeared from the shadowed space between two weather-beaten buildings. He was dressed in flowing green robes bound at the waist by a leather belt. The belt buckle was set with an amber stone. The leather boots on his feet looked well worn, as if they had seen a great deal of hard wear.

He held a large, hand-lettered sign attached to a narrow wooden post. The sign read, PREPARE FOR THE GLORIOUS DAWN. ARE YOU READY FOR THE RETURN OF THE ANCIENT ONES?

He strode rapidly toward Alice, Drake, and Karen, a man on a mission.

"Welcome, travelers," he intoned. "Do you bring news of the Aliens? Have they returned?"

"Haven't seen any Aliens," Drake said.

"Good." The bearded man nodded solemnly. "You still have time to prepare. You must seek the third level of psychic enlightenment before it is too late. Only those who arrive at the third level will be able to accept the Glorious Dawn that is coming."

"Who are you?" Alice asked.

"My name is Egan. I was sent here with the others to warn the people of Rainshadow that the Glorious Dawn will arrive here first. Many fled. But those who remain will not listen to me. If we are not prepared, the Aliens will take back this world and destroy us in the process. There is very little time left."

"Do you have a plan to reach the third level?" Drake asked.

"The answer lies in dreams," Egan said. He swept out a hand to indicate the dark fog hanging at the edge of the harbor. "Those who cannot or will not achieve the third level will meet their doom in the nightmare fog."

"How do you know all this, Egan?" Alice asked gently.

"The dreams," Egan whispered. He stared at the psi-fog. "I see it all in my dreams. Soon you will know the truth, too."

"Where are the other people in this town?" Karen asked.

Egan frowned, briefly confused by the change of topic. "Those who did not flee are making preparations for the night. With darkness comes the fog, you see." He pointed down the street to the door of one of the shops. "Some of the unenlightened are gathered there. They said that soon others would arrive to join them. You must be the ones they're waiting for. They feared that you wouldn't be able to get to the island in time because of the fog."

Alice realized that he was pointing to a shop illuminated with the light of an amber lantern. The sign over the door read: SHADOW BAY BOOKS.

"Where will you sleep tonight, Egan?" she asked.

"In the marina warehouse," Egan said. "I have a lantern to protect me."

The door of Shadow Bay Books opened. A big, bearded bear of a man came out onto the sidewalk.

"Thought I heard someone out here," he said. He looked at Drake. "I'm Jasper Gilbert. You must be Drake Sebastian. About time you got here. Don't mind telling you that we were starting to get a little worried."

"I'm Drake," Drake said. "This is my wife, Alice. And this is someone we picked up along the way, Karen Rosser."

It was, Alice realized, the second time that

day that Drake had introduced her as his wife, first to Karen and now to a stranger. For some reason she found it unsettling. She was almost overcome with the urge to explain. *I'm not his real wife. It's just an MC and not even a real MC, at that.* Except that it was a real MC.

"Pleased to meet you, ladies," Jasper said. "Good thing you got in ahead of the fog." He glanced back through the doorway. "They're here, Fletch."

An elegant, silver-haired man appeared on the doorstep. The wedding ring he wore matched the ring that Jasper had on his hand.

"Name's Fletcher Kane. I can't tell you how relieved we are to see you." He turned his head to call back into the shop. "Drake Sebastian is here. He's got a couple of friends with him."

"A new friend and my wife," Drake corrected.

Alice glanced at him, wondering why he was putting so much emphasis on her legal status. He gave a small, almost imperceptible shake of his head, making it clear he wanted her to keep quiet about the MC.

A handful of other people rushed out onto the sidewalk. Introductions went quickly.

"Charlotte Attridge now." An attractive,

dark-haired woman with fashionable glasses smiled. "My husband is the chief of police here in Shadow Bay."

A red-haired woman stepped forward. "I'm Rachel Blake. I own this bookstore." She gave Drake an apologetic look. "I'm Harry's fiancée, Drake. Sorry we had to meet like this."

"A pleasure," Drake said.

Rachel gave Alice a quizzical look. "We didn't know that Drake was married. Congratulations."

"Thanks," Alice said, "but it's a little complicated —"

She broke off because Drake was giving her another hard look. She couldn't see his eyes, but it didn't take any psychic talent to know that he wanted her to shut up.

She closed her mouth on what would have been a convoluted explanation of the MC.

"Oh, you have a dust bunny pal, too," Rachel said, delighted.

"This is Houdini," Alice said.

She reached up to take Houdini from her shoulder. But he surprised her by chortling excitedly. Avoiding her hands, he bounded gleefully down to the ground and fluttered through the front door of the shop. Alice heard a responding chortle from inside.

She glanced at Rachel. "You've got another dust bunny here?"

"Darwina. She'll be ecstatic to have a new playmate. But it doesn't take much to make a dust bunny ecstatic."

There was more wild chortling from inside the bookstore and then a sudden silence. "Darwina must have given him one of her last chocolate zingers," Rachel said. "He and Darwina will both be bouncing off the walls in a few minutes."

Charlotte waved everyone indoors. "Come on inside and have some tea. You didn't arrive by boat here in the marina, so I'm guessing you have a story to tell."

"Where is Harry?" Drake asked.

Rachel paused in the doorway to look at him.

"You didn't know?" Rachel asked. "No, I guess you wouldn't have heard. Harry said the last time he talked to you was several days ago. The phones and computers have been down since Monday."

Alice was aware that the others had gone very quiet.

"What's wrong?" Drake asked.

It was Fletcher Kane who answered.

"Harry and Chief Attridge left about forty-eight hours ago. They had to go into the Preserve to track a bunch of those Glorious Dawn twits who decided to go

176

through the fence to get enlightened. They got lost, of course. Harry and Slade went in to pull them out."

"They haven't returned yet," Jasper said. "We're getting concerned, to tell you the truth."

"They're okay," Rachel insisted. "I'd know if something had happened to Harry."

"And I'd know if anything had happened to Slade," Charlotte declared.

Both went into the shop.

Jasper looked at Drake and lowered his voice. "Like I said, we're worried about Harry and Slade."

Chapter 17

"You got caught in the open when that fog rolled in last night?" Rachel Blake asked. She poured tea into the three cups she had placed on the table. "That must have been an absolutely horrible experience."

Alice indicated the amber lantern sitting in the center of one of the tables. "Not nearly as bad as it would have been if Drake hadn't realized that the boat's emergency lantern and a nice big fire muted the effects of the fog's energy. But I have to tell you, it was the mutant insects that made for a long night."

Everyone at the table, with the exception of Drake, stared at her.

"Damn," Charlotte said. "You're not kidding, are you?"

"No," Alice said. "It wasn't a joking matter, believe me."

They were gathered in the café at the back of Shadow Bay Books. It was a motley crew that had come together to figure out how to stop whatever was going on inside the Preserve, Alice thought. The weird thing was that, although she told herself she was part of the group only because she needed the job and because Drake had promised to find Fulton's killer, she felt oddly comfortable with the others. Maybe it was because she had some genuine family history on Rainshadow. In a way, she had a right to be here; make that a responsibility to be here.

It wasn't much in the way of family history, of course. She had not even known that Nicholas North existed until a year ago, let alone her connection to him. In addition, he had evidently been a failure at just about everything except the pirate business. She was pretty sure the only reason he had been successful in that line was because of his partner, Harry Sebastian the first, who had no doubt been the brains of the outfit. Still, North had been involved in burying the crystals that were now causing so much trouble, and Alice was his direct descendant. That linked her to the island and the situation — for better or worse. Either way, she belonged here with these people, at least for now, she thought.

Besides, she liked her new friends. They had welcomed her even though she'd had a hand in creating the problem they now faced. She wanted to help them and undo the damage she had unwittingly caused.

Rachel had prepared a special tisane for the weary travelers. Alice was amazed at how much better she felt after a few sips of the herbal brew. She could see that the tisane was also having a soothing effect on Karen Rosser, who now appeared more composed.

The two dust bunnies, high on chocolate zingers, were dashing around the floor of the bookshop. They appeared to be engaged in some version of a dust bunny game. Darwina clutched a small Amberella doll dressed in a sparkly ball gown. There were occasional crashing sounds when books or other small objects fell to the floor.

Drake picked up his cup and inhaled the aroma of the tisane with obvious appreciation. "Figured the amber lantern might be useful, but the fire worked better because with it for illumination I didn't have to wear my glasses. That gave us an advantage when the insects came out of the Preserve. We used a couple of fire-starters modified for use inside the fence to zap the bugs."

Charlotte shuddered. "Giant mutant insects. How much worse can things get?"

"I don't think we want to find out,"

Fletcher said.

Jasper shook his head. "Gotta say, it's amazing that you both survived the night."

"We spent it watching each other's back," Drake said. "Literally." He looked at Alice across the table. "We maintained physical contact. That helped. And we had Houdini, who functioned as an early warning system."

Fletcher nodded, understanding. "Sounds like the three of you made a good team."

"Yes," Drake said. He did not take his mirrored gaze off Alice. "We do make a good team. Nothing like spending a night zapping giant roaches to find out if you were meant for each other."

He said it very seriously, but the crowd around the table — with the exception of Alice — laughed. The sudden rush of heat into her cheeks told her that she was blushing.

"Probably a more accurate compatibility test than those questionnaires the professional matchmakers use," Charlotte said dryly.

"Yes," Drake said. It was clear he took the comment very seriously. He looked at Alice. "A hell of a lot more accurate."

Frantically, Alice searched for a way to change the conversation.

"When did the Glorious Dawn crowd ar-

181

rive?" she asked quickly.

"That lot came in on the last ferry," Rachel said. She made a face. "No one was expecting them. Slade and Harry were getting as many people off the island as possible. Not everyone was willing to leave, but most of the folks with kids did want to evacuate. Slade and Harry let the Dawn crowd stay because they needed space on the ferry for the Shadow Bay families. They figured they'd get rid of the Dawners on the last run. But there were no more runs. The ferry was never able to get back to the island. Several of the families did not make it off."

"Thus, we got stuck with the Dawners," Jasper explained. "And the first thing they did was head into the Preserve." He sighed. "Slade and Harry thought it would only take a few hours to find them and pull them back out. But that was two days ago."

No one spoke for a moment.

Rachel exchanged a look with Charlotte.

"We keep telling you, they're okay," Charlotte said quietly. "Trust me, Rachel and I would know if that wasn't the case."

Fletcher eyed Karen, who was sitting very quietly and drinking her tea.

"You said that this Dr. Zara Tucker stuck a couple of Old Earth crystals into an Alien ruin to jump-start it and now the place is overheating?"

Karen lowered her cup. "Yes. She wants to get off the island before it blows but she's trapped, too, just like us."

Alice cleared her throat. "I think you should all know that I'm the one who located the Keys."

Charlotte stilled. "The Keys? You mean those three crystals?"

"I was told that's what my great-grandfather called them in his diary," Alice said. "Why? Does that mean something to you?"

"Nothing terribly useful," Charlotte admitted. "But it may explain something I've always wondered about. My aunt Beatrix, who died and left me Looking Glass Antiques across the street, spent the last years of her life searching for something she called the Key. Singular, not plural, but she may not have realized there were three of them. I don't think she even knew what the Key looked like or what it opened."

"Dr. Tucker used those crystal Keys to fire up the Chamber," Karen said. "That's all I can tell you."

Drake finished his tea. "Alice and Karen and I all need some food and some sleep." He looked out the window at the unnatural dark that had fallen in the past half hour. "We need to pull together the information we've got and come up with a plan, but there's nothing we can do until morning."

"You've got that right," Fletcher said. "Shadow Bay was never what you'd call a lively town after dark. We roll up the streets around nine o'clock most nights. But lately it's gotten real quiet at night. You can move around to some extent with an amber lantern, but that fog makes people nervous as hell."

"Folks think they see things in it," Rachel said. "And now that we know about those mutant insects in Deception Cove, we have to take the hallucinations a little more seriously."

"Everyone who couldn't get off the island or who refused to leave is staying here in town," Fletcher explained. "Jasper and I are sleeping in our shop."

"Rachel and I are staying at the B-and-B at the end of the street," Charlotte said. "We can squeeze Karen in there, but the place is really full. I think Burt Caster, who owns the Marina Inn and Tavern, mentioned that he had one room left. Drake, you and Alice can have it."

Alice went very still. She did not dare look at Drake.

"That works," Drake said.

Rachel gave Alice a commiserating smile. "I'll bet you didn't expect to spend your honeymoon on Rainshadow, did you?"

"Actually," Alice said, "it's become something of a tradition for me."

CHAPTER 18

"You know," Alice said, "if we hadn't already spent a couple of nights together, this situation would be somewhat awkward."

Room Number Five at the Marina Inn had seen better days. The curtains, carpet, bedspread, and towels were faded and a bit frayed, but the bathroom and the sheets were clean, and that counted for a lot in her opinion. During the past year she had learned to establish priorities. Nevertheless, in the low, mellow light of the amber lantern on the table, the place didn't look all that bad. Under other circumstances, it might even have been romantic in a retro sort of way. The kind of place where a young, broke, eloping couple might spend a honeymoon.

But she could not remember a time when she had felt young, and she was married — temporarily at least — to one of the wealthiest men in the four city-states. True, they had eloped, but not for the usual reasons.

When they had entered the room a moment ago, Drake had done a methodical walk-through of the small space. Houdini had followed at his heels, evidently taking the job of checking out the room as seriously as Drake. There was none of the usual dust bunny obsession with turning the nearest bright, shiny object into a toy; no trying to swing from the drapery cord. At first Alice had wondered if the effects of the chocolate zingers had simply worn off, but now she sensed that, like Drake, Houdini was in sentry mode.

"Charlotte and Rachel probably could have made space for you over at the B-and-B," Drake said. "But I didn't want to go into detailed explanations of exactly why we got married, not in front of a lot of people we don't know very well." He shrugged out of the pack and dropped it on the small table near the window. "Figured that would be even more awkward."

"You're right." Alice smiled ruefully. "Explaining to a bunch of strangers that you married me to protect me from Ethel Whitcomb, who thinks I murdered her son, would have been a tad difficult."

"That wasn't the part that worried me."

"No?"

"No." He opened the pack. "I held off on the explanations because this is a small town. It's even smaller now that the few locals who are still here are all hunkered down. I trust everyone at that table tonight, primarily because Harry told me that he trusts them. But there are no secrets in small towns. If word gets out that our marriage is a fake, there's no telling who will find out."

Alice looked out the window. The dark mist had closed in on Shadow Bay. Here and there she could see the weak light of an amber lantern in a window or the flames of a hearth fire, but the rest of the scene was drenched in dark, disturbing energy.

"I don't think that any gossip will get off this island as long as it's locked in this fog," she said.

"We can't be sure of that. I'd rather not take any chances."

"Are you going to tell your brother the truth about our marriage when he returns?" she asked. *Assuming he does return,* she thought. But there was no reason to sound pessimistic. Drake had enough to cope with at the moment.

"I'll have to explain the situation to Harry." Drake removed his overnight kit from the pack. "He'll know there's something off about the marriage as soon as he finds out about it."

Alice wrinkled her nose. "Because we don't look like a happily married couple?"

"No." Drake studied the fog-bound scene through the window. "Because in our family we don't do MCs."

Her insides clenched but she tried not to let him see the effect his words had on her.

"I suppose MCs are way too tacky for the Sebastian family," she said, going for flippant. "Always nice to meet a man with such high standards." Guilt flashed through her. "Sorry," she said gruffly. "That was uncalled for under the circumstances. Our MC is certainly not typical."

"It's not so much a question of standards — more like a definition. In my family, marriage is marriage. An affair is an affair. There is no middle ground."

"In other words, in your family, when it comes to making a commitment, there's no gray area. You either make a commitment and keep it or you don't."

He gave her a wary look. "Something like that."

"What a lovely, noble tradition. Very admirable. Yet here you are, stuck in a low-class MC thanks to me. Yep, I can see why you feel like you have to explain things to your brother. Sorry about that, but if you will recall, it was your idea."

"Yes," he said a little too evenly. "It was my idea. And it's not like Harry did things perfectly, either. He went through a full-blown Covenant Marriage ceremony, but his wife divorced him three weeks after the wedding."

"Really?" Alice stared at him, astonished. "I didn't hear about that."

"Probably because a lot of money was spent keeping the scandal out of the media."

"I see. Wow." Alice thought about that. The dissolution of a Covenant Marriage was not unheard of, but it was rare because it was a legal and financial nightmare that always left a social stigma. "Mind if I ask what the grounds for the divorce were?"

"It was granted under the new laws governing divorce. Harry's ex claimed intolerable psychical incompatibility."

"Geez. Must have cost a fortune."

Drake smiled wryly. "Like I said, money can't buy everything but it comes in handy at times."

"That's for sure." Alice took a deep breath. "Okay, thanks for the family background. That makes me feel a little better about getting you into this mess."

Drake stopped smiling. "You didn't get

me into it. The MC was my idea, remember?"

"I know, but —" She stopped because she did not know where to go with that.

Drake surveyed the room with a grim expression. "And while we're on the subject, I apologize for the accommodations."

"Not a problem." Alice sat down on the bed, leaned back, and braced herself on her hands. "I've lived in worse places. You saw that apartment I was renting in Crystal City. This is a real step up. It's . . . cozy."

He watched her through his glasses. "I was apologizing for the lack of privacy, not the lack of luxury."

"Oh, well, that can't be helped. You heard the woman at the front desk. This is the last available room. We're lucky we're not going to be sleeping on the floor in the lobby. What do you say we go downstairs to the tavern and get some dinner? Don't know about you but I'm hungry."

Drake seemed to relax. "Sounds like a plan."

"Also, I could use a drink."

"That, too, sounds like an excellent idea."

The Tavern on the first floor was lit with amber lanterns and crowded with locals who were spending the night at the inn. The mood was that of a community under siege, Alice thought. In spite of the fact that almost every table was filled, a dark, subdued atmosphere pervaded the rustic space. Some of the booths and tables were occupied by families. The parents talked in hushed tones. The kids were unnaturally quiet.

A boy who appeared to be about thirteen sat at a table with a woman who looked the right age to be his grandmother — a young grandmother. She was blonde with a fit, athletic figure and she wore a police uniform complete with a mag-rez pistol. There was another person at the table, a young man in his early twenties. He, too, wore a uniform with a patch embroidered SBPD.

The kid brightened when Alice walked in with Houdini on her shoulder.

"Hey, look, the lady has a dust bunny," he said to a friend.

The other youngsters in the restaurant turned around to look at Alice. The little ones jumped up and came running.

"Can we pet him?" a small, dark-haired girl asked eagerly.

"What's his name?" an older boy asked.

Sensing that he had an audience, Houdini went into high-rez cute mode. He bounced a little and chortled a greeting.

Alice found herself surrounded by a small throng of excited children. She took Houdini off her shoulder and set him on the back of a chair.

"His name is Houdini," she said. "And I don't think he would mind if you pet him."

Drake looked at her. "You and Houdini entertain the kids. I'll get us some food."

He went to the counter to put in an order. There was a harried-looking cook laboring over an old-fashioned stove that was operating off an ancient amber-fueled generator.

The kids gathered around Houdini's chair. The small girl reached out to give him a tentative pat. Houdini chirped encouragingly.

"Houdini is a magician," Alice said. "He can disappear."

"Yeah?" The boy who had been sitting with the police officers looked skeptical. "Will he do it for us?"

"I think so, if you ask him nicely. What's your name?"

"Devin Reed. That's my grandmother over there. She's a police officer. Her name is Myrna Reed. And that's Officer Willis with her. They're in charge because the chief is gone for a while."

Alice glanced at Myrna, who nodded and gave her a grateful smile. The adults in the room were quietly scared, Alice thought, and trying not to show it for the sake of the children.

She turned back to the small audience and put a hand on Houdini. "What do you say, Mr. Houdini? Will you do your vanishing act for us?"

Houdini chortled happily.

"That means yes," Alice said.

She kicked up her talent, generating a little energy through her hand.

There was a collective gasp when Houdini vanished. He chortled again. The sound, coming as it did out of thin air, caused an excited murmur to run through the crowd. Alice realized it wasn't just the kids who were watching now. Several of the adults in the room were also paying attention.

"How did he do that?" Devin asked. "Tell us how the trick works."

"Professional magicians never give away their secrets except to students of the art who are serious about becoming professional illusionists," Alice said. "Besides, if you knew how it worked, it wouldn't be any fun. Houdini, please reappear."

She lowered her talent. Houdini popped back into view.

"Can he make other stuff disappear?" one of the kids asked.

"Oh, sure," Alice said. She picked up a spoon and held it out to Houdini. They had done the trick many times before. He gripped the end of the spoon in one paw. Alice kept her hold on the other end and generated a little energy. The spoon vanished.

A chorus of oohs and aahs swept through the crowd of youngsters. There were more suggestions from the audience.

"Make the dish vanish," someone said.

"No, make the whole table disappear," the dark-haired girl pleaded.

Alice and Houdini went to work. Together they made the saltshaker, the small bouquet of artificial flowers, and a paper napkin vanish. When Drake started back toward the table with a tray of pizza and a couple of beers, Alice decided to go for the wow factor. She positioned Houdini on the table.

"Mr. Houdini will now make the table vanish," she intoned. "Leaving him suspended in midair."

The kids waited, breathless with anticipation. Alice heard several chairs scrape on the floor as a number of adults moved closer for a better view.

"Are you ready?" Alice asked.

There was a chorus of yesses.

She touched the table. "Mr. Houdini,

please make the table vanish."

Houdini chortled and bounced up and down. He knew the applause line. Alice sent a heavy pulse of energy through her fingertips. The table vanished, leaving only Houdini and the artificial flowers.

The kids shouted with glee. Houdini was in the zone now. He dashed in circles around the top of the table, looking as if he was running in midair. He paused to pull one of the artificial flowers out of the little vase. He waved the flower madly at his audience, who responded with gleeful shouts.

Drake stopped a few steps away and met Alice's eyes. He smiled.

"And the crowd goes wild," he said.

Alice lowered her talent. The table popped back into view. There was a round of applause, much of it coming from the adults.

"But how does he do it?" a boy asked.

"I told you, Houdini's a professional magician," Alice said. "He has his secrets. But between you and me, I'm pretty sure it's just a trick of the light."

Drake set the tray of pizza and beer down on the table. He gave one of the slices to Houdini, who set to it with his usual enthusiasm for anything edible. Alice took her seat and reached for a slice.

She was about to take a bite when Devin's

grandmother stopped at the table.

"I'm Myrna Reed," she said.

There was a short round of introductions.

"I'd say welcome to Rainshadow," Myrna said, "but I imagine that, under the circumstances, you'd both rather be anywhere else but here. The chief told Officer Willis and me to expect you. He said the two of you were going to help out with the problem in the Preserve. I just wanted to say thanks."

"You're welcome," Alice said. "But I'm not the one who is going to fix whatever is going down inside the Preserve. Drake and his brother are the magicians on that job. I'm just the box-jumper."

Myrna frowned. "Box-jumper?"

"The magician's assistant." Alice glanced at Houdini, who had devoured his pizza and was now table-hopping madly around the room, enjoying his stardom. "Pretty much the same job that I have with Houdini."

Myrna smiled. "What you did just now with the kids, that was good. They loved it. The parents appreciated it, too. Things have been a little tense here. You can feel the difference in the mood now. You lightened up things for a while."

"Magic," Drake said.

He wasn't looking at Houdini. He was looking at Alice.

CHAPTER 19

The sound of the door opening and closing brought Alice out of a restless sleep. She came awake on a hot tide of energy, leaping from the bed and instinctively rezzing her talent.

By the time she was fully awake she was on her feet, facing the door.

"It's okay," Drake said. He spoke calmly, as if her over-rezzed reaction was perfectly normal. "Houdini wanted out. He was very clear about it. I assumed it was all right so I opened the door for him."

She felt the energy level rise a little in the atmosphere and knew that Drake had jacked up his talent so that he could see her. If he found that necessary, it meant she was doing a fade.

She took a deep breath and dropped back into her normal senses. She had to give Drake credit, she thought. Most men would have freaked at the sight of a woman jumping out of bed and disappearing into thin air. But it would take a lot to make Drake freak.

"Sure, that's fine," she said. "I told you, he often goes out at night. He'll be back before dawn." She hesitated. "Sorry about the disappearing act a minute ago."

"No problem."

Drake rezzed the lock and moved toward the chair in front of the window. He was wearing the trousers and clean T-shirt that he had produced from his pack. For her part she was still in the long-sleeved black pullover and the black trousers she had stuffed into her own pack. In the morning she was going to have to do some hand washing in the bathroom sink.

Earlier she had stretched out on top of the bed to get some sleep. She had expected Drake to settle down beside her. The bed was certainly large enough for two. It should not have been any more complicated than sitting back-to-back until dawn last night, she thought. Then again, maybe it would have been more complicated. Something about a bed changed things. In any event, Drake had insisted on dozing in the reading chair, his feet propped on the small hassock.

He came to a stop in front of the window

and looked at her. "Good thing no one can see either of us now. We're not exactly dressed like honeymooners, are we?"

She wrinkled her nose. "No, but we're not your typical honeymooning couple."

"And Rainshadow is not your typical honeymoon destination."

"It certainly is for me," Alice said.

"There is a pattern developing," Drake conceded.

They both smiled. Alice relaxed somewhat.

Drake looked at her for a moment longer and then turned away to contemplate the night on the other side of the window. "The fog has gotten a lot heavier in the past hour."

"It's midnight." She came to stand beside him. "According to the legends, they used to call this time of night the witching hour on the Old World."

"This is the paranormal equivalent of high noon. If you don't understand the science of para-physics, the effects can look a lot like magic."

They stood together in the sphere of golden light produced by the amber lantern and looked out at the darkness.

Alice folded her arms. "It's not nearly as bad as it was last night in the cove," she said. "It helps being indoors."

"It also helps that this sector of the island isn't nearly as hot as the Deception Cove region."

"But this area will get hotter if we don't find Zara Tucker and those missing crystals."

"We'll find her," Drake said.

"Good."

"And then we'll take care of Ethel Whitcomb."

"Excellent."

"Alice?"

"Yes?"

"About that kiss in the garage after we got our MC papers."

She went very still. "I thought we agreed to pretend it never happened."

"That was your plan, not mine. I've never been very good at pretending. I'm more of a facts-on-the-ground kind of guy."

"You're the guy in the audience who can't enjoy the magic because he's always trying to figure out how it's done."

"Yeah, that's me, the boring guy who just wants to know what's real and what isn't."

She pursed her lips, uncertain how to react to the edge on his words.

"That's not quite what I meant," she said.

"That kiss in the garage felt real to me. Just wondered how it felt on your end."

"It *was* real." She unfolded her arms and spread her hands wide. "I never said it wasn't. But a kiss is just a kiss."

In the shadows she could see that his mouth was etched with amusement. "Why does that sound familiar?"

"I have no idea. Look, what I'm trying to say is, it's the *reason* I kissed you that's complicated."

"Has it occurred to you that you're the one who's making it complicated? There is such a thing as overanalyzing."

She stared at him in disbelief. "This from the facts-on-the-ground man?"

He put his hands on her shoulders. "Let's just stick to what we know to be true."

"Which is?"

"That kiss in the garage was a really interesting kiss," he said.

"It was?" She was suddenly a little breathless.

"Very high-rez," Drake said. "At least, that's how it felt on my end."

"It was sort of over the top, wasn't it?" She frowned. "I really can't explain that aspect of things. I mean, there was the stress factor and all, but, generally speaking, that's not my usual style when it comes to kissing."

"What is your usual style?"

"I'm not sure I've got one, to be honest. I've been told I'm repressed."

"Repressed."

"I'm unable to commit emotionally to a relationship," she explained. "Therefore I can't really enjoy sex. Something to do with a combination of abandonment issues and my weird para-psych profile."

"Who told you that?"

"A para-psychologist. After I got rejected by three matchmaking agencies it was suggested that I seek counseling."

"Did the shrink offer any guidance?"

"He suggested sex therapy. With him. I declined."

"I'm glad to hear that," Drake said. "Can I ask why you declined?"

"There were little velvet handcuffs and small whips involved. I'm not opposed to little velvet handcuffs and small whips in principle, you understand. At least, I don't think I am. I haven't actually tried any of those things. But somehow in that particular context they did not appeal."

"That particular context being the para-shrink's office?" Drake asked.

"And the fact that he was in a Marriage of Convenience," she said. "That sort of pissed me off, if you want to know the truth. Sure, it was just an MC, not a full Covenant

Marriage, but an MC is supposed to be some sort of a commitment, isn't it? At least while it lasts?"

"Yes," Drake said. "It's supposed to be a commitment while it lasts. Mind if I turn off the lantern?"

She stilled. "Okay."

He de-rezzed the lamp, plunging the room into darkness. But this was normal darkness and with her talent she could see well enough to make out shadows and shapes. She knew exactly when Drake removed his glasses and set them down on the table because she could see his eyes. They were psi-hot with a silvery energy that made her catch her breath.

"And while we're on the subject," he said, "I'd like to say that you're wrong about not having a style. Judging by that garage kiss, your style is very high-rez."

"Thanks, but I'm pretty sure it was just an anomaly." Her voice sounded husky, even to her own ears. "I mean, I've never kissed anyone like that before in my whole life. Doubt if I ever will again."

"Let's run an experiment and see what happens."

She stared at him, dazed. "You really want to do this?"

"Oh, yeah," he said. "More than anything

else in the world."

"Well, okay, but just so you know, according to my para-psych profile, I'm not a very passionate person by nature."

"A number of people have labeled me as cold-blooded."

"Your competitors and business rivals, no doubt." She braced her hands on his shoulders. "That's not quite the same thing as sexually repressed."

"You know what? I don't give a damn about our para-psych profiles right now."

She sucked in a deep breath and took the leap.

"Neither do I," she said. "I mean, how bad could it be if we had sex?"

"That's it, think positive."

He took her mouth, slowly, deliberately, completely. This time he was fully in charge of the kiss. He was not asking for a response; he was seducing one from her.

This was not the reckless wildfire of a kiss that she had ignited in the parking garage when she had gone a little crazy. This was an intense, smoldering kiss infused with the energy of Drake's talent.

There was definitely nothing cold-blooded about this kiss, she thought. A thrilling rush of heat swirled in the atmosphere and sizzled in her blood. This kiss was warming all the cold places inside her, setting fire to her senses. That made it a truly dangerous kiss, and the full measure of the peril in which she found herself was that, in that moment, she did not give a damn about the potentially disastrous aftermath. She would worry about the fallout later.

There was always time to regret a mistake, but a woman did not often get an opportunity to make a mistake as exciting as this one promised to be.

She closed her hands very tightly around Drake's shoulders and let the raw power of the kiss sweep through her.

Drake tightened his hold on her until she was pressed so intimately against him she could feel the fiercely rigid outline of his erection through the fabric of their clothing. Everything about him was hard and compellingly male. His scent stirred things deep inside her. She wanted him in ways she had never wanted any man. Most of all she wanted to leave her mark on him. When this was over she wanted him to remember her.

Maybe in the future he would think of her as that woman in the parking garage, the one he'd zapped giant bugs with one memorable night. But that was better than having him forget her.

She felt his hands slide down her rib cage until his fingers settled around her waist under the pullover. He was so much bigger and stronger than she was. More to the point, he could see her even when she did her disappearing act, rendering her primary defense mechanism useless. She was here with him tonight only because he believed she could help solve the problem on Rainshadow — a problem she had helped cause. It was hardly the most romantic reason for a one-night stand.

All things considered, she probably should have locked herself in the bathroom. Instead she was locked in a senses-searing embrace.

There would be a price to pay later but not tonight. Tonight was about learning to fly.

He seized the hem of the black pullover and hauled it upward, tugging it over her head. He tossed the garment over the back of the chair, then reached behind her and unsnapped the clasp of her bra. He added the lingerie to the growing pile of discarded clothing.

At that point he paused, closed his powerful hands around her waist, and looked at her.

"You are perfect," he said. His voice was rough around the edges and his eyes were molten. "So perfect."

That was not true, she thought, but it was very sweet of him to say it. No one else had ever said those words to her.

Tears filled her eyes. She blinked them away and managed a misty smile. "Not perfect, but thank you."

He tightened his hands around her waist and lifted her straight off her feet and into the air. Suddenly she was dangling above him, looking down into his blazing eyes. Startled, she instinctively clutched his shoulder with one hand to steady herself and used her other hand to push her hair out of her face.

"What the heck?" she gasped.

"You are perfect," he repeated. "Perfect for me."

The words sounded more like a vow than a simple statement.

Delight flooded her senses. She loved the feeling of his strong shoulders. She laughed and kicked her feet a little in midair.

"That's good," she said. "That's very good. Because I have to tell you that you are perfect for me, too."

"That's good," he said. "That's very good."

She could not see him clearly enough in the deep shadows to be certain of his expression, but she could hear the wickedly male smile that edged the words.

He carried her across the room and set her on her feet beside the bed. She was shivering with the thrill of what was happening. She grabbed the headboard to steady herself while Drake yanked aside the faded bedspread and quilt.

In an effort to show that she was not just a passenger on this high-risk ride, she fumbled with the fastening of her pants but for some reason her fingers were not functioning properly.

Drake caught her wrists and put her arms around his neck. He went to work getting her out of her pants.

"Just hang on to me," he whispered into her ear. "I'll take care of the details. I'm good with details."

"I know," she said.

He stripped her pants and panties down over her hips and let the clothes fall to her ankles. His hands closed around the curves of her rear. He squeezed gently, flexing his fingers. She heard him groan. The sound came from somewhere deep inside, a low, husky growl of raw male desire. The knowledge that he wanted her so fiercely sent her into the hot zone. She was already wet and he had not even touched her down there.

Energy danced in the atmosphere. There was power in the room — hers as well as his. Her senses sparked and flashed the way they had in the parking garage. She was suddenly free in a way she had never before experienced. She kissed Drake's throat, inhaling his scent, and grabbed the bottom edge of his T-shirt. He laughed a little when she practically tore off his shirt and flung it aside.

She flattened her palms on his chest. He was hard and sleek and very warm to the touch. She knew that some of the heat was paranormal in nature. He was running hot. The wavelengths generated by sexual desire came from the paranormal as well as the normal ends of the spectrum — the more one was aroused, the more heat infused the aura.

Not that it took psychic talent to recognize serious lust in a man. But if a woman happened to have a fair amount of paranormal sensitivity, the fires of a very strong passion were all the more evident. Alice looked into Drake's eyes and glimpsed the cauldron that burned below the surface. Heat lightning flashed through her. She had this effect on him. Her sense of her own feminine power acted like an aphrodisiac.

Dazed and nearly euphoric with excitement and an aching anticipation, she wrapped her hands around Drake's neck and kissed him with all the sultry energy that was shuddering through her.

"That's it," he said. "That's what I've been waiting for. That's what I want from you. That's what I need."

He lifted her out of her clothing, swung her around, and set her on the bed. She pulled up the sheet to cover her lower body and braced herself on her elbows to watch him undress. He made short work of getting out of his pants and briefs.

He came to her fully, heavily aroused, his body hot with the psi-fever of desire. She was wet and achingly full and clenched. A great sense of urgency tightened everything inside her.

Drake stretched out on top of her, bracing himself on his arms, caging her on the bed. He kissed her mouth and then her throat and then her breasts. When she struggled, trying to make him move more quickly, he used his greater strength to gently overwhelm her, forcing her to let him set the pace. His hands went lower, finding the damp, hot, throbbing place between her legs.

He eased one finger inside her and then another. She moaned and clawed at his shoulders. She took a savage feminine satisfaction in discovering that his back was slick with sweat. The act of self-restraint was not easy for him. He was paying a price.

He found the tight bud at the top of her sex with his thumb and pressed upward. She gasped and clamped herself around him, straining for more, demanding more.

He stroked her, his mouth wet and hot on her breasts, until she sank her nails into his shoulders, until she drew up her knees and reached down to take him in her hand.

"Alice," he groaned. *"Alice."*

He abandoned the sensual battle and pushed himself slowly, carefully, into her, forging a path that stretched her so tightly she wondered if she would be able to hold him. For a moment the intense sensation hovered on the thrilling borderline between pain and pleasure. She was not sure which would prevail.

"So damn good," he got out on a grating whisper.

He rose on his elbows and began to move in and out of her in a slow, relentless cadence that maddened her senses.

It was neither pain nor pleasure that prevailed. Instead it was a deep need for something more; it was a need for release.

She raised her hips to take him deeper,

her whole body clenching around him.

"Yes," she whispered. Her nails scored his back. "Yes."

He surged into her again and again, angling his thrusts so that he was constantly pushing against that special, swollen place just inside her, until she could not stand the mounting pressure any longer.

The climax struck in a small explosion of sensation that rippled through her in waves.

She heard Drake's half-muffled roar of satisfaction, felt him lock into her one last time, and then the heavy waves of his release spilled into her, blistering her senses.

In that moment she could have sworn that the room was illuminated with a shimmering aurora of dark light. It ignited a breathtakingly intimate resonance between their auras. It seemed to Alice that, for a moment, she and Drake were connected in a way that seemed to defy the laws of para-physics.

Just a trick of the light, she thought.

CHAPTER 20

The bastard was on the island. With a wife, no less. It was obvious that Drake had seduced Alice North into a Marriage of Convenience to gain her cooperation. It was too much.

Zara Tucker snatched up the nearest object — a small green quartz bowl — and hurled it against the nearest green quartz wall. There was a sharp crack of sound when the indestructible dish struck the impervious quartz wall.

The bowl dropped to the quartz floor, undamaged. The wall showed no evidence of the impact. Nothing humans had ever devised, not even heavy earth-moving machinery, could put so much as a dent in the psi-infused quartz. The Aliens had used the stone to construct not only many small artifacts like the bowl but also entire cities and the network of catacombs beneath the surface of Harmony.

Zara ignored the bowl on the floor and started to pace the vast underground cavern. Nothing had gone right since the two-story pyramid that occupied most of the space had begun to overheat. The energy coming off the Dream Chamber was now so intense she knew it was only a matter of time before it exploded.

At first she had been convinced that she could shut down the process. But after several attempts using her two research assistants, she was now forced to accept the reality of the situation. It was infuriating to realize that she — the brilliant Dr. Zara Tucker — had made a terrible mistake by inserting only two of the Keys. The result was a chain reaction of unstable paranormal energy that had gone undetected until a few weeks ago.

It was only after the dark fog had developed that she had been forced to acknowledge that the energy inside the pyramid was affecting the ocean currents, tides, and weather around the island. And now the wildlife as well.

The arrival of Harry Sebastian a few weeks ago had thrown her into a near panic, but she had hoped that he would leave after he discovered one of the Keys. Instead he had not only remained on the island, he had opened up an investigation into the bizarre changes that were affecting everything inside the Preserve.

Whatever was happening inside the pyramid had reached a critical point. The fog had settled in with a vengeance, cutting off the island from the outside world. Sebastian and Attridge were evidently trapped somewhere inside the Preserve along with the Glorious Dawn crowd. At least they would not be a problem now. If the disorienting effects of the fog did not send them plunging into a crevasse or one of the flooded caves to be devoured by the bizarre sea creatures lurking inside, sooner or later they would encounter a few of the rapidly evolving spiders and insects. It was a known fact that mag-rez pistols and other high-tech weapons were worse than useless inside the psi-fence.

So, no need to worry about Harry Sebastian and Attridge, she thought, trying to steady her nerves. *That leaves the day-blind bastard and his wife.*

The roiling fever of her long-festering hatred of Drake Sebastian threatened to overwhelm her. She thought she had taken her revenge. Drake did his best to keep a low profile, but as the president and CEO-in-waiting of Sebastian, Inc., he could not entirely avoid the public eye. Every time she saw a picture of him in the business pages of the newspapers or caught a video showing him at a social event or a fund-raiser, she got a rush of satisfaction.

Drake was condemned to wear the special mirrored sunglasses that were the mark of her vengeance. Every day when he faced a new dawn he was forced to remember her. For Drake, it was always night.

"I told you that you would never forget me," she said.

A lot of high-rez talents who suffered a catastrophic loss of their para-senses plunged into deep depression. Suicide was not uncommon. So were hallucinogenic drugs. She had anticipated that Drake would self-destruct after she destroyed much of his talent. She had looked forward to watching him spiral down into a bottomless pit of despair.

Instead, he had become the man the business world called the Magician — the brilliant strategist that Sebastian, Inc. relied on to close the deal. The man who was slated to take over the family empire.

Bastard, she thought.

How he had successfully piloted a boat through the bizarre currents around the island and navigated the nightmarish fog was anyone's guess. The only explanation was sheer luck. But not even luck could explain how Drake and Alice North had survived the night out in the open on the beach, rescued Karen Rosser, and hiked around the coastline all the way to Shadow Bay.

It was as if the universe was conspiring against her.

Nothing had gone right. The only good news was that Drake was trapped in Shadow Bay and cut off from the outside world just like everyone else in the small town.

"Just like I am." She managed a grim smile. "We're star-crossed lovers, you and I, Drake. If Rainshadow blows, we will die together. Wouldn't that be romantic?"

If things went that far south, she would make certain that — come hell or nightmare fog — Drake Sebastian knew that she was the one responsible for his death and the death of everyone else on the island.

But she was far from ready to give up. In some ways, just knowing that Drake was on Rainshadow was energizing. She would find a way out of this situation. Afterward she would destroy the bastard.

No half measures next time.

CHAPTER 21

Drake felt Alice slide out from under his arm and get to her feet. Energy shivered in the air. He knew that she had jacked up her senses a little.

"Hang on, I'll light the lantern for you," he said.

"It's okay. I've got some paranormal night vision thanks to my talent."

He put on his glasses and hit the lantern button, anyway. A soft glow illuminated the room.

"Thanks," Alice said.

She disappeared into the bathroom. He heard water run in the sink. The toilet flushed. Alice reappeared wearing a towel wrapped around her body.

He folded one arm behind his head and admired the view of Alice lit with paranormal energy. The towel was not an over-sized luxury spa bath sheet. It was a cheap little towel and it did not cover much. That was a good thing, he thought. He immediately got hard.

She scrambled back under the covers. In the process she lost her grip on the front of the towel. It slipped off altogether. When she finally got the sheet pulled up to her chin, she glared at him.

"Don't you dare laugh at me," she warned.

"I'm not laughing."

"You're smiling."

"Okay, I may be smiling," he conceded.

"Hah. I knew it." She was quiet for a moment. "I hope Houdini is all right."

"He'll be fine." Drake shoved aside the covers, swung his legs over the side of the bed, and got to his feet. "You're pretty shy for someone who spent the past year on the stage."

"I don't go on stage naked." She fluffed up her thin pillow. "And for your information, I've got a right to be shy at this particular moment. I barely know you and here I am in bed with you."

He was surprised by the flash of irritation that zapped through him.

"Here you are married to me," he corrected.

"That, too. Boy, this has turned into one strange road trip. My life is starting to remind me of that children's story *Alice in*

Amberland. You know, the one where the heroine falls down a dust bunny hole and winds up in a sort of alternate universe where everything is weird."

"You think this situation, you and me here together, is weird? Looks pretty damn straightforward and normal to me. We're married. We had excellent sex. At least it was excellent from my standpoint."

To his surprise and further irritation, she gave that some close thought.

"Yes, it was," she finally agreed, sounding somewhat astonished. "That's the first time I've had an orgasm without the assistance of a small personal appliance."

"Yeah?"

"You know, you're right," she said.

"I am?"

"I'm overreacting. A man and a woman are thrown together in stressful circumstances. They are attracted to each other and they wind up in bed together. It happens."

"Right," he growled. "It happens. But you left out the part about the man and the woman getting married."

He stalked into the bathroom.

When he came back out, he settled down on his side of the bed, very aware of the distance between himself and Alice. He turned off the lantern and took off his glasses.

"Don't," he said.

She turned her head on the pillow to look at him. "Don't what?"

"Don't try to blame what happened between us on stress."

There was a small silence.

"I would think that a facts-on-the-ground guy would want explanations for everything," she said after a moment.

"Some things don't need explaining."

"Okay."

"Some facts are just facts," he said.

"Right."

"You said it yourself, the sex was pretty fantastic. That's a simple, straightforward fact. It doesn't need any further analysis."

She put her fingertip on his chest and drew an invisible line straight down to his serious erection. She encircled him with her fingers.

"No more analysis," she promised.

She started to kiss him, her wet, warm mouth following the path that she had traced with her fingertip.

"Alice," he whispered. He reached down and tangled his fingers through her hair. "Alice."

CHAPTER 22

The scratching at the door and a soft, muffled chortle brought Drake out of a dream that involved an endless hallway lined with doors. Each time he opened a door he was blinded by a blazing sun. Somewhere in the hall, Zara Tucker laughed.

"Houdini," Alice mumbled into the pillow. "About time he got home."

"I'll let him in," Drake said.

"Thanks."

Dawn was approaching. Drake groped for his sunglasses and got them on before he opened his eyes.

He climbed out of bed and opened the door. A single amber lantern glowed at one end of the hall near the stairs. Houdini bustled into the room, chortling a cheerful greeting. He hopped up onto the bed.

"Hey there, pal." Alice stirred and reached out to pat him. "I was getting worried."

Houdini submitted briefly to a few pats

and then stretched out on his back at the foot of the bed, all six paws in the air. He closed his baby blue eyes.

Drake took off his glasses and went back to the bed. He stood there for a moment, studying the sleeping Houdini.

"What are you thinking?" Alice asked.

Drake got back under the covers and folded his arms behind his head. "I'm thinking that you don't know where Houdini goes when he disappears, but he always knows how to find you."

"So?"

"The same is true of Zara Tucker. We don't know where she's hiding, but she knows where Shadow Bay is located. If she can move about inside the Preserve, she can probably get here, or more likely send someone here, assuming she's still got that one security guard left."

Alice sat up, alarmed. "Why would she do that?"

"One thing I know about Zara: she hates me. She also knows I'm the one person on the island who might be able to help her retrieve those two Keys. When she finds out I'm in Shadow Bay, she'll make a move. She won't be able to help herself."

"How will she find out you're here? From

the sound of things, she's as cut off as we are."

"According to Karen Rosser, Zara always seems to know what is going on here in town. She's probably using the flutes to navigate the Preserve."

"Wouldn't someone in Shadow Bay notice if a gorgeous mad scientist showed up on occasion?"

He thought about Zara's uncanny ability to charm the male species. "Not if she's using some man in town as her spy."

Alice regarded him with a somber expression. "If you're right, her spy could be any man in Shadow Bay. Officer Willis, the cook in the tavern tonight, one of the men we saw in the restaurant. And then there are the folks staying at the B-and-Bs."

"True. But we aren't without our own resources. Harry says Rachel has a talent for aura reading. And Charlotte's a high-level talent. Her intuition is probably way above average. Both of them are well acquainted with the locals. They'd know if someone was acting out of character. We've also got Fletcher Kane and Jasper Gilbert. They're former hunters, according to Harry. He trusts them. And they know the locals, too."

"Yes, but they are men. According to you,

they'd be vulnerable to Zara's charm."

Drake smiled. "I think they're safe. From what I've witnessed, Zara's talent for seduction is based on opposite-sex attraction. Kane and Gilbert are married."

Understanding brightened Alice's expression. "You think the fact that they're gay makes them immune to her?"

"Yes. Trust me, I've had good reason to delve into Zara Tucker's background. I found no record of her using women or gay men for her purposes."

"So your plan is to alert Charlotte, Rachel, Fletcher, and Jasper to the possibility that there's a spy here in our midst and ask them to vet every hetero male left in town."

"Not much of a plan, is it?"

"Actually, it sounds brilliant." Alice hugged her knees. "We've got the perfect locked-room mystery setup, except that our locked room is a small town. Same principle, though. All the suspects are gathered together in one convenient place. What's more, we've got a motive. Our spy is the victim of a calculated seduction. He thinks he's in love, or at least in lust. The task now is to start working through the list of straight men in town to see which one is acting like a man who is bewitched."

"Don't forget the ticking-clock angle,"

Drake said. "That always adds to the drama. If there's one thing we know for sure, Rainshadow is a bomb waiting to explode."

Chapter 23

"Drake Sebastian married her." Outrage shivered in Ethel Whitcomb's refined, private-school voice. "I can't believe it. The woman is a witch, I tell you. Alice North is nothing but a cheap little gold digger with nothing to recommend her. No family, no social connections, not a dime to her name. She's not even beautiful. Just an ordinary-looking woman who one wouldn't glance at twice on the street. How does she manage to attract the attention of men like my son and Drake Sebastian?"

"You said the marriage is only an MC, according to the investigator." Aldwin Hampstead struggled to keep his tone calm and soothing. It wasn't easy. He was seething inside with something akin to panic. But his task now was to keep Ethel under control. "We both know that a Marriage of Convenience is nothing more than an affair that's been given a sham of respectability. It won't

228

last long."

He had to be careful, he reminded himself. Judging by the last message he had received from Rainshadow, the situation on the island was shaping up to be a disaster. He knew now that would be the best possible outcome for him. He wanted nothing more than to cut his losses.

It had all seemed so brilliant at the start. Zara Tucker had dazzled him with the promise of riches and power beyond his wildest imaginings. But in the past few days the scales had fallen from his eyes. He had awakened that morning with the sure and certain knowledge that he had been a fool. The best thing that could happen would be for the whole damn island to explode in flames and take the bitch with it.

But the immediate crisis was Ethel Whitcomb. She was obsessed with the death of her son, but obsession did not equate with stupidity. He must not forget that, not for an instant. Everything depended on Ethel. She was the matriarch of the Whitcomb family. She controlled a fortune, and now that things were falling apart on Rainshadow, he needed access to the money more than ever.

They were sitting in the living room of Ethel's home in an exclusive gated community on Emerald Sunset Drive. The front windows had a panoramic view of the Old Quarter of Resonance City. The ethereal green towers of the Alien ruins were clearly visible, sparkling in the sunlight. But the interior of the Whitcomb mansion was shrouded in gloom.

When he had arrived a short time ago, he had been shown into Ethel's study. The room was decorated in an elegantly neutral mix of off-white and cream with discreet touches of rich, dark amber for counterpoint. The space had been designed to showcase a few pieces from Ethel's rare collection of Old World antiquities and First Generation art.

Ethel was a formidable woman, straight-shouldered, tall, arrogant, and regal. She wore her graying hair in a refined chignon. Her black silk trousers and pale blue silk blouse had been hand-tailored. She'd had a little work done on her patrician face, very good work. She could afford a fortune in jewels but she always kept her jewelry to a tasteful minimum. Today that amounted to a pair of gold and amber studs in her ears and a gold necklace.

She had been widowed for several years but she still wore her wedding band. Ethel had never remarried. Aldwin was quite sure that was because she enjoyed having full control of the Whitcomb money. And she handled it brilliantly. In the years since her husband's death, she had become something of a legend in the business world. While Whitcomb Industries could not match the Sebastian, Inc. empire in size, scope, and power, it was certainly a force to be reckoned with here in Resonance City.

Aldwin had been a little unnerved at first by Ethel's obsession with the murder of her son. It was not as if she didn't have four other offspring, he thought. The Whitcombs were a prolific family. In any event, it was a known fact that Fulton Whitcomb had been the Whitcomb family screwup. That was, of course, what had made it so easy to manipulate him. Fulton's obsession in life had been to prove to himself and his mother that he could be a smashing success.

Ethel's fixation on Fulton's death and her unwavering conviction that he had been murdered in spite of the lack of evidence struck Aldwin as over the top. But then, he did not really get the whole heavy-duty family-bond thing. Hell, his own mother probably wouldn't have noticed if he'd gone missing. She had spent most of her time lost in an alcohol-and-drug-induced haze until the crap had finally killed her.

Family, he thought. *Gotta love 'em.* It was that attitude, of course, that had helped cement the bond between Zara Tucker and himself at the start of their association. They both saw family ties as sentimental weaknesses to be exploited. They had done exactly that, first with Fulton and then with Alice North.

It was not that he did not have his own passions, Aldwin thought. He was only human, after all. But those passions were centered on one objective — making a place for himself in the rarefied social circles in which Ethel and her family moved. He had a right to enter that world. His father had come from that world — a realm where money and connections could buy a reckless young man out of any problem, including those that resulted from a one-night stand with a cheap, drug-addicted whore.

No doubt about it, his unknown father was his true, if unwitting, inspiration, Aldwin thought. He wanted nothing more than to follow in the footsteps of dear old dad. His talent had already brought him a long way. He had started out as a low-rent drug dealer from the Old Quarter slums and today he was the curator of the most exclusive private museum in the city.

But he had allowed himself to get suckered into the doomed project on Rainshadow, and now he was engaged in some serious damage control. He could not afford to lose Ethel Whitcomb's patronage, not now that his own fantasy of a brilliant future was about to crash and burn.

He had to maintain his connection with Ethel, and that meant he had to nurture her obsession with avenging her son's death. Ethel had vowed to make Alice North's life a living hell and she had spent a great deal of money to do that.

Ethel was the ultimate stalker, Aldwin thought — a head full of obsessive revenge fantasies and all the money in the world to make those fantasies come true.

He suppressed a sigh. *Just because you were rich, connected, and powerful didn't mean you weren't a whacko.*

"When I discovered that Fulton was in an MC contract with Alice North, I told myself it wasn't important," Ethel said. She rose from her chair and went to stand at the window. "He certainly was not the first man of his class to use an MC to placate a mistress. When I confronted him, he assured me that it was just a short-term fling. He said she had insisted on the arrangement and he saw no harm in it. The MC was supposed to be a trinket, like a nice piece of jewelry, to satisfy her. But she wanted more."

"I understand," Aldwin said. Surreptitiously he checked his watch. He had heard the story many times.

Ethel clenched one hand into a fist. "Alice North wanted a full Covenant Marriage. As if a Whitcomb would marry a woman of her sort. When she realized that she was not going to become Fulton's CM wife, she murdered him. Why couldn't the police see that she killed him?"

Because there was no evidence, Aldwin thought. Thanks to a useful item of Alien technology that killed without a trace. But he didn't say it out loud. He and Ethel had been over this territory a thousand times in the past year. Ethel had run up against one thing her money had been unable to buy — the criminal justice system. Which was actually rather astonishing, in Aldwin's opinion. A year ago he would have bet good money that with Ethel Whitcomb pushing for an arrest, the system would have obliged. It had come as a bit of a shock when Alice North had walked free. Evidently not everything was for sale down there at the Resonance City PD. He would have to keep that in mind.

"I just cannot comprehend Drake Sebastian entering into an MC with that woman," Ethel said. "Everyone knows the Sebastian men don't do MCs with their mistresses."

Aldwin cleared his throat. "The family standards may be slipping. There was that divorce a while back. The Sebastians tried to keep it hushed up, but everyone in their circle knew about it."

"Yes, I know," Ethel said. "But this tacky MC coming on the heels of that dreadful scandal just makes it all so much worse. Drake's mother, Samantha, must be furious. I can't even imagine what Drake's grandfather is thinking. And as for Drake, it's no secret he is set to take over the business next year. Why would he embarrass his family like this?"

Aldwin was quite certain he knew the answer to Ethel's questions. There was only one logical reason why Drake Sebastian would have gotten himself involved in an MC with Alice North. It was the same reason that Fulton had married the woman. The Sebastians had concluded that they needed Alice's assistance to find the crystals. The fact that Drake had whisked her off to Rainshadow immediately after the ceremony said it all. *Not like the island is any woman's dream of a honeymoon paradise,* he thought.

He did not want to contemplate what

would happen if Drake was successful. If the Sebastians found the two crystals, they would also find the Dream Chamber and the bitch, Zara Tucker. That could not be allowed to happen. Aldwin knew that Zara would take him down with her in a heart-beat.

It was all falling apart. Aldwin was now in survival mode. He hoped that Rainshadow blew sky-high and soon, taking Zara Tucker with it. The biggest mystery in this whole mess was why he had allowed Tucker to drag him into the project in the first place.

The panicky feeling was getting worse. He was not claustrophobic, but Ethel's study seemed to be closing in around him. It was getting hard to breathe.

"You've got other things on your mind, Mrs. Whitcomb," he said gently. "We can discuss the plans for the new wing of the museum some other time."

"Yes," she said, bleak and bitter. "Some other time."

"I'll see myself out," he said.

Ethel did not respond. Aldwin left her standing at the window as she gazed out at the spectacular view.

CHAPTER 24

"The first step is to make a list of men who might be vulnerable to Zara's talent," Drake said.

"That shouldn't be difficult," Fletcher said. "Not that many people left here in town, and between the four of us we know them all."

They were gathered in Looking Glass Antiques. It was early morning but the sky was once again dark and heavy. Alice knew there would be no sun that day. The lights were still off, leaving the shop steeped in shadows. The place was crammed with antiques, and all of them had a paranormal provenance. The combined currents that emanated from the objects infused the atmosphere with a faint, hair-lifting buzz.

Alice stood quietly, lounging against a counter with Houdini tucked under one arm. Drake laid out his plans to Charlotte, Rachel, Jasper, and Fletcher. She was glumly aware that she had nothing to contribute to the strategy. Her brief moment of feeling like a member of the group had dissipated. She could not assist with the task of winnowing down the list of suspects because she was not well acquainted with anyone on the island. She had no talent for aura reading, like Rachel. And she had only arrived yesterday, so she could not determine various timelines and alibis. The best she could do in a pinch was bend a little light and vanish. She was just the magician's assistant.

Drake was the magician in this situation. He had taken charge with the ease of a natural leader. No one had even blinked when he had announced that he had a strategy and he wanted help implementing it. Alice had the distinct impression that the others were relieved that someone had a plan. There was nothing worse than sitting around waiting for disaster to strike.

"Are you sure you don't want to bring Officer Willis in on this?" Rachel asked.

"I wish we could," Drake said, "but I don't think we should take the chance. Unfortunately, for now he's on the list of suspects. He's an ideal target for Tucker — young, single, male, and well positioned to know what is going on here in Shadow Bay."

"What about Myrna Reed?" Charlotte asked. "I know that Slade trusts her. She's been a police officer here on Rainshadow for years. She knows all kinds of secrets."

"Her input would be valuable," Drake said. "But informing her of this project would put her in a difficult situation with Kirk Willis. In addition, because of her close ties to the community, we can't be sure where her loyalties lie. She might feel bound to protect some of the people on the list. For now, this stays with the six of us."

"Understood," Jasper said.

"I agree," Fletcher added. "We'll get started on the list immediately."

Charlotte looked at Drake with a speculative expression. "What happens if we come up with a likely suspect?"

"I'll have a short conversation with him," Drake said.

Jasper raised his bushy brows. "And if he isn't feeling chatty?"

"He'll tell me what I want to know," Drake said without inflection. "I'm sure of it."

Jasper nodded, satisfied. "You need any help with that conversation, feel free to call on Fletch and me."

In that moment, Alice glimpsed a few of the hard edges under the surfaces of the two retired ghost hunters. They might be an artist and a gallery owner now, but they had survived for years in the underground catacombs. It was tough, dangerous work and it had left its mark on both men.

Drake smiled. "Count on it, you will be in on that conversation."

"That's it, then," Charlotte said. "We're all on the clock here, not that any of the clocks in town are working. Let's get started on our list. Rachel and I can supply the names of all the men staying at the B-and-Bs."

Houdini chose that moment to wriggle free of Alice's grasp. He made it up onto the counter and started examining a display of marbles.

"While you're working on that," Drake said to the group, "I'm going to start a few rumors in town."

Rachel raised her brows. "Rumors about what?"

"I want to get the word out that, thanks to Alice, I've got some old North family records that describe a method of de-escalating the unstable frequencies generated by the crystal Keys."

Jasper nodded. "Trying to build a fire under whoever is behind this?"

"No harm in giving our man an incentive

to move quickly," Drake said.

Charlotte shot him a thoughtful look. "You're making yourself a target."

Drake's smile was cold. "One I'm hoping Zara Tucker won't be able to resist."

Fletcher smiled. "This is a pincer-move. Between us narrowing down a list of suspects and you setting yourself up as a target, we're going to force someone's hand."

"That's the idea," Drake said.

There was a short silence. Alice heard a small noise behind her. She whirled around in time to see five colorful glass marbles roll across the counter.

"Houdini, no," she yelped.

She dove for the marbles and managed to snag two. The other three sailed off the edge of the counter and landed with three loud, sharp cracks on the wooden floor.

Houdini chortled euphorically.

Alice looked at Charlotte. "I'm sorry. Are they, uh, very valuable antiques?"

Charlotte smiled. "Don't worry about it. I'm sure the marbles will be fine."

"If they aren't, send the bill to the Foundation," Drake said.

Charlotte laughed. "Deal."

Alice whisked up Houdini and started toward the door. "If you'll excuse us, I have to get to work."

Everyone, including Drake, looked at her with varying degrees of surprise.

Drake frowned. "Where are you off to?"

"You could say that I'm engaged in some behind-the-scenes work," Alice said.

CHAPTER 25

The lunch rush hit early.

"More like the morning rush took a coffee break and then turned into the lunch rush," Burt Caster grumbled. He angled his head toward the tables where a number of people were still drinking coffee and chatting with neighbors. "Some of these folks never left after breakfast."

"People are bored," Alice said. She stacked the last of the newly washed plates on a shelf. "I think that may be one of the problems with being under siege. There's not much to do."

"Except eat." Burt opened a cupboard and eyed a row of industrial-sized can goods. "Good thing the Foundation is picking up the tab for all the food costs here and down the street at Madge's place until they get this business in the Preserve settled. Lot of the folks we're feeding couldn't afford to dine out three times a day, I can tell you that."

"Seems to me it's the least the Foundation can do under the circumstances," Alice said. "Besides, any way you look at it, a few days' worth of free meals is just pocket change to the Sebastians."

"That may be true," Burt said. He closed the cupboard door. "But at the rate things are going, we may have to start rationing canned soup. Which reminds me, the power has been off for almost a week now. I managed to keep the freezer going for a while with my old amber-based generator, but it gave up the ghost two days ago. We need to start using up the frozen food and fast. Figure it won't last more than another day at best."

"I'll go downstairs and assess the situation," Alice said. She wiped her hands on her apron and headed toward the steps that led to the basement. "The kids will be thrilled when we tell them they have to eat ice cream for dinner tonight."

"Whatever you do, don't leave the locker door open any longer than necessary."

"I won't," she promised.

"And Alice?"

She paused in the doorway. "Yes?"

"Thanks for volunteering to help out here in the tavern. I don't mind telling you, it's been a tough few days. Betty, my waitress, and Carl, my bartender, both made it off the island in the first wave of evacuations. I've been holding down the fort alone since they left. Feels like all I do is work eighteen hours a day, get a few hours' sleep, get up, and repeat the process."

"I'm just happy to have something to do," Alice said. "Nothing worse than doing nothing in circumstances like this. Besides, I've done a fair amount of food-and-beverage work in the past."

Burt nodded approvingly. "Yeah, I can tell you've had some experience." He reached up to a shelf and took down a large can of tomato sauce. "Sure hope Sebastian and Attridge get back here soon. That fog was worse than ever last night."

"Drake has a plan to put a stop to what's happening inside the Preserve," Alice said.

Burt glanced over his shoulder, his brows elevated. "Is that right?"

"It has to do with some information he found in the old North records," Alice explained.

Burt's expression lightened. "Yeah?"

"You'll be hearing more about it soon," she assured him in her best breezy accent.

She grabbed a small amber lantern and started down the steps. An eager chortle behind her made her pause and look back over her shoulder. Houdini was in the doorway. He fluttered down to where she stood and then zipped past her to the bottom of the stairs. He disappeared into the shadows of the basement. She followed him on down.

Burt had cause for concern about supplies. Many of the shelves holding canned goods, boxes of cereal, and crackers were less than a third full. Some were already empty. She did not want to think about what might happen if Drake's plan did not work. She also did not want to think about what would happen if it did work. She was quite certain that Drake could take care of himself, but the knowledge that he was deliberately making a target of himself unnerved her.

She crossed the concrete floor to the frozen food locker and used both hands to haul open the heavy door. Cold air rushed out. She could tell that the temperature was well above the freezing point.

She carried the lantern into the locker and set it on an empty shelf. The yellow glare cast odd shadows among the packages of frozen goods.

Houdini chortled and raced in after her.

"Suit yourself," she said. "But it's still

246

pretty cold in here."

She pulled the door shut, wrapped her arms around her midsection to ward off some of the chill, and looked around, taking stock. The packages of frozen meats, pizza dough, and other items were all starting to show signs of thawing. She moved closer to one shelf and poked at a carton of ice cream. It gave slightly.

"The ice cream won't last another day," she informed Houdini. "Definitely ice cream for dinner tonight." She went to the shelves that held the hamburger meat. "Some of this will last another twenty-four hours or so if we keep the door closed, but no longer."

Houdini scrambled up onto her shoulder and muttered.

"I warned you it was cold in here," she said. She took down a large package of hamburger meat. "We'll need this for dinner."

Reasoning that the remaining items might stay colder longer if she positioned them closer to one another, she started rearranging the shelves. Although the temperature was no longer freezing, it was the equivalent of working in a refrigerator. The chill was starting to get to her.

"Should have brought gloves," she told

Houdini. She reached for a large carton of partially thawed sausages, struggling to push it up against the remaining packages of meat. When she got it moved, she saw that there was another bulky, oddly shaped object behind the sausages.

Houdini rumbled a warning. She knew that growl. Hurriedly, she stepped back, her breath tightening and her senses spiking.

"What is it?" she asked, scanning the interior of the frozen food locker for threats.

Houdini growled again. Then she saw what had focused his attention. A man's shoe extended out from behind one of the cartons of sausages. A terrible dread descended on her.

She made herself push the next carton aside. The eyes of a very dead, partially frozen man stared back at her. The face was horribly familiar.

CHAPTER 26

"His name is Samson Crisp," Alice said. "He was the private investigator I told you about, the one I hired to look into Fulton's death. No wonder he never got back to me or bothered to send me a bill. I feel absolutely terrible about this. All the time I was thinking he had scammed me he was in that freezer, dead. And it's probably my fault."

Drake watched her stalk past him as she made another circuit of the small space. He was seriously annoyed by the distress and the guilt that he saw in her eyes.

"Alice, pay attention. This is not your fault."

"But I'm the reason he wound up on Rainshadow," she said.

"He was a professional. You employed him to investigate the murder of a very wealthy man. He had to know that might be dangerous work."

They were in their room at the Marina

Inn. The location was the only place Drake could think of that guaranteed them some privacy. News of the discovery of the body had flashed through the tiny community like lightning. The rumors that Alice had been acquainted with the victim had riveted everyone's attention. Kirk Willis and the town's only doctor, Ed Forester, had taken charge of the rapidly thawing Crisp. Forester had made it clear up front that he was a family practitioner, not a forensic pathologist, but he had agreed to examine the body to see if he could determine the cause of death.

Drake was sprawled in one of the room's two chairs, mostly because it was the only way he could stay out of Alice's path. She had begun pacing the room almost as soon as he had gotten the door open. Every so often she started to fade a little around the edges, enough so that he had to use some energy to bring her back into focus.

Houdini was hunkered down on the window ledge watching Alice. Whenever she went past his perch, he made small, comforting noises.

"I had no idea that Crisp had come here," Alice said. "He never told me that he planned to do that." She came face-to-face with a wall, spun around, and started back toward the opposite wall. "He must have traveled here to see if he could verify my version of events."

"That's a possibility," Drake said. Personally, he had his doubts.

"I must say, Crisp's investigation was certainly a lot more thorough than I gave him credit for," Alice continued. She locked her hands behind her back. "I expect that when he started asking questions, he alerted the killer, who followed him here and murdered him."

"When confronting new facts, the first rule is, don't jump to conclusions," Drake said. "We don't know for certain what Samson Crisp was doing here on the island."

Alice stopped and turned to face him, startled. "It's obvious why he was here."

"No," Drake said evenly. "Nothing is obvious, not yet. But we may know more when we read his notes."

Alice looked at the leather-bound notebook on the table. She had notified Drake first after discovering Crisp in the freezer. Drake had done a quick search of the body before Kirk Willis and Myrna Reed had arrived. He had found the notebook inside a waterproof pocket of Crisp's trench coat. Making an executive decision, he had quietly confiscated it before Willis and Reed got to the restaurant.

There was no telling what Samson Crisp had discovered in the course of the investigation, but whatever it was had most certainly gotten him killed. It was Crisp's motive for being on Rainshadow that made Drake suspicious. It was a long and expensive trip for a low-rent PI to make without checking to be sure the client would pay for all costs.

"Maybe he found out who really killed Whitcomb," Alice said. She watched the notebook with an expression of wary hope. "Maybe he also came up with some proof. But why would the killer stick him in Burt's frozen food locker?"

"I can think of two possibilities," Drake said.

Alice blinked. "Two?"

"The murder may have been an impulsive act that left the killer with a body to dispose of in a hurry. Evidently Burt's freezer was the most convenient place to stash it."

Alice gave that a moment's thought. "What's the other possibility?"

"The murder was premeditated but it did not go according to plan. Same outcome. The killer is stuck with a body."

"And Burt's freezer was the most convenient place to stash it," Alice concluded.

"It wasn't a great option because sooner or later someone was bound to discover the body. But it wasn't a bad choice, all things considered."

"How can you say that?" Alice widened her hands. "Who knows how long poor Mr. Crisp's body has been lying there behind the breakfast sausages?"

"Long enough to give the killer plenty of time to get off the island undetected," Drake said.

Alice winced. "I see what you mean." She frowned, her brows scrunching. "I hired Crisp about two months after Whitcomb was murdered. That's how long it took me to realize that the cops probably were not going to find the real killer. I'll bet he came here immediately to start his own investigation."

"Let's see what Crisp has to say for himself," Drake said.

He sat forward and picked up the notebook. The freezing process had done very little damage, but nevertheless he turned the pages cautiously.

Alice hurried across the room to look over his shoulder. "Oh, damn, it's in code."

"Not exactly." Drake studied the somewhat cryptic entries that had been made in cramped handwriting. "Some sort of personal shorthand. Since we know the names of several of the people involved in this thing, as well as the locations where the events took place, the initials should be easy enough to identify." He pointed to the letters *A* and *N*. "That's you. This looks like the date you initially contacted him. And the *W* has to stand for Whitcomb."

"Yes. Hang on, I'll get a pen and take some notes while you read."

Drake waited until she was settled at the table with a pen and a pad bearing the legend *The Marina Inn* on each page. Then he started to read aloud. It didn't take long to pick up the telltale signs.

"Crisp was looking for an angle, right from the start," Drake said.

Alice frowned. "What do you mean?"

"He realized that the real money involved in the case was the Whitcomb fortune. He started hunting for a way to tap into that the minute you walked out of his office."

"You mean he tried to sell his services to Ethel Whitcomb?"

"No, at least not yet." Drake turned another page. "But he did what the cops should have done more thoroughly — what I plan to do as soon as we get the computers up and running again. He looked into the background of everyone who was closely associated with Fulton Whitcomb."

"Well? Don't keep me in suspense. Did he find anything that might point to the killer?"

"Do the initials *AH* mean anything to you in connection with the Whitcomb Museum?"

Alice went still. "The director of the museum is Aldwin Hampstead. He was the one who hired me to work in the gift shop."

"If I'm interpreting these notes correctly, it looks like Hampstead was operating a thriving business in black market Alien antiquities out of the basement of the museum."

"Good grief, are you sure?"

"Looks like Crisp was certain about it, which is the critical point." Drake flipped another couple of pages. "I think it's safe to say that, after a short but evidently solid investigation, Crisp believed that he had found a way to turn a handsome profit on the Whitcomb case."

"By finding out that Aldwin Hampstead was dealing in illegal antiquities?" Alice asked. "How does that — ?" She broke off, her eyes widening. "Yes, of course, he intended to blackmail Aldwin. But that makes no sense. Aldwin wasn't the one with the money."

"No, but Aldwin Hampstead had a pipeline into the Whitcomb money. He had evidently been convincing Ethel to spend a fortune on fake antiquities for years. Looks like Crisp figured Hampstead could find a way to get more money out of Ethel and use it to pay Crisp for his silence."

"So how did Crisp wind up on Rainshadow?"

Drake turned another page. "Here we go. At some point along the way Crisp realizes that Hampstead and Fulton Whitcomb are into something very, very big here on Rainshadow, an important Alien find. Compared to the potential profits of a discovery that yields a substantial amount of Alien technology, blackmail would be penny ante stuff."

Alice put down her pen. "He wanted in on the project?"

"Yes. Hampstead agrees. They set up a meeting here on the island to show Crisp the ruin."

"Instead of taking Crisp on a tour of the ruin, Aldwin Hampstead murdered him," Alice concluded.

"Looks like it." Drake turned the last page. "Crisp notes that he made a reservation here at the Marina Inn."

"Well, it's not like there are a lot of options here in Shadow Bay," Alice said. "There are a handful of B-and-Bs, but people tend to remember you in small establishments. The Marina Inn would have seemed much more anonymous."

"Given that Crisp's body was found in the basement of the tavern, we can assume he was killed at the inn."

"It still seems strange that the killer stashed the body in the freezer."

"He was probably killed there," Drake said, "or somewhere close by. It's not easy to dump a body in a small town like Shadow Bay. The obvious location is inside the Preserve, but that would require the killer to carry the corpse through the inn and outside to a vehicle. There would have been too much risk that someone would see something suspicious."

Alice tipped her head to one side. "We're assuming that because Crisp came here to meet Hampstead, Hampstead is the killer. But what about Zara Tucker?"

"Zara is a very petite woman. She would not have had the upper body strength to lift Crisp up onto that shelf in the freezer where you found him."

"Petite, huh? And I think you also said she was beautiful."

Alice's tone was a little too neutral and her expression was unreadable.

Drake suddenly felt as if he was walking

on eggshells. He cleared his throat. "Take it from me, Zara is not the one who stuffed Crisp into the freezer. She never does her own dirty work if she can avoid it."

"Which leaves Aldwin Hampstead as our most likely suspect."

"If Hampstead and Zara are both in on this, which seems likely, you can be sure that Hampstead is taking orders from Zara Tucker. She's the one running the show."

Alice nodded once. "I believe you. What's our next move?"

Drake got to his feet and went to stand at the window. "That's obvious, isn't it?"

"Excuse me?"

"Crisp's body wound up in Burt's freezer, not the freezer at the grocery store or the one at the fish market."

"Good heavens, surely you don't think Burt Caster killed the investigator." Alice hesitated. "Unless he's Zara Tucker's spy here in town."

Drake shook his head. "I don't think Burt is the killer. He wouldn't have sent you downstairs to clean out the last of the frozen hamburger meat if he had stashed a body inside the locker."

"Right. *Whew.* That's a relief. Okay, let's see what we've got." Alice held up one hand and ticked off facts. "Samson Crisp came here to Rainshadow to meet with Aldwin Hampstead. Crisp wanted a piece of the action at the ruin that Zara Tucker is excavating somewhere on the island. The meeting between Crisp and Hampstead took place at the Marina Inn where Crisp was killed."

"It seems likely that Hampstead would have been staying here at the inn for the same reason that Crisp got a room there," Drake said, thinking it through. "It's the largest and most anonymous motel in Shadow Bay."

Alice jumped to her feet, excitement sparking in her eyes. "If they both stayed here, there will be a record."

"The killer would have used a fake name," Drake warned her. "Rainshadow isn't a major tourist destination in the Amber Sea, but it gets a fair number of day-trippers during the summer months and on the weekends."

"But we've got dates and descriptions of both men."

Drake smiled slowly. "We also know that one of the guests never checked out, at least not in person. In a community the size of Shadow Bay, you can be sure that someone will remember something."

Alice made a face. "Small towns. Gotta love 'em."

CHAPTER 27

"I remember the dead guy now." Sylvia Benetz peered at the card she had taken out of a file box. "Checked in as Fred Smith. Paid cash. Didn't see him the next morning. Just assumed he left on the early ferry. I didn't worry about it at the time. After all, he'd paid for the room."

Alice studied the card that Sylvia set on the inn's front desk. She was not the only one examining it. A sizeable crowd was gathered around the desk. In addition to Drake, Kirk Willis, Myrna, Rachel, Charlotte, and Dr. Harrison were present.

Houdini and Darwina were the only ones who did not show any interest in the murder investigation. They were out in the street in front of the inn, learning how to play hide-and-seek with the half dozen children left in town.

The fog had retreated for the day, leaving behind another heavy sky. The parents of the kids had all agreed that the little ones needed to work off excess energy, and the dust bunnies were thrilled to take on the role of camp counselors. With a natural talent for turning anything and everything into a game, they had picked up the essential concepts of hide-and-seek almost immediately. Shouts of laughter interspersed by short bursts of hushed silence were followed by excited chortling and more giggles echoing through the partially deserted town.

"That's not the address of Samson Crisp and Associates," Alice said.

Kirk glanced at the card. "He was using a fake name so he went with a fake address, as well. Not that it matters now that we've got a positive ID. Damn. This is a genuine homicide. Too bad the chief isn't here. He was FBPI. He knows how to run a murder investigation."

"Well, Slade isn't here, so we're on our own," Myrna said. She gave Drake a narrow-eyed look. "But this is Foundation Security business, isn't it?"

"Yes," Drake said. "It is. Normally Harry would handle a Preserve-connected murder, but since he and Attridge aren't around, I'll take the lead." He paused for a beat. "If that's okay with you and Kirk?"

"Fine by me," Myrna said. "Crisp wasn't

a local and it doesn't look like the perp was from the island, either. Not our problem."

Kirk gave a clipped nod of his head. "As the only representative of the Foundation available at the moment, sir, you're in charge. But you need to keep Myrna and me in the loop. The chief will want a full report when he gets back."

"Understood," Drake said. He turned to the doctor. "What can you tell us, Dr. Forester?"

"Call me Ed," Forester said. "And I don't have squat for you. No visible wounds. If Sylvia had found Crisp's body in one of the rooms upstairs, I would have said the guy had suffered a heart attack or a stroke."

"Just like Fulton," Alice said quietly.

With the exception of Drake, everyone looked at her.

"My ex," she explained.

"Oh, right," Rachel said. "The guy you spent your first honeymoon with here on Rainshadow."

Alice flushed. "It was just an MC."

Drake stepped into the short, awkward silence. "Given the facts, I think we can assume that Crisp was killed with the same weapon that was used on Fulton Whitcomb."

Kirk's jaw hardened into a grim line.

"Alien technology?"

"I think so," Drake said. "A couple of the people involved in this thing — Zara Tucker and Aldwin Hampstead — had access to a lot of Alien artifacts."

"I don't get it," Charlotte said. "If the killer knew the death would look like natural causes, why would he go to the trouble of concealing the body in the freezer?"

"I can think of a couple of reasons," Drake said. "First, he wanted to buy some time. He had to know that the body would be identified fairly quickly once it was discovered. It wasn't like Crisp was working under deep cover. He just checked in with a fake name and address."

Alice nodded. "And once the body was identified, there was a strong possibility that someone back in Resonance — Crisp's last client, for example — would start asking questions about why he had gone to Rainshadow and what he'd found there. Said client might have gone to the police with her suspicions and convinced them to reopen the investigation."

Myrna arched her brows. "Crisp's last client being you."

"Yep."

Sylvia shook her head. "Told Burt ages ago that he needed to clean out that freezer."

"What about the killer?" Drake said. He studied the handful of cards on file. "Doesn't look like there were a lot of other folks staying here the night Crisp checked in."

"It was off-season," Sylvia said. "We weren't booked solid. Looks like mostly couples, though." She paused. "Here's a single man. Roger Carter. Gave a Resonance City address and paid cash, too. One night only. Left early the following morning."

"We think the killer is a man named Aldwin Hampstead," Alice said. "He's a museum director and he looks the part. Mid-thirties, slender, blond hair, good looking in a polished, classy sort of way. He would have been well dressed and rather aloof."

"Huh." Sylvia snapped the registration card against the desktop a couple of times and looked thoughtful. "I don't think this is your guy. Hampstead sounds like someone I would remember. But I can't recall anything in particular about Roger Carter. Medium height, medium build. Very ordinary type, I guess."

"Damn," Drake said softly. "Sounds like Zara Tucker found herself a pro."

Everyone looked at him.

"A professional hit man who knows how

to fade into the background," Drake explained. "The kind of guy no one remembers."

Alice shook her head. "That's definitely not Aldwin Hampstead."

CHAPTER 28

Drake stood at the window of the lantern-lit room, watching the shadows of the paranormal fog roll through the main street of Shadow Bay.

Alice was still in the bathroom. He could hear water running in the sink. It seemed to him that she had been in there for an inordinate length of time. Something told him that their second night together at the Marina Inn was going to be a lot more complicated than the first.

Last night had been simple because they had both been exhausted. The sex had come out of nowhere, blindsiding them. Like the torrid kiss in the parking garage, the fiery passion last night had hit hard and fast. It was not the kind of sex that implied a commitment to another such encounter tonight.

He was sure that when they climbed the stairs to their room a short time ago they had both been thinking about the bed that awaited them. He certainly had been thinking about it. But he could not get a read on Alice. He should not push her, he thought. She'd had a rough day. Finding a dead body was a traumatic experience made even worse in this case because she had known the victim. He should give Alice some space tonight.

Too bad Houdini had taken off a short time ago. The dust bunny served as a sort of chaperone.

The bathroom door opened. Drake turned around and watched Alice emerge in the robe and nightgown that she had borrowed from Rachel. Her hair was tumbled down around her shoulders. In the glow of the lantern she looked freshly scrubbed and sweetly vulnerable.

His wife. For now, at least.

His blood heated. He fought the nearly overpowering impulse to take her down onto the bed and lose himself in her arms. She was a dazzling drug to his senses, and he was completely and utterly addicted.

He really should give her some space tonight.

She stopped and looked at him. "Anything going on outside?"

"No," he said. Intensely aware of his fierce erection, he started toward the bathroom.

"Be out in a minute."

Give her some space, he thought.

When he emerged a short time later, he discovered that Alice was in bed. She had turned the lantern down very low. To his eyes, the room was still fully illuminated, but he knew the shadows that she perceived gave her a sense of privacy. At least she could not see how aroused he was.

He went around to the far side of the bed and stripped off his trousers and shirt. He climbed under the covers wearing only his briefs, folded his arms behind his head, and concentrated on the ceiling.

There was a short silence.

"You can turn off the lantern," Alice said.

"It's all right. I don't mind sleeping in my glasses."

"That's not necessary, really."

"You're sure?"

"I'm sure."

He hesitated and then reached out and de-rezzed the lantern, plunging the room into what he knew was utter darkness for Alice. He took off his glasses and put them close at hand on the bedside table.

There was another short silence. Alice stirred.

"You can still see me, can't you?" she asked.

"Yes."

"As if I'm lying here in broad daylight?"

He turned onto his side and looked at her. "No, not unless I jack up my talent a little. But I'm not doing that now. I'm just looking at you with what passes for normal vision for me."

"What do you see?"

He looked at her with a sense of wonder and tried to find the words. "It's as if you were lit by moonlight and shadow, but the hues and shades are all from the far end of the spectrum. You look . . . beautiful. Magical."

She twisted onto her side, facing him. Her eyes were open but he knew from her unfocused gaze that she could not make him out in the darkness.

He sensed energy shifting in the atmosphere and realized that she had rezzed her talent. She looked straight at him with luminous eyes.

"You can see me," he said.

"A little. You're drenched in deep shadows."

"Just a big shadow, huh? Doesn't sound too interesting."

She put out a hand and touched his bare shoulder. "You're wrong. You look incredibly interesting."

Her fingers burned on his skin, thrilling his senses.

"Is that a polite way of saying I look better in the dark?" he asked.

"No," she said, very serious now. "You are the most interesting man I have ever seen in the dark or in daylight. "You are . . . amazing, Drake. Last night was amazing. I will never forget it or you. I just wanted you to know that."

He stopped breathing for a beat. His pulse thudded in his veins. His whole body felt tight and hard and heavy with desire. He reached under the covers and put a hand on her thigh.

"Alice?" he said.

His voice sounded thick and harsh to his ears.

But she levered herself up on her elbow, leaned forward, and kissed him. His talent spiked and the night was ablaze in dark light.

The kiss ignited his senses, but he made himself hold back. Last night had been fast and hot. His intuition told him that tonight she wanted to explore him, learn him, discover more about what was happening between them.

She moved her lips to his throat, his shoulder, and then his chest. Her soft, warm hand glided over him as if she were trying to memorize him with her sense of touch.

He wanted to give her time and for a while he succeeded in his goal. He gripped her carefully, as if she were made of delicate porcelain. He flattened his palms on the contours of her sleek, elegant back. She was warm to the touch. Then he went lower, seeking the cleft between her legs.

He found her melting and hot. He caught the scent of her arousal and it took him over the edge. He eased her onto her back and came down on top of her, making a place for himself between her legs. She welcomed him, lifting her hips to meet him.

He entered her slowly, deliberately, intensely aware of the tight little muscles that guarded her core. She gasped, cried out softly, and sank her nails into his shoulders.

"Drake. *Drake.*"

He went deep and the night blazed around them.

CHAPTER 29

When he emerged from the bath room for the second time that night, he automatically looked out the window. The unnatural darkness still cloaked the town.

He started to turn away and go back to the bed but a flicker of light at the far end of the street made him pause. He took a closer look. The golden glow of an amber lantern appeared briefly again in the distance.

"What's wrong?" Alice asked.

"Looks like someone is wandering around outside in the fog with an amber lantern," he said.

"That's strange." Alice got out of bed and made her way to the window. "I can't see anything."

He draped an arm around her bare shoulders and rezzed a little of his talent. "How's that?"

"Much better. Okay, now I see the light

bobbing around at the end of the street. It's a lantern, all right. Whoever is out there must be terribly disoriented. Probably scared out of his wits."

"I'd better go see what's going on."

"I'll bet that accounts for the ghost," Alice said.

He turned away from the window and grabbed his pants. "What ghost?"

"Today I heard a couple of the kids talking about the ghost that haunts Shadow Bay. I assumed they were just telling stories to scare each other as a means of dealing with their fears. But maybe one or two of them happened to see someone walking around at night with a lantern."

"I'll check out our ghost," Drake said.

He dressed swiftly, took one of the fire-starters out of the pack, put on his glasses, and opened the room door.

"Drake," Alice said urgently.

He paused in the doorway. "What?"

"Be careful."

She looks so serious, he thought, smiling.

"I will," he promised.

He let himself out into the lantern-lit hall, descended the stairs to the lobby, unlocked the door, and went outside into the foggy night. Eerie, menacing visions swirled in the atmosphere. Fragments of his dream of the endless hallway lined with doors that opened onto blinding sunlight as well as Zara's laughter whispered to his senses.

He removed his glasses, put them in his shirt pocket, and jacked up his talent to suppress the hallucinations. He started toward the spot where he had last seen the lantern.

But there was no sign of the flickering light now. Whoever had dared the night with a lantern had disappeared. *Probably gone back indoors,* Drake thought.

He walked the length of the street through the senses-chilling fog and turned the corner. In the dark light of night he could make out two stone pillars that formed an entryway.

The words engraved in the sign above the gate read: SHADOW BAY CEMETERY.

CHAPTER 30

Alice emerged from the tavern in mid-afternoon after the lunch rush. The laughter at the end of the street drew her attention. She looked around and saw Houdini and Darwina playing yet another game of hide-and-seek with the kids. The dust bunnies were chortling happily and the children's laughter rang true. She smiled. It wasn't just the mood of the youngsters that seemed elevated today. The adults she had served at lunch were also in a more positive, optimistic frame of mind.

Somehow Drake had managed to convince everyone that the situation on the island was under control and that progress was being made.

Drake did his own kind of magic, Alice thought.

She spotted Egan when she turned to walk toward the Marina Inn. He stood in front of the window of the Kane Gallery, gripping his Glorious Dawn sign. He was trans-fixed by whatever he saw in the darkened window.

Curious, she walked toward him.

"Hello, Egan," she said when she got close.

He did not turn toward her or acknowl-edge her existence. The picture on the other side of the window held his complete atten-tion. She stopped beside him and studied the painting propped on an easel. The gal-lery lights were off but there was enough weak, gray daylight left to make out the landscape.

The focal point of the picture was what appeared to be a frozen waterfall. The hot, seething brushstrokes and the surreal aspect of the image somehow conveyed the impres-sion that the scene could only exist inside the Preserve.

"It's a very interesting picture, isn't it?" Alice ventured after a while.

Egan did not respond. He just stood there, staring at the image.

A figure moved in the shadows on the other side of the window. The door of the shop opened. Jasper came out onto the side-walk.

"Hi, Alice," he said. "Taking a break before the dinner rush?"

"Yes. Just so you know, I think there will be hamburger on the menu again tonight."

"The last of the meat from the freezer?"

"Don't worry, it wasn't anywhere near the body and Burt has big plans for it."

"The body or the hamburger?" Jasper asked.

"Ha-ha." She shot him a severe glare. "The hamburger. I think the recipe involves canned mushroom soup." She gestured toward the painting. "Your work?"

"Yes." Jasper looked at the riveted Egan. "Hey, buddy, how are you doing today?"

"The ghost that doesn't kill you only makes you stronger," Egan intoned. He did not take his eyes off the painting.

Alice looked at Jasper. "An old hunter saying, I assume?"

"Yeah." Jasper blew out a long sigh. "Egan is a former Guild man — at least, that's what Kane and I think. Once in a while when Egan is coherent and not rambling about the return of the Aliens, he talks like a hunter who spent a little too much time in the tunnels. We think maybe he got burned real bad somewhere along the line."

"By one of those energy storms Guild men call ghosts?"

"Right. Ghosts are a hazard of the job. The new Guild bosses are shaking things up with stricter safety codes and security measures. But back in the day when Egan was working the tunnels, things were different. Guys took chances they shouldn't have taken. A lot of 'em still do, come to that. Now there are the added risks of the rain forest work."

"It's no secret that a lot of hunters get singed one time too many and end up on the streets," Alice said.

Egan stirred, hoisting his sign. "Those who do not seek the third level of Enlightenment will be swept away when the Aliens return."

He turned and walked down the street. Alice glanced at Jasper.

"Egan seemed quite taken with your painting," she said.

"I've noticed him checking it out a few times." Jasper watched Egan move down the street. "I don't know why it fascinates him so much."

"The picture is stunning," Alice said. "I can feel the energy in it even out here on the sidewalk. A scene from inside the Preserve, I assume?"

"To be more precise, it's a scene of a dream about the Preserve," Jasper said.

"One of your dreams?"

Before Jasper could answer, Fletcher

emerged from the gallery.

"Not in this case," he said. He looked at the picture with a critical eye. "It's an interpretation of one of Rachel's dreams. She says Jasper got it pretty much right."

"It looks like a frozen waterfall," Alice said. "Or maybe a waterfall made of crystal."

"That's close," Jasper said. "It's actually a dream vision of what turned out to be an Alien storage vault made of frozen rainstone."

"Rainstone?" Alice asked.

"It's a kind of stone that has the properties of both a crystal and a liquid. It's harder than mag-rez steel in one state, but if you can work the currents locked in the rock the way Rachel does, it can be transformed into a liquid."

Alice shivered. "That rainstone vault is where Drake's brother, Harry, and Rachel found one of the missing Keys, isn't it?"

"That's right," Fletcher said. "They nearly got killed in the process, but at least they bought us some time to find the other two Keys."

"Do they have any idea how one of the Keys ended up in that rainstone vault?" Alice asked.

"Nope." Jasper shook his head. "It's a mystery, like so many other things here on

Rainshadow."

Fletcher gave Alice a sympathetic look. "I'll bet you didn't expect to spend another honeymoon on Rainshadow."

Alice winced. "I'm really hoping this one goes more smoothly."

"Way I heard it, this honeymoon couldn't be as bad as the first one." Jasper snorted. "Rumor has it your first husband tried to kill you."

"Word gets around," Alice said.

"That's the way it is in small towns," Jasper said.

"I know," Alice said.

"You don't need to worry about history repeating itself here in Shadow Bay," Fletcher said quickly. "Not with Drake Sebastian."

"Hell, no," Jasper said. "We've seen enough of the Sebastian men to know they take care of their own."

"I'm sure they do," Alice said politely. "But I'm not a real member of the Sebastian family. As I keep explaining to people, Drake and I are in an MC, not a CM."

It dawned on her that Fletcher and Jasper were not looking at her. Instead, they were focused on something over her shoulder. She heard boot steps approaching behind her.

Drake came to a halt and looked at her. The gray light glinted somewhat ominously on his mirrored glasses.

"Did I hear my name?" he asked very softly.

She raised her brows, refusing to be intimidated.

"Jasper and Fletcher were assuring me that my second honeymoon on Rainshadow would end on a more upbeat note than the first one did," she said.

Drake studied her for a long moment. She could not see his eyes but she knew there was some heat in them. She could sense it in the atmosphere. Her intuition warned her that he was recalling hot sex and damp sheets.

After a couple of beats, Drake's mouth curved slightly in a sensual, deeply satisfied smile.

"Oh, yeah," he said. "This honeymoon will be different."

Alice narrowed her eyes, shoved her hands deep into the pockets of her windbreaker, and started walking toward the three men who blocked her path.

"If you'll excuse me," she said crisply, "I need to go help Burt get ready for the dinner rush."

The three men got out of her way. None

of them said a word. There was no need. Jasper's and Fletcher's hastily suppressed grins said it all.

Alice kept walking. *Men.*

CHAPTER 31

Burt eyed the gloomy view from the front window of the tavern. "Looks like that damn fog is already starting to roll in. I swear, it comes in earlier every day."

Alice did not look up from refilling the row of empty ketchup bottles that she had arranged on the counter. She had already added an inch and a half of water to each bottle and was now in the process of pouring in actual ketchup from another jar. She used a funnel to get the thick stuff into the bottles.

"Maybe it just seems like the fog is earlier today because it's been so dark and gray all day," she said.

"Nope." Burt turned away from the window. "Pretty sure it's darker out there over the bay than it was yesterday at this time. Means the dinner crowd will be arriving earlier, too. They'll probably stay longer and eat more food."

"Don't worry, you said the Foundation is picking up the tab."

"I'm not concerned about the money, it's the supply end of things that's starting to worry me. We're going through food like crazy. I'm telling you, we'll have to start rationing."

"Already on it, Boss." Alice fit the narrow tip of the funnel into the first bottle. "Starting with the ketchup."

Burt watched her use a spatula to push the thick ketchup into the bottle. When it was full, she removed the funnel, set it aside, and screwed the cap back on the bottle. She picked up the bottle and shook it vigorously until the water was thoroughly mixed with the ketchup. When she was finished, she held up the bottle for inspection.

"There you go, a nice full bottle of ketchup," she said.

Burt took the bottle from her and examined it with an expression of deep admiration. "Good work. No one will know that you thinned it with water. You are a pro. Where'd you learn the trick?"

"I told you, I've worked in the food-and-beverage business off and on my whole life," she said. "But I must admit that I picked up the ketchup-stretching trick in the orphanage."

Burt's forehead furrowed. "You were an orphan?"

"I know, we're a rare breed." Alice smiled ruefully. "We're not supposed to exist. There is always supposed to be some family around to take in a kid who finds herself alone in the world. But once in a while you get someone like me, someone with no next of kin, at least no kin that the authorities can find."

"But you're Nicholas North's great-granddaughter."

"True, but I didn't discover that until last year. And come to find out, I'm the last of the line."

"Geez, that's gotta be tough," Burt said. He brightened. "But you've got a new family of your own now. You're a Sebastian."

"It's just an MC," she said lightly. "The family thing is temporary."

"Yeah, but —"

"The ketchup will pour a little more easily now, but I doubt that anyone will notice the difference." Alice eyed the row of bottles. "I estimate that with a couple of inches of water in each bottle we can make the ketchup supply last another few days. By that time, Drake will have sorted out the problems in the Preserve."

At that moment Drake was in a meeting

with Jasper, Fletcher, Charlotte, and Rachel. They were holed up in the Kane Gallery, going through the list of men in town,
searching for a possible spy. Acutely aware
that there was nothing she could do to help,
she had returned to the tavern.

"Sure hope you're right." Burt put down
the ketchup bottle. "Now if you could just
do something about the hamburger supply.
I'm using up the last of the meat from the
freezer tonight. Tomorrow we start in on
the canned goods." He hesitated. "Sure as
hell hope that nothing has happened to
Harry Sebastian and the chief."

"They're okay," Alice said.

"Yeah?" Burt cocked a bushy brow. "What
makes you so sure of that?"

"Rachel told me she would know if something bad happened to Harry," Alice said.
"Charlotte said the same thing about the
chief. I believe them."

*Because I would know if something bad
happened to Drake,* she thought.

The sudden certainty of that knowledge
stopped her cold — literally. A true chill of
deep awareness shifted through her, stirring
all of her senses. For the first time she
forced herself to face head-on the fact that
she had been avoiding since she had met
Drake in the alley behind the theater. There

was a powerful, very vital, very intimate connection between them. It had been there from the start. The sex had simply intensified the bond, making it so much harder to ignore.

Until now she had tried to tell herself that the connection she felt was a product of her imagination. She had made up all sorts of plausible explanations, seeking logical answers — any answers — other than the obvious. But there was no longer any way to avoid the truth. She was in love with Drake Sebastian. He was the one man in the world who could break her heart.

Burt studied her with a worried expression. "You okay, Alice?"

She pulled herself together. "Yes, I'm fine." She picked up two of the newly filled ketchup bottles and positioned them on nearby tables. "I was just thinking about the culinary possibilities of canned beans."

Burt snorted. "Personally, I'm praying that Drake shuts down that damn fog machine before we have to start feeding beans to the entire population of Shadow Bay."

She winced. "I take your point. I vote we move to canned soup and peanut butter crackers first. Keep the beans as a last resort."

"That'll work. The kids will eat anything

with peanut butter on it." He looked out at the bay again. "That fog isn't just coming in earlier this afternoon, it's darker, too. I swear you can *feel* the damn stuff."

He's right, Alice thought. She could sense the eerie whispers of energy that always preceded the incoming tide of fog. She went to stand beside Burt. Together they looked out the window. The seething mist that was crouched just a short distance offshore did seem closer and darker than it should have at that hour.

"This is not good," she said quietly.

"No." Burt turned away from the window. "But there's nothing we can do except hope that Drake is making progress. Meanwhile, you and I had better get ready for an early dinner rush."

"I'll make up the peanut butter crackers," she said.

She started to turn away from the window, but a flicker of movement at the edge of her vision made her pause for a closer look. As she watched, two young boys dashed across the street and ran toward the entrance of the marina warehouse. She recognized the youngsters.

"I thought all of the kids were down at the library this afternoon," she said.

"Last I heard, that was the baby-sitting

plan for today," Burt said.

"Well, it looks like Billy Walters and Mark Snyder snuck away to play a game inside the warehouse. I'd better go get them."

"Good idea. If they get caught in the fog, they'll panic and so will their parents and everyone else."

Alice hurried through the maze of tables to the door and let herself out onto the street. The amber lantern in front of the tavern burned steadily, but the glow could not stave off the disturbing currents of darkness that emanated from the fog. The water in the bay was eerily quiet.

Night was going to fall fast and hard this evening.

She went quickly along the empty sidewalk and crossed to the entrance of the warehouse. The boys had left the door ajar. She looked through a grimy window, but the interior was heavily shadowed. Egan was out somewhere, walking his lonely patrol on the outskirts of Shadow Bay.

A loud chortling stopped her just as she gripped the door handle. She turned to see Houdini rushing excitedly toward her. All four of his eyes were open. She scooped him up and tucked him under her arm.

"You're still playing hide-and-seek with Billy and Mark, aren't you?" She opened the door and stepped into the gloom. "I'm surprised you and the kids haven't grown tired of that game."

Houdini made encouraging noises and wriggled madly. She put him down on the floor. He took off and promptly disappeared into a canyon created by two rows of wooden crates.

"Billy, Mark, the game is over," she called into the stillness. "The fog is coming in early today. Your parents will be worried."

Houdini chortled madly somewhere in the shadows. Two small figures popped up.

"He found us," Mark said. "I told you he could, even this far away."

"We're over here, Ms. North," Billy said. "We were testing Houdini. We think the cops should use dust bunnies for tracking criminals."

"Not a bad idea," she said. She went toward the boys, her sense of anxiety intensifying. "You can talk about that with the chief when he returns."

"*If* he returns," Billy said.

There was a new note in his voice now. He was no longer a happy-go-lucky kid playing a game. He was a scared kid playing a game, hoping that game would distract him from his fears.

"Chief Attridge will return soon, and so

will Mr. Sebastian," she said firmly.

"I heard Dad talking to Mom last night," Mark said. "Dad told her that if Drake Sebastian can't stop whatever is causing the fog, we're going to have to make a run for it in our boat. I could tell Mom was really scared. But Dad said we may not have any choice."

Alice thought about the treacherous currents and the impenetrable fog that formed a paranormal moat around Rainshadow. She and Drake had barely made it through. The forces in the mist and the water had only grown stronger in the intervening time.

She looked down at the boys and remembered what it had been like to be young and scared of things over which you had no control. The terrifying part about growing up was the dawning realization that the adults who were responsible for protecting you did not always have control over the scary stuff, either. She knew that Billy and Mark did not want more soothing platitudes from her. They needed to be reassured that someone over the voting age knew what he or she was doing about the problem.

"I know you're scared," she said. She crouched down in front of the boys. "We all are. But I can promise you that Mr. Sebastian and the chief are still safe out there in the Preserve. They are both professionals. They know what they are doing."

"But how do you know they're safe?" Billy asked.

"I know they're safe because Charlotte and Rachel know they're safe."

"But how can they know that?" Mark demanded.

"Because Charlotte has a psychic link with the chief. And Rachel has a similar connection with Harry Sebastian. Trust me on this, Charlotte and Rachel would know if something terrible happened to the men."

"Huh." Billy looked dubious. "Sounds kind of weird."

"I dunno," Mark said. "Mom says both the Sebastians and the chief have unusual para . . . para . . ."

"Unusual para-psych profiles?" Alice asked.

"Yeah, that's it," Mark said. He studied Alice. "She says you're different, too. She says those tricks you do — making things disappear — aren't like the tricks that real magicians do."

"Your mother is a very wise woman," Alice said. "She's right. And because Harry and Drake Sebastian and Chief Attridge are a little different, they are going to take care of the bad guys. Meanwhile, we need to get you back to your parents. It's almost time for dinner."

"Ah, just one more game with Houdini," Mark wheedled.

"Nope. Houdini will be wanting dinner, too. He never misses a meal or a snack." Aware of an unusual silence, she looked around. "Where is he?"

"Hey, I'll bet he's figured out that he can reverse the game and hide from us," Billy said. "He wants us to find him."

"Houdini," Alice called. "Game over. Seriously." She clapped her hands lightly together in the signal they used on stage. "Come on out. Dinner time."

There was a brief, muffled chortle in response to the word "dinner," but Houdini did not dash out of the gloom. Alice walked through the crowded space, her unease spiking.

"Houdini," she said. "Please, come out."

There was a scratching noise. Houdini appeared on top of a nearby crate. He chortled at her and then scampered down off the crate and disappeared back into the gloom.

"Oh, for pity's sake." Alice marched toward the spot where she had last seen him. "I really do not have time for this. We need to get Billy and Mark back to their parents."

She made her way cautiously through the warehouse, Billy and Mark at her heels. She rounded the far end of a row of neatly stacked kayaks and stopped when she saw Houdini. He was on the concrete floor and all four eyes were wide open. He was not sleeked out but he was definitely in alert mode. There was just enough of the failing gray light filtering through a dingy window to enable her to make out what had captured his interest: a bedroll composed of several ragged blankets and a well-worn khaki backpack that bore the faded emblem of the Resonance City Ghost Hunters Guild.

"That's Egan's stuff," Mark said. "This is where he sleeps. We shouldn't touch it. Everyone says he's crazy."

"Yeah, Dad says Egan must have got burned real bad by a ghost down in the tunnels," Billy said. "Mom says that's why I can't be a ghost hunter when I grow up."

"I agree, we are not going to touch Egan's things," Alice said. "But not because he might be psi-burned. We're not going to touch them because they are his personal property. Everyone has a right to his privacy. Come on, it's past time to leave."

She bent down to collect Houdini. He rumbled as though in warning but he did not try to evade her. He dropped the object he had been playing with. It landed on the concrete floor with a small clink. Alice straightened, Houdini in her arms, and glanced down.

When she saw the object at her feet, everything inside her went cold.

"Oh, crap," she whispered. "Houdini, where did you find that?"

But of course there was no answer. Nor did she need one. It didn't matter now. The only thing that mattered was getting Billy and Mark out of the warehouse.

She picked up the object that Houdini had found, straightened, and looked at the boys.

"We're leaving," she said. She spoke very quietly. "Come with me. We'll go out the back door, it's closer."

Something in her tone must have gotten through to Mark and Billy. They followed her out the rear door of the warehouse without asking any questions. She breathed a sigh of relief when they were safely outside and hurried them around the corner of the building.

A moment later they were on the sidewalk and no longer alone. Lanterns bobbed in the gathering dusk. They passed several people who were on their way to various places of refuge for the night.

Billy's parents and Mark's father appeared out of the fog.

"There you are," Mrs. Walters said. "I was starting to worry."

Mr. Snyder glared sternly at Mark, but his relief was palpable. "Didn't I tell you not to wander off alone?"

"I wasn't alone," Mark said quickly. "Billy and I were playing with Houdini. And then Ms. North found us."

Mrs. Walters looked at Alice, gratitude in her worried eyes. "Thanks for rounding them up."

"No problem," Alice said. "Almost time for dinner. I'll see you at the tavern in a few minutes."

"Where are you going?" Billy asked.

"To find Drake," Alice said. "Is he still at the Kane Gallery?"

"No," Mr. Snyder said. "I saw him a while ago. He was heading down to the police station."

"Thanks," Alice said.

With Houdini under one arm, the object he had discovered in her other hand, she hurried along the empty sidewalk. The windows of the unlit shops glittered darkly in the gathering dusk.

Her intuition was screaming at her now. She focused on finding Drake. The first tendrils of the mist wreathed around her like the tentacles of some monstrous sea creature rising from the depths to hunt on the shore.

She did not sense the dark shadow in the narrow alley until Houdini hissed a warning and went into full combat mode. Instinctively she pulled hard on her talent, trying to go invisible and take Houdini with her.

But it was too late. Neither she nor Houdini could move fast enough to evade the chilling radiation from the Alien weapon. Houdini went limp in her arm.

"Houdini," she whispered. *"No."*

She tried to run but she could not move. Instead the icy psi-light forced her to her knees. Her heart was pounding. Consciousness was slipping away. She managed to put Houdini on the ground. His paws twitched. His hunting eyes were closed but his baby blue eyes were still partially open. She dropped the object in her other hand on the ground next to him.

"Drake." She did not know if she said the name aloud or not. "Get Drake."

Drake would come to this place eventually, she thought. He would retrace her steps from the warehouse and find the object. He would understand why it was important.

Egan took no notice of the small object.

Perhaps he never even saw it. He was too busy focusing energy through the Alien weapon.

For a terrible moment Alice locked eyes with him. But he was already pocketing the weapon and reaching down to catch hold of her. She tried to scream but she could not manage so much as a whisper.

She plummeted into the abyss. Egan's hands and the terrible fog closed around her.

CHAPTER 32

"Tucker's connection here in town is Egan," Drake said. He tossed the notes that he and the others had made down onto Myrna's desk. "None of the other suspects even come close."

"Crazy Egan?" Myrna frowned at the handwritten notes in front of her. "But that makes no sense."

"Not so sure about that," Kirk said, his expression tightening. "When you think about it, he's the one person who can move around town at any time, day or night, without drawing more than a passing glance. Hell, none of us even sees him after dark because he sleeps in the warehouse."

"The kids have seen him at night," Drake said.

Myrna raised her brows. "What do you mean?"

"They've been talking about the ghost in the graveyard," Drake said. "I saw one the other night, too. Pretty sure now that was Egan."

"Get real," Kirk said, looking uneasy. "No such thing as ghosts."

"No, but there are ghost hunters," Drake said. "Egan is one. He must be the person I saw prowling around the old cemetery last night. I tried to find him, but by the time I got downstairs to the street he had disappeared."

"Why would he go to the graveyard?" Myrna asked.

"I don't know," Drake said. "What can you tell me about him?"

"Nothing that you don't already know," Myrna said. "He arrived on the ferry a few days ago with the rest of the Glorious Dawn crowd. According to you, Zara Tucker has been running her operation inside the Preserve for nearly a year. If Egan is her spy and he's been in Shadow Bay all this time, where's he been hiding?"

"I don't know," Drake said again. "What I can tell you is that Rachel and Charlotte and Fletch and Jasper have taken a close look at every man in Shadow Bay who fits the profile I drew up. Egan is a perfect match."

"Except that he just arrived on the island," Kirk pointed out.

"Look, I admit there are a lot of questions that need answering here, but I'm convinced that Egan has the answers," Drake said. "Whether he knows it or not."

Kirk frowned. "You think maybe he doesn't know what he's doing? Maybe he's an innocent victim who Tucker is manipulating?"

"Maybe," Drake said. "Regardless, I need your help. We've got to bring him in."

Kirk and Myrna exchanged brief glances. Drake could see that the decision had been made.

"You got it," Myrna said. "Not like we have any better ideas."

Kirk came away from the desk. "Let's pick him up."

"What charges?" Jasper asked dryly.

"Hell, I don't know," Kirk said. "We'll call him a person of interest for now."

Drake glanced out the window, trying to suppress the rising sense of urgency that was eating at him. A moment ago he'd gotten the gut-wrenching feeling that something had happened to Alice, but there was nothing going on out in the street that indicated trouble. He was on edge like everyone else. He had to control his imagination. *Stick to the facts, Sebastian.*

The fog was coming in earlier that afternoon and people were reacting accordingly. The amber lanterns in windows and over doorways had been lit even though it was not yet dark. Parents had already hauled kids off the swings in the small park. The softball game had ended. In the town square the door of the library opened. Those who had spent most of the day inside trooped out.

Everyone headed toward the B&Bs or the Marina Inn. By now Alice would be fully occupied with the evening dinner rush. She was safe indoors. So why was his intuition waving red flags of warning?

Because something bad had happened, of course. When you were born with a psychic talent, you learned to pay attention to your intuition. He headed for the door.

"Where are you going?" Rachel asked.

"I need to find Alice," he said.

"She'll be at the tavern," Jasper called after him.

Drake ignored him and went out onto the front porch of the station. He jacked up his senses a little, looking deeper into the gathering shadows. One of the shadows, a small one with four eyes, rushed toward him down the middle of the empty street.

Houdini's fur was plastered against his small frame. He was running on his four hind legs and clutching a small object in one front paw. Drake's blood turned to ice.

"Houdini." Drake went down the steps and crouched on the pavement. "What's wrong?"

Houdini vaulted up onto his shoulder, yammering madly. He waved the object in his paw. Drake rose and took the object.

The door of the police station slammed open. Jasper and Fletcher emerged and Myrna and Kirk followed.

"What is it?" Fletcher asked.

Charlotte came down the steps, peering through the gloom. "Looks like eye makeup." She took the flat plastic box and looked at the label. "It's not a standard cosmetic counter brand. This is stage makeup, the kind actors wear."

Drake looked at Houdini. "Where did you find this?"

Houdini rumbled in agitation.

"I saw Houdini playing with some kids a short time ago," Kirk said. "Maybe they can tell us where he found the stage makeup. The families will all be down at the tavern by now."

Ten minutes later Drake stood in the gloom-filled warehouse, looking at Egan's ragged bedroll and the "Prepare for the Glorious

Dawn" sign. He found the rest of the stage makeup and some fake eyebrows stashed in a nearby crate.

"He's got her, doesn't he?" Jasper asked.

Houdini growled.

"We'll find her," Drake said.

Fletcher was grim-faced. "How are we going to do that?"

Drake looked at Houdini. "Time to play hide-and-seek for real, pal. Find Alice."

Houdini needed no second urging. He took off at a run. Drake followed, Jasper and Fletcher on his heels.

"Where's he going?" Jasper asked. "I can't see more than ten feet in this fog and the stuff is getting worse."

"He's heading for the graveyard," Drake said.

CHAPTER 33

Alice came awake on a surge of panicky energy and the sound of a low, moaning litany infused with resigned despair.

"Oh, shit, oh, shit, oh, shit."

The voice was male, she decided.

She realized she was lying on what felt like a very hard cot. She opened her eyes and discovered that she was on her back looking up at a green quartz ceiling that glowed with the unmistakable radiance of Alien psi. The ambient, senses-ruffling currents of energy in the atmosphere confirmed that she was in a chamber that could only have been built by the ancients.

For a few tense seconds she listened for Houdini's reassuring chortle. But all she got was the bleak, toneless litany.

"Shit, shit, shit."

She sat up slowly and looked around. It came as no surprise to discover that there were no windows. The Aliens had avoided sunlight and fresh air as if both were poison. There was a door that was a heavy, man-made mag-steel gate fitted with prison-style bars. It was mounted on steel rails at the bottom and top so that it could be slid aside. Through the bars she could see a portion of a glowing green hallway.

She was not alone in the Chamber. A young man was huddled in the corner. He was visibly pulled in on himself, his arms locked around his knees. He rocked numbly. His long sandy-brown hair was dirty and unkempt. There was dull fear in his eyes, as if he had seen one too many ghosts. Alice was quite certain that he had not eaten or slept well in a long time.

"You must be Pete," she said.

He stopped rocking. His eyes widened. "I'm officially whacked now, aren't I? Flat-out crazy."

"I doubt it." She waved a hand to indicate their surroundings. "But I can certainly understand why you might think so. Living in this place would make anyone a little nuts. Karen Rosser told us that Tucker had probably sent you into the Chamber a few more times since you helped her escape. She says it's a real nightmare trip."

Disbelief flashed in Pete's eyes. It was followed by a faint glimmer of hope.

"You saw Karen?" he whispered. "She's okay? She made it to Shadow Bay?"

"She's fine. We found her in Deception Cove. She's safe in Shadow Bay now."

"You're for real?" Pete came out of his huddled position and got slowly to his feet. "You're not a ghost?"

"What makes you think I'm a ghost?"

"You've been asleep ever since they brought you in here. I was waiting for you to wake up. But a minute ago you sort of disappeared and then you reappeared. I figured I was hallucinating."

"Oh, yeah, the disappearing thing," Alice said. "Sorry about that. Instinct, I guess. I woke up in a bit of a panic. I'm a light-talent, like you and Karen. But you know how it is with talent. No two people get the same version. Mine is only good for vanishing temporarily."

"I'd give a lot to be able to disappear from this place, believe me. You're sure Karen is okay?"

"You have my word, she's safe. I can also assure you that no matter what you've been told, Zara Tucker's operation is not an authorized Foundation excavation. But Foundation Security — the real deal — is here on the island. Just a matter of time before help arrives."

She infused her words with all the confidence she could muster. But Pete wasn't buying the act.

"If Foundation Security is on Rainshadow, what are you doing here?" he asked.

She winced. "That's a little harder to explain. I managed to get myself kidnapped by a cult guy named Egan. Everyone in Shadow Bay believed he was harmless. Evidently we were wrong. He's working with Dr. Tucker, isn't he?"

"I don't know anyone named Egan, but the witch does have one security guy left. The others bailed a while ago but the last one stuck around. He's crazy about Tucker. I mean literally crazy about her."

"Any idea why Tucker had Egan kidnap me?"

"You said you're a light-talent, right?"

"Right."

Pete grimaced. "She needs light-talents to go into that damned Chamber. I'm not strong enough to find the Keys. Neither was Karen. Maybe Tucker thinks you can do it. She's desperate."

Crisp footsteps echoed in the hallway. A woman appeared on the other side of the barred door. She was dainty and delicate, with fine bones and exquisite features. Her big blue eyes were shielded by a pair of very serious black-framed glasses that somehow made her appear absolutely adorable. Her blonde hair was pinned in a severe knot at the back of her head. She wore a camp shirt embroidered with the Sebastian, Inc. logo as well as khaki trousers and boots. The swashbuckling jungle gear only served to enhance her adorableness. She held a clipboard and a leather-bound volume in one hand.

"Let me take a wild guess here," Alice said. "Dr. Zara Tucker, Professional Mad Scientist, I presume."

The woman blinked, frowning ever so slightly as if she had not expected quite that reaction. Her expression smoothed out almost immediately. *Probably afraid of getting frown lines,* Alice thought.

"I'm Dr. Tucker and I assure you I'm not mad," Zara said calmly. "I expect that Drake Sebastian has been feeding you that line. He's the one who is unbalanced. His parapsych profile has been terribly unstable ever since the accident."

"It wasn't an accident. You attacked him with an Alien weapon."

"Is that what he told you?" Zara sighed. "Well, I'm not surprised. He was furious because I wanted to end our relationship. He threatened to kill me. I had to defend

309

myself. We were in one of the artifact labs when the argument occurred. I grabbed the laser device and fired it in self-defense."

"Geez," Alice said. "You're not just a mad scientist, you're also a pathological liar, aren't you? Wow, talk about a warped para-psych profile. You'd make a terrific case study for the shrinks. And by the way, I'll bet that's my great-grandfather's diary. It belongs to me."

Something that looked a lot like rage burned in Zara's eyes. But she got control of it quickly.

"I don't have time for this," she said. "The reason you are here is because there is a possibility that you are my ticket off this damn island."

Alice got to her feet. "How am I supposed to get you off Rainshadow? I can't even drive a boat. Not that anyone is going to be leaving by boat until that fog clears."

"According to my calculations, the fog will clear as soon as the two crystals are removed from the Chamber." Zara's fine brows puckered briefly in another barely there frown. "I am convinced now that the problems began when the oscillation pattern became unstable. The effect was so subtle at first that the instruments missed it. The crystals did ignite the forces inside the

Chamber, as your great-grandfather theorized in this diary, but the currents became unstable."

"Blah, blah, blah," Alice said. "In other words, you screwed up. Mad scientists do that a lot. Ever hear about a guy named Dr. Frankenstein?"

Once again Zara's eyes went hot with fury. Like the tiny frown lines, however, the fierce emotions were quickly veiled.

"You're a real bitch, aren't you?" Zara smiled. "And a not very bright bitch at that. For your information, that damn fog and everything else that has gone wrong here on Rainshadow is your fault."

"How do you figure that?"

"You were supposed to marry Fulton Whitcomb, you stupid woman. Not just an MC, a full Covenant Marriage."

"After which I was scheduled to suffer a lethal accident, leaving my Rainshadow inheritance to Fulton, right?"

"That was the original plan. Aldwin and I needed Whitcomb from the start because he was the one who had the kind of money it takes to underwrite a full-scale excavation of an Alien ruin. We also assumed that, with his looks and his social status, he would have no problem convincing you to marry him. Instead, you only agreed to an MC."

"Lucky me, marrying up like that."

"Still, he was sure he could get you pregnant and force you into a Covenant Marriage. Instead, the day you found those crystals, you told him you wanted a divorce. From then on, things kept going wrong."

"Why did you murder Fulton? He returned from Rainshadow with the three crystals and you said you needed his money. Why get rid of him?"

"Whitcomb decided he didn't need us any longer. He was planning to go to the Sebastians and offer to tell them what I had discovered on Rainshadow if they would agree to let him conduct the excavation. All Fulton cared about was having his name attached to the project."

"So you killed him."

"I didn't kill him. The head of my security team took care of that aspect of things. No choice really. For a time everything was put on hold. But Aldwin managed to get enough money out of Ethel Whitcomb to finance my work. She thinks she's building a new wing on her precious museum."

"But the money has been going into your project here on Rainshadow," Alice said.

"Unfortunately, I haven't had the budget I needed to hire the kind of professionals I wanted, the kind I deserve to work with. I was forced to make do with low-rent talents like Pete, here, and Karen Rosser."

"To summarize, you've been running an illegal, off-the-books operation here on Rainshadow and you've screwed it up so much the whole island is about to blow." Alice nodded. "Nice work, Dr. Tucker. This should certainly earn you a place in the journals of para-archaeology, not to mention a nice long vacation in prison, assuming you survive."

"Shut up." Zara's eyes were chips of ice. "You have no idea what you're talking about."

"Then let's cut to the chase. How am I supposed to rescue you?"

"You're a light-talent, a strong one, evidently. We didn't know just how strong you were back at the start." Dr. Tucker clicked her teeth in mild disapproval. "You certainly kept your ability to bend light a secret from Fulton and the rest of us. I didn't believe you were anything but a run-of-the-mill talent until you started doing your little magic tricks for the kids in Shadow Bay."

Alice smiled.

Zara raised her brows. "No, you won't try that magic act with me. For one thing, although I know that you can go invisible, it's just a trick of the light. You certainly can't walk through walls or the door of this cell. And just to make sure you don't try anything clever, you will be handcuffed to Pete, who will be closely guarded by the head of my security team."

"You are no doubt referring to your last remaining thug-for-hire," Alice said. "That would be Egan."

"Egan Quinton," Zara said. "He has proved to be an extremely useful and versatile employee."

"Okay, so I can't escape. What do you expect me to accomplish?"

Zara's hands clenched around the clipboard and the diary. Her eyes narrowed. "You are going to go into that overheated Chamber and retrieve the two crystals. Once they're out, I'm certain that the Chamber will cool down. When the energy levels start to fall, the fog will recede and I will be able to get off the island."

"What makes you think I can get the crystals out of the Chamber?"

"Only a light-talent can enter that Chamber now. But it's going to take one with a lot of power to find the crystals and bring them out. Let's hope you're stronger than Pete or Ms. Rosser."

"And if I refuse to give it a whirl?"

"In that case, Egan will start killing people

in Shadow Bay. One by one." Zara glanced at Pete. "But we'll let him start with Pete so that you can be certain that I mean business. Egan?"

There were more footsteps in the glowing hall, heavy boots this time. Egan Quinton appeared on the other side of the steel bars. He was no longer in costume and he had removed his makeup. Minus the scraggly, long-haired wig, heavy eyebrows, and the facial prosthetics that had altered the lines of his face, he looked remarkably ordinary; remarkably unremarkable.

"How's that enlightenment thing working out for you, Egan?" Alice asked. "Any insights into Zara, here?"

Egan gave her a brief, irritated look and then fixed his ghost-gaze on Pete.

"Want me to do him now?" he asked. There was no trace of emotion in the question. He might as well have been asking Zara if she wanted him to take out the trash.

Zara removed her geeky glasses. "That depends on Alice. It's her decision."

Pete watched Egan the way a small creature watches a cobra. "Please, don't."

Egan reached into his jacket and pulled out the Alien weapon he had used on Alice and Houdini.

"At full power it causes the heart to stop,"

he explained.

"Forget it," Alice said. "I'll try to get those crystals for you but only if you leave Pete alone."

Zara gave her an approving smile. "Excellent. I assure you, I have no wish to kill Pete or anyone else. I would prefer not to waste the time or the energy in the weapon. No telling how long it will last. My only goal now is to get off Rainshadow and disappear."

"Probably a good idea," Alice said. "Because it won't be long before the Sebastians come looking for you."

"I vanished once, quite successfully. I can do it again." Zara turned away from the cell gate. "Egan, bring them both to the Chamber. Time is running out."

CHAPTER 34

Drake came to a halt at the gravestone. The others caught up with him, breathing hard. The weeds and grass around the weathered grave marker had been trampled by a pair of heavily booted feet on more than one recent occasion.

Houdini jumped up and down on the stone, making urgent noises.

Fletcher frowned at the name on the stone. "William Bainbridge. Why does that sound familiar?"

"Because it's engraved over the front door of the library and it's the official name of the town park," Myrna said. "Bainbridge was a smuggler who worked the Amber Sea area years ago. Technically speaking, he's the guy credited with founding Shadow Bay."

Fletcher grimaced. "Oh, yeah, right."

Houdini continued to bounce up and down. He was becoming increasingly agitated.

Drake crouched beside the flat stone marker. Methodically he ran his hands around the edges. It didn't take long to find what he was looking for. He pushed the concealed lever.

The gravestone opened ponderously with only the faintest of groans. Someone had been keeping the hinges well oiled, he thought.

Currents of Alien psi wafted out of the opening. He looked down at the flight of glowing quartz steps that descended into a tunnel illuminated with eerie green light.

"Son of a ghost," Jasper said. "So there are some catacombs here on the island, after all. Always figured we'd find them someday."

"Looks like old Bainbridge stumbled into a hole-in-the-wall," Fletcher said.

"If Bainbridge isn't buried here, what happened to him?" Rachel asked. "Not that it matters now."

Houdini darted down the steps, pausing expectantly.

"I should have done a more thorough investigation after I saw that so-called ghost wandering around here in the middle of the night," Drake said.

Jasper shook his head. "Not like you've had a lot of spare time to investigate anything. Doubt if you would have found this trapdoor, anyway. Hell, Fletcher and I have been living here for a couple of decades — spent our former careers in the tunnels — but we never stumbled onto this entrance."

"Well, at least we now know how Egan managed to contact Tucker frequently without having to go through the Preserve," Charlotte said.

"And how he kidnapped Alice without having to carry her through the fence and across a lot of psi-hot territory," Drake said. "I'm betting that this tunnel is a shortcut to the Chamber ruin. He can't be too far ahead. I'm going after him."

"This island has never been under the control of the Guilds," Fletcher said. "That means the catacombs down below have never been cleared of ghosts. Egan is a hunter. He can handle ghosts. But you don't have that kind of talent. Looks like you are going to need some backup."

"I'd appreciate it," Drake said.

He started down the glowing staircase. Jasper and Fletcher followed him into the catacombs.

CHAPTER 35

Alice sensed the seething energy emanating from the pyramid before they walked into the subterranean chamber. The instant she saw the glowing ruin she knew that it was only a matter of time before it exploded. The dark, heavy currents coming off the crystals that formed the pyramid felt inherently unstable. They flooded the atmosphere with an invisible sea of hot psi.

The only part of the structure that was man-made was the heavy mag-steel door at the entrance. Under most circumstances, mag-steel was strong enough to block paranormal radiation, but Alice had a feeling that in this case the door would not last much longer.

The fierce, wild energy swirling in the outer chamber lifted Alice's hair as if she were floating in water. Goose bumps prickled her skin. The waves of psi were both unnerving and exhilarating. She did not know how it was possible to be terrified and at the same time thrilled, but she did know how to conceal her emotions. She kept her stage face in place.

"I gotta tell you, Zara, as a research scientist, you're a real loser," she said. "What did you think you were doing, fooling around with Alien technology this powerful? That pyramid feels like it's going to blow at any moment."

"You can save the sarcasm," Zara said. "Because if it does blow, all of us, including you, are going with it."

Alice glanced at Pete. His right hand was handcuffed to her left hand. A two-foot-long chain connected them. Egan gripped Pete's upper arm.

Pete was probably even more frightened than she was, Alice thought, because he had been inside the pyramid and knew what they were about to encounter. But he was doing his best to appear calm and stoic. Maybe he actually had some faith in her promise that rescue was on the way.

Alice turned back to Zara. "That Chamber is big, and according to what I've been told, I'm not going to be able to see my hand in front of my face once I'm inside."

"That's correct," Zara said. "You'll be completely blind. One step past the entrance and you won't even be able to look back and see the opening. The para-energy inside overwhelms light from the normal end of the spectrum. It's like going into a cave."

"How am I supposed to find the crystals?"

"Trust me, you'll sense them. They're so hot now that even someone without much talent can pick up the energy emanating from them."

"So why don't you send Egan in after them?"

Fury and frustration flashed across Zara's face. "Because only someone with a strong light-oriented talent can get through the force field at the entrance without going unconscious within seconds. Back at the start, it was possible for any talent to come and go from the Chamber. It was similar to walking through the psi-fence that surrounds the Preserve. But now it's a thousand times worse."

"Because you heated things up with the crystals. You're a real twit, aren't you?"

Zara's eyes were hot with rage, but she pulled herself together with visible effort. "Egan will put a rope around your waist. He'll hold the other end. When you have the crystals, signal him by yanking on the rope a couple of times. He'll pull you out."

"We both know if it was that easy, you

would have done it yourself. You're a light-talent. But you can't even get past the entrance, can you?"

Zara gave her a thin smile. She was still in control, but cracks were appearing in her icy composure. "You are wasting time, Ms. North. Egan will slide open the door for you."

"What a gentleman," Alice said.

She walked slowly toward the entrance of the Dream Chamber, drawing Pete with her.

"Shit," Pete whispered. "I hate this place."

Egan followed. He picked up the rope that was coiled on the floor at the entrance and looped the noose-like end around Alice's waist. She shuddered in revulsion when he touched her. He did not appear to notice, let alone take offense.

Satisfied that the line was secure around her, he grasped the other end firmly in one hand. Then he used both hands to haul aside the heavy steel plate blocking the entrance.

Night and energy from the farthest end of the spectrum swirled just inside the opening. Fog-like tendrils of power stormed in the Chamber.

"Hurry," Zara shouted. "There isn't much time left."

"Too bad you didn't think of that before

you started fiddling around with those crystals," Alice called over her shoulder.

"This is your fault, damn you," Zara shrieked. "Get those crystals out of there or we are all dead."

A frisson of awareness whispered through Alice. Drake was somewhere nearby. She could sense it.

She glanced toward the vaulted opening at the far end of the cavernous room. She could not see anyone, but the certainty that Drake was close was growing stronger.

She was equally certain of another fact. Zara and Egan would not hesitate to use Pete and her as hostages.

Not yet, she thought. *Too dangerous.*

There was no such thing as telepathy, or so the experts claimed. But she shared some kind of psychic connection with Houdini. On stage he always seemed to get his cues right. As for her bond with Drake, that was a lot more complicated, but she no longer doubted that it existed. He certainly could not read her mind but he had a gift for strategy. If she gave him an opening, he would seize it.

Step one was to keep Zara and Egan distracted for a few more minutes.

"It's going to be okay, Pete," she said quietly.

She reached back for his hand, gripping his fingers tightly, and moved to the entrance. She needed physical contact for what she was about to do.

Pete looked as if he might be ill but he stumbled forward with her.

"Trust me," she whispered.

"Not like I've got a lot of choice," Pete said. "Sure hope you know what you're doing."

"I'm the box-jumper," she said. "The magician's assistant. That means I know the secret of the trick."

"Yeah? So where's the magician?"

She was careful not to look back over her shoulder. "He'll be on stage any minute now."

"What part am I playing in this performance?"

"You're the volunteer from the audience."

"I was afraid of that."

She tightened her grip on his hand, kicked up her talent, and pulled him with her through the wall of midnight.

CHAPTER 36

The green ghost fire blocked the quartz tunnel, forcing all of them to a halt. The ball of Alien energy was fueled by the chaotic currents that burned at its core. It had no doubt been blazing just as fiercely ever since the Aliens had vanished.

Drake watched the ghost through his mirrored glasses. He could have removed the shades because all of the energy that emanated from the quartz catacombs was paranormal in nature. But he did not know what surprises Zara might have in store. Even a simple amberrez flashlight could temporarily blind him.

Houdini, stationed on Drake's shoulder, rumbled impatiently and blinked his hunting eyes.

"No way Egan could have made it past that ghost," Fletcher said. "It's possible that it drifted in from a connecting passage after he went through, but more likely he deliberately planted it here on the off chance that someone found the gravestone entrance and tried to follow him."

Although they were called ghosts, the balls of psi-fire that floated through the maze of Alien catacombs were not the remnants of sentient beings. The technical name for the phenomena was Unstable Dissonance Energy Manifestations, also called UDEMs. They were one of the many hazards of the tunnels and the primary reason for the enduring power of the Ghost Hunter Guilds. Only those with a talent for dealing with the unique psi of the UDEMs could neutralize the dangerous, unpredictable storms of psi that drifted randomly in the eerie underworld.

"Are we sure this is the right passage?" Jasper asked. "What if Houdini is wrong?"

Houdini bounced on Drake's shoulder, agitated by the delay.

The vast array of green catacombs was a bewildering maze to human senses. Only a small portion of the Underworld had been mapped. No one knew how far the passages extended. The Guild did its best to guard the known entrances and restrict unauthorized access, but there were thousands of secret holes-in-the-wall that were used by illegal antiquities hunters, thrill-seekers, and the occasional serial killer.

"Houdini is leading us in the right direction," Drake said. "He's got some kind of psychic connection with Alice. Dust bunnies have no trouble navigating underground."

He did not add the obvious point: Houdini's guidance was their best hope — make that their only hope — of finding Alice in time to save her. His intuition told him that if Zara Tucker and Egan managed to get off the island, Alice would be dead within hours.

"We've seen how some dust bunnies bond with humans," Fletcher said to Jasper. "Drake's right, got to trust Houdini here. Not like any of us can track a man through the tunnels."

Jasper stepped forward. "I'll take care of this sucker. Haven't done this kind of work in a while. Got to admit, sometimes I miss it."

Drake felt energy shift in the atmosphere and knew that Jasper was raising his talent. A second, smaller ghost flashed into existence directly in front of the blocking storm. Jasper's UDEM oscillated with hot energy at its core, but unlike the wild ghost it was under his control.

Jasper used his talent to maneuver the

second ghost until it collided with the furnace of hot psi that blocked the tunnel. There was a flash of green lightning. Energy roared in the atmosphere. A moment later the wild ghost winked out.

Jasper quickly extinguished the ghost he had created. He was grinning.

"That was fun," he said.

"Good to know you haven't lost your touch," Fletcher said. "Nice work."

Houdini bounced up and down and rumbled ferociously, urging everyone forward.

They moved swiftly, but distances underground were difficult to gauge. Drake reasoned that the Chamber could not be too far from Shadow Bay via the Underworld tunnels because Egan had evidently come and gone frequently between the two locations. But there was no way to be certain how their position belowground related to the aboveground terrain.

They rounded a corner. Houdini abruptly stiffened on Drake's shoulder and growled a warning that brought them to a halt in a large, high-ceilinged chamber. A dozen glowing passages branched off on all sides. Houdini was gazing intently at one of the corridors. He was tensed with the anticipation of a predator.

"We're close," Drake said.

Jasper glanced at Houdini. "Yeah, the little guy looks ready to go for someone's throat."

They moved along the corridor that Houdini appeared to favor. At the far end Drake could see more intersecting passages. Alice was not far away. The whisper of intimate awareness on the back of his neck told him that she was somewhere nearby.

Instinct prompted him to move as quietly as possible. He noticed that Jasper and Fletcher did the same. Their caution was probably unnecessary. The reality was that sound, like other kinds of energy, was always distorted and quickly overwhelmed by the Alien psi that emanated from the tunnel walls, ceiling, and floor. It was possible to be within fifteen feet of someone who was talking in a normal voice and not be aware of his or her presence if the person happened to be out of sight around a corner.

"I know the three of us have a plan," Fletcher said. "But I doubt that Houdini understands human strategy. If we're close to Alice, he's liable to take off at any moment to try to get to her. If Egan spots him, he'll realize that we might be in the vicinity."

"Every plan has a weak point," Drake said, glancing at Houdini. "The good news is that we know ours. That means that we can compensate. On second thought, that's not the only good news."

Jasper raised his brows. "But, wait, there's more?"

"Oh, yeah," Drake said. "We've got two ghost hunters on our team. Zara Tucker only has one."

"One hunter who just happens to be armed with an Alien weapon," Fletcher pointed out.

"I'm counting on your ghost-fighting talents to neutralize Egan's weapon," Drake said.

"Right." Jasper automatically touched the amber he wore around his neck. "No problem."

They hugged the wall of the tunnel as they approached the intersection. Drake took Houdini off his shoulder and tucked him under one arm, silently trying to convey the need to stay out of sight until the last minute. Houdini wriggled a little but he stayed put. Maybe he had gotten the message, Drake thought. Or maybe when it came to hunting instincts, all predators relied on the same basic strategy — don't let the prey see you coming until you're ready to make the kill.

Drake was in the lead, so he arrived at the

vaulted entrance of the passage first. Now, at last, he could make out voices. He motioned Jasper and Fletcher to a halt. They all listened intently.

". . . They've been inside a full minute and they haven't collapsed," Zara said. Relief and excitement vibrated in her voice. "It looks like Alice can handle the psi."

"What if they don't find the crystals?" Egan asked.

"She's still conscious. This is going to work."

"But if it doesn't?"

"You had better hope that it does," Zara said. "Because if this fails there is only one last option."

"You never said there was another option." Egan sounded uneasy. "What is it?"

"We'll have to send someone else in," Zara said, impatient now.

"Yeah? Who?"

"You."

"Are you crazy? I'm not going in there. I can't handle that kind of energy. I'm a ghost hunter, not a light-talent."

"According to my calculations, there is a seventy-percent possibility that a non–light-talent can survive the experience for a short time. Hopefully, long enough to bring out the crystals."

"But you said the energy buildup inside the pyramid would drive a non–light-talent mad."

"That is a complication," Zara said. "Let's hope that Alice can pull off one last magic trick."

CHAPTER 37

The nerve-shattering darkness screamed around them. *And this is with my senses at full throttle,* Alice thought. No wonder Zara Tucker and Egan had not been able to get through the storm. It took everything she had to forge a path. She did her best to protect Pete as well as herself but she could tell from the death grip he had on her hand that he was struggling.

A few more steps and they were through the psi-barrier. Alice realized she had been holding her breath. She finally managed to inhale. Not that the situation was greatly improved.

A storm of dark light roared and crashed and churned around them. There were occasional flashes of paranormal lightning, but they did nothing to illuminate the interior of the pyramid. Bizarre images appeared and disappeared in the depths of the seemingly impenetrable night.

The utter darkness was disorienting. No normal light filtered in past the narrow entrance. They had taken only a couple of steps inside, but Alice could not see anything, not even Pete standing so close that his shoulder brushed against hers.

"Oh, shit," Pete said. Dread edged his words. "It's gotten even worse than it was yesterday when she sent me in here, a lot worse."

"It's okay," Alice said with a cool certainty she did not feel. "It's just light — really, really dark light — but light is light and I can work with that."

"I used to think I could work with light, too. But this stuff isn't like anything I've ever seen."

She kept her grip on Pete's hand and focused on altering the currents of her aura so that they formed a shield, forcing the dark wavelengths of the nightmare energy to bend around the two of them.

"What's happening?" Pete whispered.

"We just went invisible. This is my one big trick. We're standing in the eye of the storm now. Too bad we don't have an audience. How are you doing?"

"Okay." Pete sounded vaguely amazed. "I'm okay, at least I think so. Or maybe this is one of the hallucinations. I'm aware of the intensity of the energy but it's as if we're in a bubble that's protecting us from the forces."

"That's a good way to describe it."

"How long can you keep this up?"

"Long enough." *I hope,* she added silently. *Never let the audience see you sweat.* "Let's find those crystals."

"Not a good idea. Once Dr. Tucker and Egan get their hands on those damn stones, you and I are both toast. Well, I am, for sure. They might keep you around until they're safely off the island, but I'm a goner as soon as I step out of here. I doubt if you'll last much longer."

"I know, but those crystals are the only bargaining chips we've got," Alice said. "Once we have them, we might be able to buy a little more time."

"Time for your husband to arrive?" Pete sounded dubious.

"Yes," she said. "Trust me, he'll get here eventually."

"Okay, it's not like I've got any plan at all."

"Can you sense the crystals?"

"Not anymore," Pete said. "The bitch sent me in here one too many times. I haven't had time to fully recover between sessions. I'm pretty burned out."

Alice went still, probing cautiously. A thin trickle of energy that felt very different from the currents of the storm danced somewhere in the darkness.

"I think I've got a fix on them," she said.

She moved forward, keeping her grip on Pete. She put her free hand out to ward off an encounter with a sloped wall.

She was walking blind but that did not stop the fractured images from swirling around her.

"It's like moving through a dream," she said.

"Yeah, a nightmare," Pete said. "But I don't feel as disoriented as I have in the past. Usually by now I start to pass out. Your light-bending trick is working."

The delicate trickle of energy was growing stronger.

"We're getting closer," she said.

The tension on the rope around her waist remained steady as Egan let out the line.

"They must be getting real excited out there," Pete said grimly. "They'll know we haven't collapsed yet. Hell, *I'm* excited because I haven't passed out."

Alice did not reply. There was no point letting Pete know that she was having to pull harder and harder on her talent to keep the shield around both of them. She was approaching her limits.

The trail of crystal energy brightened. For the first time she could perceive a pale, shadowy light flickering in the utter darkness, a weak paranormal candle flame. As she and Pete moved closer a second current of eerie radiance appeared.

"The crystals," Pete said. He sounded stunned. "I think I can see them."

Alice stopped. Pete stumbled to a halt beside her. They looked down. At least Alice thought they were looking down. In the disorienting darkness it was impossible to know.

Regardless, she could make out two flat slabs of crystal, each slightly larger than a man's hand. They glowed with paranormal energy.

"They look harmless," she said. "Guess I was expecting something more dramatic."

"A hot stove looks harmless, too, until you put your hand on it."

"Good point." She reached out and touched one stone very carefully. A frisson of energy flashed through her but there was no pain. She picked up the slab. "You take the other one."

Pete did as instructed. "Now what?"

"Now we hang on in here as long as possible to give Drake time to deal with Zara

Tucker and Egan."

"And if he doesn't come to the rescue?"

"We go to Plan B. If worse comes to worst, we'll pretend we found one of the stones but that we need a break before we go back in after the second crystal. I told you. It's all about buying time."

"Too bad you're not a real magician," Pete said. "We could use one of those about now."

Chapter 38

Drake moved around the corner and saw Zara and Egan. Egan looked very different without his disguise, remarkably unremarkable. Zara and Egan were hovering close to the entrance of the crystal pyramid, which was the size of a two-story house. He could feel the energy of the Chamber from where he stood.

Egan gripped the end of a long length of rope in one gloved hand. The cord was stretched taut. It disappeared into a deep darkness at the entrance of the Chamber. Drake was very sure that Alice was on the other end of the line.

He set Houdini free.

"Get him," Drake whispered. He doubted that Houdini could understand, but with luck he would serve as a distraction.

As if he had sized up the situation and had recognized the primary source of danger in the room, Houdini dashed across the cavernous space, heading straight for Egan.

Sensing that they were no longer alone, Zara whirled around. When she saw Drake, alarm exploded into fury.

"Bastard," she said. "Kill him, Egan."

Egan dropped the end of the line he had been holding and yanked the Alien weapon out of his belt. He leveled it at Drake.

Houdini arrived at his target and scampered up Egan's pant leg.

"Shit." Egan reeled backward, frantically swiping at Houdini with the weapon.

Houdini bounded off Egan to evade the vicious swipes but he immediately circled to find another opening. Egan brought the weapon up again and fired it, aiming for Houdini. The ray missed Houdini's tail by scant inches.

"Egan!" Zara screamed.

Egan finally realized he had been paying attention to the wrong threat, but it was too late. Jasper and Fletcher were already moving forward, initiating the strategy they had devised during the trek through the tunnels. Both conjured hot, powerful ghosts that closed in on Egan, driving him back toward a wall.

There was nothing like having a pair of energy storms chasing you to help concentrate your attention. Egan had spent time in the tunnels. He recognized lethal-sized ghosts when he saw them.

"Drop the gadget," Fletcher ordered.

Egan came up against the wall. There was nowhere to run. He tossed the weapon aside. It rolled across the floor.

But Zara was running and she was not headed toward the nearest exit. She went toward the entrance of the pyramid. For a beat or two Drake thought she was going into the Chamber.

He was wrong.

When she reached the entrance, she bent low, scooped up the trailing end of the rope, and hurled it through the wall of energy that sealed the pyramid.

The line vanished into the darkness.

"Your little MC wife will never find her way out," Zara said. "Neither will Pete. You can't possibly come up with a way to rescue them or retrieve the crystals — not in time to keep this whole island from drowning in that damn fog. You and I are going to go together, my love. Isn't that romantic?"

CHAPTER 39

The tension on the line around Alice's waist went abruptly slack.

"Oh, crap," she whispered softly.

She tucked the crystal under her arm and tugged slightly on the rope. There was no resistance.

"He let go of the rope, didn't he?" Pete said in the voice of doom. "He might as well have dropped us down a bottomless mine shaft."

"There's only one reason why Egan would have dropped the rope," Alice said briskly. "Drake is out there."

"Even if you're right, it doesn't matter now. No one is going to be able to find us before this place blows."

"The trick isn't over yet," Alice said.

"Got any ideas?"

"It's up to the magician now," Alice said. "I told you, I'm just the box-jumper."

CHAPTER 40

"Keep an eye on both of them," Drake said.

"No problem," Jasper said.

He sent his ghost closer to Egan, who opened his mouth on a soundless scream when the fierce energy brushed against him. He crumpled to the ground and lay very still.

"Is he — ?" Drake asked.

"Just unconscious," Jasper assured him. "Easier to keep an eye on him this way."

"Same treatment for Dr. Tucker?" Fletcher asked.

"No," Zara shrieked. "You can't do this to me. You don't understand. This was important research."

"Just tie her hands behind her back," Drake said. "Unless she starts to give you any trouble. In which case, feel free to zap her."

Fletcher took a length of leather cording out of a pocket and went toward Zara.

"Please," she entreated. Energy shivered in the atmosphere around her. "You must help me. Drake Sebastian hates me. He wants to kill me. You've got to stop him. Together you and I can save this island."

"Forget it," Fletcher said. He snagged one of Zara's wrists and then the other. "I'm married to that guy over there." He angled his head toward Jasper. "We're both gay."

Houdini chortled excitedly, fully fluffed once more with all four eyes still open. He dashed through the entrance of the pyramid and disappeared.

Drake went swiftly to the opening and looked into the thick, impenetrable darkness that barred the way.

"You're psi-blind," Zara taunted. "There's no way you can enter that pyramid. One step inside the door and you'll be lost. You'll never find her or those Keys."

Drake ignored her. He took off his dark glasses and slipped them into the pocket of his jacket. He jacked up his senses and walked through the gate of midnight energy and into a brilliantly lit crystal chamber that glowed with the dark light that came from the farthest end of the spectrum. Dazzling waves of energy stirred his senses.

Somewhere in the distance he thought he heard Zara scream in rage, but he paid no attention. The scene inside the pyramid riveted his full attention.

This was a world lit by the energy of darkness. Walking into it was the equivalent of waking up to a new dawn. The crystal walls of the Chamber were radiant with energy — energy that he knew intuitively he could channel. And when he did focus the currents in the walls of the pyramid, he knew he would see wondrous things.

Alice stood in the center of the Chamber, illuminated in the enthralling light. She clutched a glowing crystal in one hand. Houdini was on her shoulder, chattering happily. With her other hand Alice gripped the fingers of a young man. Pete, Drake decided. The kid looked scared but hopeful. He, too, held one of the crystals.

Drake realized that neither Alice nor Pete could see him. They stood close together, shoulders touching, and gazed blindly into space.

"I'm here," Drake said.

"I know." Alice turned partially toward him, relief and joy on her face. "I could sense your presence."

"He's really here?" Pete asked. "That voice isn't a hallucination?"

"He's here," Alice said. "The magician pulled off the trick. Told you he would."

"Alice," Drake said.

He took her into his arms. It was an awkward move because she did not drop Pete's hand or the crystal. And then there was Houdini bouncing around as if they were playing some new game.

But Alice rested her forehead against Drake's shoulder. "I knew you would come for me."

"You're sure this guy is your husband?" Pete asked.

Alice raised her head, smiling, even though Drake knew she could not see him.

"Yes," she said. "This is really my husband. Trust me, I'd know him anywhere."

CHAPTER 41

At ten thirty that night Alice and Drake sat at a table in the Marina Inn Tavern. Alice had Nicholas North's diary safely stowed in a bag that she kept close to her side.

She and Drake were not alone. Rachel, Charlotte, Jasper, and Fletcher were with them. They were the only people left in the restaurant. Houdini and Darwina had disappeared shortly after the kids had been sent upstairs to bed. Alice was fairly certain that the dust bunnies had gone hunting inside the Preserve. She wondered where they got the energy. She was exhausted but still too worked up to sleep. She doubted that she would sleep at all that night. She wanted to read her great-grandfather's diary.

Earlier, Burt had fixed her a large bowl of canned vegetable soup accompanied by crackers. She had eaten everything he put in front of her and asked for seconds.

The power had come back on an hour ago. There was no sign of the dark fog. A few brave souls who had been staying at the inn had returned to their own homes, but many of the Marina Inn rooms were still occupied and the B&B was doing a brisk business. There were those who did not entirely trust that the threat was over.

But the lights were on and phones and computers were functioning. Communications with the mainland had been restored. Ferry service was scheduled to resume in the morning, conditions permitting. The proprietor of the service had promised to bring supplies, including toilet paper and groceries, on the early run.

Alice studied the two crystal slabs on the table. "So much trouble for such dumb-looking stones."

"Not very impressive, are they?" Charlotte observed.

The crystals no longer glowed. Shortly after being removed from the pyramid they had reverted to a murky, unremarkable gray.

Rachel looked at Drake. "What are you going to do with them?"

"I'm tempted to drop them offshore into a deep-sea ravine but I'm not sure that would neutralize them," Drake said. "It might have the opposite effect. These damn rocks have an affinity for geothermal energy. Be my luck they'd land in an undersea volcano and cause an eruption. For now they'll be safer in a mag-steel-and-glass strongbox where the energy levels can be monitored."

"In hindsight, it's a wonder that the crystals were dormant for decades, sitting in a box in a cave here on the island," Rachel mused. "Rainshadow is a nexus, a real hot spot where geothermal psi-forces intersect."

"That's probably why the Aliens chose it to set up their bio-research labs in the first place," Alice said.

"According to the Old Earth records, the crystals have never caused any problem as long as they were properly stored aboveground in a strongbox," Drake said. "But taking them underground into a hot psi environment was a hell of a mistake."

Charlotte folded her arms on the table. "I assume you'll store them in one of the Foundation labs?"

"Right," Drake said. "We've got special vaults for the volatile specimens."

Jasper looked thoughtful. "Think there's any way to destroy them?"

"I don't know," Drake said. "It might be possible to pulverize them and scatter the bits and pieces over a large stretch of the ocean. Theoretically that would limit the resonating power of each individual shard. But I'm not even certain that would work."

"Something else to consider here," Fletcher said. "We humans have only been around on Harmony for a couple of hundred years. No more than a fraction of the planet and the Alien underworld has been explored. Got a hunch there are a lot of surprises waiting for us in the oceans and the catacombs and the rain forest. We might need some real firepower someday. Could be a good idea to have these stones in our hip pocket, so to speak."

"Kind of like having spare tuned amber when you go into the tunnels," Jasper added.

"My family has been guarding these rocks for a few hundred years, first on Earth and now here on Harmony," Drake said. "Guess we'll have to keep on doing that for a while. But once we get these back to the lab we can do some serious research on them. We need to know what we've got here."

Drake started to say something, but a faint, muffled sound stopped him. Alice heard it, too. Chanting.

". . . The Ancients will return, the Ancients will return.

Glorious dawn, glorious dawn, glorious
dawn.
The Ancients will return, the Ancients will
return.
Bringing wonders, bringing wonders,
bringing wonders to behold . . ."

Burt came out of the kitchen, wiping his
hands on his apron. "Sounds like Harry and
Slade found that bunch of Glorious Dawners who went missing."

"Not sure that's a good thing," Fletcher
said.

"Look at it this way," Drake said. "Tomorrow morning we can put them on the first
ferry off the island and send them home."

"Good idea," Jasper said.

The door of the tavern opened, bringing
in the fresh air of a fog-free night. Two men
walked into the room. Energy whispered in
the atmosphere around them. Men of talent, Alice thought. Slade Attridge and Harry
Sebastian had returned.

Chairs scraped on the floorboards. Rachel
and Charlotte leaped to their feet. Both
women were glowing with relief and delight.
They rushed forward, each hurtling into the
arms of one of the men.

Three dust bunnies scurried into the
tavern and began chattering enthusiastically.

A small gaggle of ragged-looking people in green robes paraded into the room. They had evidently lost their signs along the way but that had not diminished their enthusiasm.

"Glorious dawn, glorious dawn, glorious dawn."

Burt planted his hands on his hips and eyed the newcomers. "Anyone who wants to eat had better shut up and stop chanting now."

A sudden hush descended.

The tall, dark-haired man, who had one arm wrapped around Rachel, looked at Burt.

"Thank you," he said. "I know I speak for Slade as well when I tell you that we are forever in your debt."

"That damn chanting was enough to make us seriously consider leaving these dudes behind in the Preserve," Slade added.

Houdini dashed toward Alice and bounced up onto the table. He made enthusiastic greeting sounds. Alice patted him affectionately.

"So that's where you and Darwina went tonight," she said. "You knew they were on the way back, didn't you? You went out to meet them."

One of the Glorious Dawners spotted the

small group at the table. He lifted a hand, palm out.

"The nightmare fog is gone," he intoned. "It's a sign that the return is near."

"You know something? I'm starting to think that I'd rather see the Aliens return than these guys," Fletcher said in low tones.

The Dawner was not deterred. *"Glorious dawn, glorious dawn —"*

The other five took up the chant.

"Glorious dawn, glorious dawn —"

Back in the kitchen, Burt banged a frying pan loudly.

The Dawners hastily went silent again and sat down at the nearest tables.

Harry looked at Burt through the opening. "Feed 'em and send the bill to the Foundation."

"Okay," Burt said. He narrowed his eyes. "But they're all leaving in the morning, right?"

"Oh, yeah," Slade said. "They're all leaving on the first available ferry."

"What about you and Harry?" Burt looked from one man to the other. "I've been saving a couple of cans of tuna fish."

"Sounds good," Slade said. "But I think we could both use a couple of whiskeys with that tuna fish."

Burt chuckled. "Help yourself."

Slade went behind the bar and took down a bottle. He found two glasses and started pouring generous quantities of whiskey.

Keeping Rachel close to his side, Harry walked to the table where Alice sat with Drake, Fletcher, and Jasper. He glanced at the two crystals and smiled, looking satisfied.

"You must be Alice North," he said.

She started to respond, but Drake spoke first.

"Alice, I'd like you to meet my brother, Harry," he said. "Harry, this is Alice, my wife."

"Your wife," Harry said, perfectly neutral.

"Yes," Drake said.

"Congratulations," Harry said in the same very even tone.

"Thanks," Drake said.

"Just an MC," Alice said quickly.

"Is that right?" Harry said. He turned back to Drake, his eyes gleaming with an unholy amusement. "In our family, a marriage is a marriage. Isn't that right, Drake?"

"Yes," Drake said. "So, what took you so long to show up here in town?"

"We were trapped by the fog. Couldn't get the Dawners through it. We knew when the mist lifted this evening that something had changed. Where did you find the crystals?"

"Long story," Drake said.

"Can't wait to hear it," Harry said, smiling. "I knew you'd make it here to the island."

Drake nodded. "Knew you'd make it out of the Preserve."

Slade brought the whiskeys to the table and sat down. He eyed the Glorious Dawn crowd.

"Idiots," he growled. "I should lock 'em up until I can put them on the ferry."

Alice smiled. "It might be hard to stuff all those Glorious Dawners into your little jail. It's sort of full at the moment."

Slade's brows rose. "My jail is full?"

"Kirk and Myrna are taking turns keeping an eye on the new residents," Drake said.

"Is that so?" Slade nodded once and downed some whiskey. He lowered the glass. "Then I'm with Harry. Can't wait to hear the story."

CHAPTER 42

Alice awoke alone in the bed. She opened her eyes and glanced at the clock on the table. Dawn was still an hour away. The room was dark because the amber lamp had not been lit. For the first time since they had arrived on Rainshadow, the space was flooded with moonlight.

She had not expected to sleep at all that night, but after reading several pages of Nicholas North's bad handwriting she had fallen asleep.

Alice could see Drake standing at the window, his broad shoulders silhouetted against the silver glow. He was naked except for his briefs. Houdini was with him, perched on the ledge. Man and dust bunny gazed pensively out into the night.

Alice levered herself up on her elbows. "Everything okay?"

"Everything is fine," Drake said. He turned to look at her. She saw that he was not wearing his glasses. "What about you? Catch up on your sleep?"

"Yep." She studied him. "You don't mind moonlight?"

"I can tolerate it but it's the equivalent of high noon for me."

She pulled the covers aside, stood, and reached for the robe that Rachel had loaned her. She crossed the room to the window. Drake put an arm around her waist and drew her close. She allowed herself to settle into his warmth and strength.

"What did you see today?" she asked after a while.

"When I walked into the Dream Chamber?"

"Yes," she said.

"The inside of a pyramid made with hot crystal."

"No nightmares?"

"No," Drake said. "No nightmares. But there is something important locked in the stones of that Chamber. We need to find out what it is."

"How do we do that? You're the only one who can actually see inside that place. Even with the energy levels lowered it's still filled with dark light."

"We'll go back tomorrow and I'll take a look around," Drake said. "I think I can handle the energy in that Chamber."

"Do you think that whatever is concealed in the pyramid crystals is dangerous?"

Drake hesitated. "What I sensed was something powerful and important. Powerful, important forces are always dangerous to some degree. But it did not feel destructive."

"Should be interesting. Well, congratulations to us, huh? We found the missing crystals. Mission accomplished."

Drake tightened his arm around her, pinning her close. "This thing isn't over yet. We still have to deal with your ex-mother-in-law and Aldwin Hampstead."

"Hampstead shouldn't be a problem. Zara Tucker has already implicated him. You heard her this afternoon. After she stopped blaming me for everything that went wrong, she started in on him. Slade said it won't be hard for the Federal Bureau of Psi Investigation people to tie him to the conspiracy. Zara turned on Egan Quinton, too."

"And he turned on her. Took him long enough to realize what she really is," Drake said. "That leaves Ethel Whitcomb."

"Once she's confronted with the facts, she'll have to accept the truth," Alice said. "I didn't murder her son."

"Obsessed people don't usually pay much

attention to facts. Exhibit A would be Dr. Zara Tucker."

"Good point. So, have you got a plan to convince Ethel to leave me alone?"

"I'm working on it. Meanwhile, we stay married."

"You really think that's the best way to deal with the Ethel problem?"

"For now."

Alice took a deep breath. It wasn't the answer she wanted to hear, but it was a good plan for the near term. She'd never had much luck with long-range planning, anyway, she reminded herself.

"Okay," she said.

"Okay?" He turned to face her, his hands closing around her shoulders. "That's all you can say about staying married to me? Okay?"

The low-burning fires of anger in his words and the heat in his eyes startled her. Bewildered, she flattened her palms on his chest.

"I said okay as in, I'm okay with going along with your plan," she whispered.

"And as in you're okay with staying in an affair with me?"

"Well, yes, I guess so."

"You guess so?"

Her bewilderment flashed into anger.

"Stop throwing my words back at me. Why are you trying to start a fight here? It's been a really long day. If you want to argue, could we save it until some other time?"

"Okay."

"Okay?" She was suddenly incensed. "What's that supposed to mean?"

"You tell me. You're the one who started this argument."

"Don't you dare blame me," she snapped.

Drake's eyes got hotter. "You're right. We'll save the argument until some other time."

His mouth came down on hers, silencing her before she could figure out where to go next.

The kiss acted like a catalyst, transmuting the smoldering flames of the incipient quarrel into the hot fires of passion. Energy flashed in the atmosphere. Alice felt the heat arcing through her blood, arousing all her senses.

The next thing she knew the room was spinning around her. Instinctively she clutched at Drake's shoulders to steady herself. It took her a heartbeat to realize that he had scooped her up and was carrying her to the bed. He dropped her onto the tumbled sheets and blankets. For a few seconds he loomed over her, his broad chest and shoulders blotting out the moonlight.

An urgent chortle and a scratching noise interrupted the scene.

Drake turned away from the bed long enough to open the door. Houdini disappeared out into the illuminated hallway.

"Damn," Drake said. There was irritation and pain in the single word. He closed the door very quickly and locked it.

"Your eyes." Alice sat up. "Are you okay?"

"I will be in a minute." He remained where he was near the door, gripping the knob. "Forgot the lights were back on out there in the hallway."

"Can I get you anything? A cold washcloth to put over your eyes?"

"No. I said I'll be okay. Takes a few seconds for my senses to calm down, that's all."

"I'm just trying to help," Alice said.

"I know. Stop."

"Okay."

"Do me a favor," Drake said.

"What?"

"Don't use that word again until tomorrow at the earliest, preferably never."

"What word? Oh. Okay. Oops. Sorry."

Drake just looked at her with silvery heat in his eyes.

She started to giggle. She rolled onto her

stomach and tried to smother the laughter with a pillow, but it was hopeless.

"You know," Drake said in ominous tones, "this isn't going quite the way I had planned."

"Sorry about that," she mumbled into the pillow.

"But if there's one thing I've learned in the past few days, it's that things rarely do go according to plan — not when you're involved."

She never heard him cross the room, but the bed suddenly gave beneath his weight. He put her on her back and came down on top of her, his eyes fierce with energy. She realized he had stripped off his briefs.

"Turns out I like that in a woman," he said.

"Really?"

"Really."

He anchored her wrists to the bed and kissed her until she stopped laughing; until she was hot and wet and excited; until all of her senses were thrilled; until a deep, demanding, aching need built inside her. When she started to struggle and twist beneath him, he freed her wrists and pulled her nightgown off over her head.

She put her hands around him and pulled him back down to her, sinking her nails into his shoulders.

He groaned and rolled onto his back, taking her with him. She kissed his mouth, his throat, and then his bare chest. She could feel the rigid length of him pressing against her inner thigh. She sat up slowly until she was resting on her knees astride him. She wrapped one hand around his erection and guided him into her heat. The pressure at first was almost unbearable, but then he was inside her and the intense fullness was exactly what she needed.

She climaxed on the third thrust.

He gripped her hips with both hands and watched her with his molten eyes.

"Alice," he said. *"Alice."*

Her name was a plea, a command, a claim.

He thrust again and again and then found his own release. Once again she experienced the sense of a deep intimacy for which there were no words.

Such magic could not last forever, she thought. But Alice knew she would remember and cherish the sensation for the rest of her life.

Drake awoke to the new day. Automatically, he groped for his glasses and put them on before he opened his eyes. He saw that Alice had left the shades down to protect him against the daylight. She was gone, however. So was the diary.

He got to his feet and headed toward the bath.

Fifteen minutes later he made the trek downstairs. Alice was in a booth at the rear of the tavern. Burt looked out through the kitchen pass-through and called out a greeting.

"Help yourself to the coffee, Drake."

"Thanks."

Drake poured a mug full of coffee and carried it to Alice's table. She looked up. He saw that she had the diary open in front of her. Houdini was perched on the table, finishing the last of a peanut butter cracker. He chortled a cheery greeting.

Drake gave him a pat and sat down. He looked at the diary.

"Are the answers all there?" he asked.

"Most of them." Alice gave him a misty smile. "I can't tell you how much it means to me to have this diary."

Drake thought about the hours he had spent in the Sebastian family archives over the years. "I understand how it feels to be able to touch your own past."

"I owe it all to you. You really are a magician."

"No," he said. "We needed each other to

get through this thing. If it hadn't been for you, Tucker would have destroyed Rainshadow."

Alice shook her head. "I'm the one who put the crystals in her hands."

"That wasn't your fault. You were trying to retrieve some pieces of your past. In my family, we don't consider that a crime."

She sighed. "Thanks. I appreciate that. Still, if I hadn't fallen for Fulton's line —"

"If I hadn't fallen for Zara Tucker's line three years ago, none of this would have happened. There's plenty of blame to go around."

"She really is a sneaky, conniving, sociopathic twit, you know. Also a total psycho. Any woman could immediately see through her."

"Maybe that was my problem, I'm not any woman."

Alice stared at him for a heartbeat. Then she laughed.

"Point taken," she said. "Think you'll have a problem seeing through women like that in the future?"

"No," Drake said. He watched her through his glasses, savoring the light and energy that danced in the atmosphere around her. "I see everything a lot more clearly these days."

CHAPTER 43

"Alice thinks she owns half of Rainshadow?"
Harry asked.

It was rare to see his brother looking
dumbfounded, Drake thought. But this was
one of those moments and he relished it.

"Half of anything of value that might be
found inside the Preserve, to be more
precise," Drake said. "And she's right.
There's a signed copy of the agreement in
her great-grandfather's diary and, according
to it, there's another copy in the Sebastian
family archives."

Harry whistled softly. "Son of a ghost.
Wait until the old man hears about this."

"Should be interesting."

Harry raised his brows. "Another person,
someone who didn't know you well, might
wonder if that's why you got involved in an
MC with Alice. Maybe trying to use a fake
marriage to get her to cooperate with you?"

"No," Drake said. His sense of amusement evaporated in an instant. He was suddenly angry and a little worried. *Was that what Alice believed?* he wondered. "That's not why we're married."

Harry nodded. "Figured it wasn't."

"I've got a strategy."

"You always have a strategy. That's why they call you the Magician back home."

"For the record, I had a hell of a time convincing Alice to go for an MC."

"Yeah?"

"Her last MC husband tried to kill her."

"That would be Fulton Whitcomb?"

"Yes." Drake looked at him. "And before you ask, I believe Alice's version of events."

Harry nodded, still thoughtful. "Okay, in that case I believe it, too. Doesn't explain why you're in an MC."

"Ethel Whitcomb has been spending a lot of money this past year trying to make Alice's life hell. The effort has been successful for the most part. The night I found Alice, I had to deal with a private investigator searching her apartment, looking for anything that could be used against her. Ethel wants Alice in jail."

"You figured Ethel Whitcomb would back off once she found out that you were in the picture."

"I thought it would send a message,"

Drake said evenly. "At the time I was concerned that Whitcomb might try to have Alice followed to Rainshadow. We didn't need the complications. That was before I found out that the island had been shut down by the fog."

"Uh-huh."

Drake looked at him. "What?"

"You're sleeping with Alice North."

"So?"

"I'm thinking you didn't need to get involved in an MC to protect her from Ethel Whitcomb. You have other resources available to you for handling situations like that."

"In hindsight, maybe it wasn't absolutely necessary. It just seemed like the most efficient way to get Whitcomb out of the picture until the problem here on Rainshadow was resolved."

Harry smiled slowly. There was a knowing look in his eyes. "Wait until Mom finds out."

CHAPTER 44

Alice put the North diary down on the table and looked at the small crowd gathered in the café at the back of Shadow Bay Books. Drake and Harry both lounged against the wall. Jasper, Fletcher, Rachel, and Charlotte sat at tables, cups of tea in front of them.

"In the years that followed the breakup of the North-Sebastian partnership, my great-grandfather returned to Rainshadow on a number of occasions," Alice said. "His light-talent made it possible for him to come and go through the psi-fence, and his copy of the psi-code treasure map allowed him to get to the cave where the crystals were stored. He ran some experiments on the stones and at some point he discovered that they could be made to function as para-normal compasses."

"Compasses that pointed toward hot spots on the island?" Drake asked.

"Right," Alice said. She put her hand on

the diary and thought about what she had read. "Properly positioned, they resonated with the energy fields coming from the various ruins on the island. But he could not navigate the terrain inside the Preserve any better than anyone else — until he found Bainbridge's personal papers that led him to the hole-in-the-wall entrance and into the tunnels."

Rachel smiled, understanding. "Once North was down in the catacombs, he set out to map them, and in the process he found the ruins of at least two Alien labs, the pyramid and the aquarium."

Drake smiled appreciatively. "Aware that the ruins were finds of potentially incredible value, he very cleverly got his old pirate partner, Harry Sebastian the First, to sign an agreement giving North and his heirs half of anything of value that was ever discovered on the island."

"That was probably the only shrewd business move my great-grandfather ever made," Alice said.

Fletcher chuckled. "Could turn out to be downright brilliant."

"At that time Harry Sebastian probably wasn't paying much attention to Rainshadow, anyway," Harry said. "He was busy building his business and starting a family.

He would have had no objection to signing the agreement. As far as he was concerned, he and North had been partners when they buried the treasure. He figured North had every right to half the value of whatever was discovered on Rainshadow. But he assumed that nothing of financial importance would be found on the island for years, if ever."

"He also assumed that if something of value was discovered, Sebastian, Inc., through the Rainshadow Foundation, would control the discovery," Alice said. She kept her tone exquisitely polite.

A quick grin came and went on Drake's face, but he said nothing.

Harry narrowed his eyes. "Your great-grandfather's version of your family history is a little different than the Sebastian family version."

"They say that happens a lot when it comes to history," Alice said. "Different people hold different views and the prevailing story is the one written by the winners."

"There are no winners and losers here," Harry growled. "Just a partnership that went bust."

Drake shot Harry a warning look and took charge of the meeting. "To continue, Nick North died before he could return to Rainshadow again after the agreement was signed. Thanks to his MC wife at the time, the diary and Nick's psi-code map to the cave where the crystals were stored disappeared into the underground antiquities market."

"There's always a market for lost treasure maps," Charlotte observed. "No telling how many people tried to find those ruins over the years."

"Tried and failed," Alice said. "Because only a descendant of Nick North, who also possessed a version of his talent, could decipher his copy of the psi-code map."

Drake folded his arms and sat back. "Zara Tucker came across North's psi-code map and the diary during the course of her research. She became obsessed with finding the ruins, particularly the pyramid, which North believed contained extraordinary secrets that only a light-talent could unravel. But first she had to locate the crystals. She landed a position at the Foundation research labs to try to get an inside track and access to the Sebastian family archives."

"Her plan worked at first because the two of you started dating," Harry said. "She even persuaded you to go to a matchmaking agency and take the test. Lo and behold the two of you were a perfect match."

Drake winced. "Don't remind me. Who

knew you could bribe a matchmaker to fake the results of the test? Is nothing sacred?"

Fletcher shook his head. "Nope."

"It soon became clear to Tucker that, in spite of what the agency test showed, you were not going to marry her and you certainly had no intention of taking her into your confidence," Harry continued. "Hell, our family has never even officially acknowledged that the Old World crystals existed. Those damn rocks were a deep, dark family secret and we intended to keep it that way."

"When I ended the relationship," Drake said, "she was furious because she saw everything she had worked for going down in flames. In her rage, she used the Alien laser on me and then she faked her own death."

Alice pursed her lips. "In hindsight, it certainly looks as if the two of you should have conducted a more thorough investigation into her disappearance."

Harry and Drake looked at her.

"Thank you for that advice," Harry said.

Drake nodded solemnly. "Have to remember that the next time I run into a mad scientist."

Alice shrugged. "Just saying."

Rachel and Charlotte smiled.

"Got any idea how hard it is to prove that

someone did not fake her own death by walking off into an uncharted section of the catacombs?" Harry asked. "People disappear into the tunnels all the time. In this instance, there was a note. There was a record of a recent para-psych evaluation in which the doctor noted that Tucker was at risk of doing herself some harm. A stash of potent hallucinogens were discovered in her bedroom. None of her bank accounts were ever accessed after she vanished. None of her credit cards were ever used."

"Okay, okay, I get it," Alice said. "You thought she was dead. I will admit that it's easier to disappear than most people assume — if you're willing to leave everything behind."

Drake cleared his throat. "Moving right along, Tucker reinvented herself as an Alien antiquities expert in the black market. It was the perfect cover. She operated freely in the shadows of that world and in the process she met Aldwin Hampstead, director of the Whitcomb Museum. They did business together but Tucker never gave up on her goal. She went looking for a North descendant who could lead her to the crystals."

"Eventually she found me," Alice said. "But I had no idea that my family history was connected to Rainshadow. All I knew was that I had a talent for disappearing."

"Tucker had to figure out a way to get you on board without letting you discover your heritage and your claim to half of anything found on Rainshadow," Drake said. "She was afraid that if you learned the truth you would go straight to the Sebastian family to demand your share. She didn't dare let that happen."

"She had another problem as well," Alice said. "She was going to need a lot of money to conduct an illicit excavation here on Rainshadow."

Fletcher raised a brow. "That's where Aldwin Hampstead came in, I suppose."

"Yes," Drake said. "He had a direct pipeline into the Whitcomb family fortune. He also knew enough about the family dynamics to realize that Fulton Whitcomb would jump at the chance to prove to his mom and everyone else that he was not a loser."

"Tucker and Hampstead decided to bring him in on the project," Alice said. "Whitcomb was thrilled when they approached him with the idea of going after the crystals and the ruins. They told him all he had to do was convince me to enter into a full Covenant Marriage in order to be able to claim half of whatever they found on the island."

Rachel gave Alice a wicked smile. "I'm sure they were all stunned when you turned down Whitcomb's offer of a CM in favor of a trial marriage."

"Yeah, well, there was this small voice whispering that it was all just a little too good to be true," Alice said.

"After Egan Quinton murdered Fulton Whitcomb, Tucker came to Rainshadow with the diary, the secret of the catacomb entrance, and the three crystals," Drake said. "Sure enough, she was able to use the stones to locate the pyramid. Thanks to Hampstead, she was able to tap into the museum endowment fund to finance a small-scale excavation."

"Thanks to her work in the antiquities black market, she had already found her pet ghost hunter, Egan," Alice said. "He was a professional killer with a talent for disguise. His job was to keep the tunnels cleared of UDEMs and serve as her spy in Shadow Bay. He rounded up a couple of his pals to handle security and bring in supplies by way of Deception Cove."

Jasper frowned. "You say Tucker had all three crystals but only two of them were found inside the pyramid. How did the third one end up in the aquarium?"

Slade sat forward. "I can answer that. I

talked to Tucker again this morning. She said she didn't want to take any chances with the pyramid until she knew more about the power of the crystals. She took them to the aquarium to run some experiments. But she made the mistake of putting one of the stones into the rainstone vault at the aquarium."

Rachel looked surprised. "She was able to work the rainstone to open the vault?"

"No," Slade said. "The vault was open when she arrived at the aquarium. She took one of the crystals inside to see if it would resonate with any of the antiquities. Her action triggered the vault's closing mechanism. When she realized that she was about to get locked inside, she panicked and ran for the exit, leaving the crystal behind. She barely made it."

"Once the vault closed there was no way to open it again," Harry said. He gave Rachel a knowing look. "Not unless you happen to have a talent for working rainstone."

"In the end, Tucker was left with only two crystals," Drake said. "She had no interest in the aquarium facility, so she went back to the pyramid chamber and planted the remaining two crystals inside. They eventually set up the unstable resonance frequencies that overheated the Chamber and ignited the fog."

Slade looked at him. "You are going to take all of those people who are currently sitting in my jail away from Shadow Bay, right? I want them out of town as soon as possible."

"Harry will handle that end of things," Drake said.

"Don't worry," Harry said. "I've already talked to headquarters. A Foundation Security team — the real Foundation Security people this time — will be here in the morning. We'll transport your guests back to the mainland and hand them over to the FBPI."

"I'll bet Zara Tucker lands in a locked para-psych ward," Rachel said. "Something really twisted in that pretty little blonde head."

"Tell me about it," Drake said. "I still can't believe I dated that crazy woman."

Alice made a face. "I can't believe I agreed to an MC with Fulton Whitcomb."

Rachel smiled. "Everyone makes mistakes when it comes to that kind of thing. What you both need to remember is that in the end you listened to your intuition and cut your losses before you wound up in a Covenant Marriage."

Alice shuddered. "Imagine being stuck in a marriage with someone like Fulton Whitcomb for the rest of your life."

Sunlight flashed on Drake's glasses. "Whitcomb and the others never intended a long-term marriage to be a problem for you."

"There is that," Alice said.

She shook off the creepy sensation that swept across her senses. She was safe now. It was over. And so was her Rainshadow honeymoon. At that thought, the creepy feeling gave way to an inexplicable sense of loss. *Not like it was ever a real marriage in the first place,* she reminded herself.

"What's next on our to-do list?" Harry asked.

Drake straightened away from the wall. Energy sparked in the atmosphere around him. "Next up is a closer look inside the pyramid."

"Right," Harry said. "We need to find out how dangerous that Chamber really is."

"And if it is dangerous?" Slade asked.

"Then we have to find a way to destroy it," Drake said. "Preferably without taking out the whole island."

CHAPTER 45

Drake stood in the center of the pyramid and opened his other vision. The translucent stones that formed the walls and the floor of the Chamber still seethed with energy, but the currents were stable now that the Old World crystals were gone. The wall of midnight that had blocked the entrance had disappeared.

"Feels much calmer in here now," Alice said. "Not nearly so dark, either. I can see some of the energy locked in the walls, but it's all sort of muted to my vision, as if this room is drenched in paranormal shadows."

"That's the way the daylight world appears to me when I view it through my glasses," Drake said.

"I understand," Alice said. "What do you see in here?"

She stood beside him, surveying the Chamber. Houdini was perched on her shoulder. He did not show any particular interest in the pyramid. Harry and Rachel stood just inside the entrance. Darwina was perched on Rachel's shoulder, an Amberella doll in one paw.

Drake turned slowly, examining the Chamber. "Each of the big blocks of crystal are made up of hundreds, maybe thousands, of smaller crystals. Each of the small crystals is illuminated in a different shade of dark light. I've never seen most of these colors before. But I think I can channel some of this energy."

"Channel it to what purpose?" Harry asked, sounding wary.

"I'm not sure yet," Drake said. "But I don't think there's any risk in running a couple of experiments. The energy in this place is stable."

"Go for it," Harry said.

Drake scanned the myriad building blocks of the pyramid, searching for one that felt *right*. The lively energy in one of the crystals caught his attention. He could not explain why but he knew intuitively that it was somehow familiar.

He walked closer to the crystal and got a fix. It was as if he had flipped a switch inside the stone. An image appeared the way images do in dreamscapes. In this case, it was a very familiar image.

Houdini chortled excitedly. Darwina joined in, waving her Amberella doll.

"Oh, my goodness," Alice whispered. "Would you look at that?"

They all gazed at the image in the crystal.

"It's a dust bunny," Harry said. "I don't get it. Why would the Aliens go to the trouble of building this place just to put up a picture of a dust bunny?"

"I think it's more than just a picture," Drake said. "It feels like an icon, a symbol indicating something else beneath the surface."

He fixed his attention on the image. The dust bunny icon dissolved into a series of subtly shifting dream-like images. They floated in and out of focus in a seemingly random pattern. It took a few tries but he finally got the hang of summoning one image and concentrating on it.

Beneath it, however, was another series of eerie, fleeting dreamlight impressions.

Eventually he found the secret to unlocking the dreamscape. The scenes suddenly sprang to life in a three-dimensional, life-sized display that occupied most of the interior of the pyramid.

"It's as if we're standing inside a hologram," Alice whispered.

"A video hologram," Rachel added. "The

images are moving."

"It's a dreamscape," Drake said, very certain now. "A waking dream that was constructed specifically to transmit information via dreamlight. In this case, the data being transmitted is about dust bunnies."

There were moving images of dust bunnies everywhere. Houdini and Darwina were thrilled. They seemed to understand that the dust bunnies were not real, but that did not stop them from chasing each other through the dreamscape.

The scenes depicted dust bunnies in the wild, dust bunnies at play, dust bunnies on the hunt. But it was the scenes of dust bunnies dashing around a green quartz room furnished with what looked like high-tech lab equipment that made Alice and Rachel cry out simultaneously.

"No," Alice said.

"Please don't tell me the Aliens used dust bunnies for experimental purposes," Rachel whispered. "I don't care if it did happen a couple of thousand years ago. It would be just too horrible."

Houdini and Darwina appeared oblivious to the menacing scenes around them. They continued to dash around the pyramid in a mad game of hide-and-seek.

Drake pulled harder on the dreamscape

lab images, making them sharper and crisper. As he did so, understanding flooded his senses.

"The dust bunnies are native to Harmony," he said. "And, yes, initially they were used in experiments involving paranormal forces. The Aliens' goal was to find a way to adapt to the poisonous environment here."

"Poisonous to them," Alice said.

"They came from a world where the paranormal forces were much stronger," Drake said. "A world lit by a sun that gave off that kind of energy. For the Aliens, the paranormal was normal. They were well adapted to their home world. Colonizing Harmony proved more difficult than they had anticipated."

"It would be like humans attempting to adapt to a planet that had a much lower level of oxygen or normal sunlight," Harry said. "The only way to survive would be to synthesize more of what was lacking in the environment."

Drake studied the myriad crystals of the Chamber, willing the information he wanted to come to the surface.

A small triangular crystal in one corner brightened. Dreamlight whispered in the atmosphere. Information came to Drake the way it did in a dream — a deep sense of knowing that required no words.

"When they realized that they would be forever trapped underground unless they found a way to bioengineer themselves, they established Rainshadow Island as a research center," he said. "But for the most part the experiments proved unsuccessful. The majority of the creatures that resulted from the research could only survive in a heavy-psi environment. If they were removed from Rainshadow, they died very quickly. There was only one viable exception."

"Dust bunnies two-point-oh," Charlotte said.

"That experiment worked. The dust bunnies thrived both underground and aboveground."

"Just like humans," Harry said. "True, we're not quite as nimble at crossing through low-psi and high-psi environments. But then, the dust bunnies have been adapting to this environment ever since they came out of the Alien labs. We humans are catching up fast, however."

"The experts have been telling us for years that something in the environment here on Harmony is encouraging the evolution of our latent psychic senses," Charlotte said.

Alice crossed her arms. "I'm very glad dust bunnies survived, but I hate knowing that the Aliens were experimenting on them."

Drake summoned more information with his thoughts. Another crystal glowed in the far corner. Once again information was transmitted via dreamlight.

"There are experiments and then there are experiments," he said, sorting through the dream data. "The Aliens were lonely."

Alice frowned. "Weren't there plenty of other Aliens around?"

"Yes," Drake said. "But there were no creatures of another species on Harmony that were capable of bonding with the Aliens."

Understanding lit Alice's face. She smiled. So did Rachel.

"It would be like moving to a world without cats or dogs or other animal companions," Harry said. "Damn lonely when you think about it."

"They probably didn't realize how badly intelligent life needs to connect with other species," Rachel said. "It's one of the ways that we define ourselves as human. We need to know on some level that we're a part of the ecosystem, not separate from it."

"Here on harmony the Aliens discovered that they were psychically isolated from all the other creatures on the planet," Drake said. "You're right, Harry. It would have been a very strange and disturbing kind of loneliness."

"They missed their connection to the animal world," Alice said. "So they set out to bioengineer a species capable of bonding with them."

Drake searched for more information. "But in the end they abandoned Harmony and the dust bunnies, too. The Aliens never figured out how to adapt."

"It's weird," Alice said. "But I'm getting the hang of this place. You just sort of think about the information you need and it comes to you in the form of a waking dream."

"Dreamlight is probably a universal language for intelligent life," Drake said. "At least it's effective for communicating information between the Aliens and us. Evidently the Aliens dreamed just like we do."

"Huh." Harry studied the crystals around them. "So this pyramid is a kind of information storage and retrieval device?"

A dazzling excitement flashed through Drake. "It's the most spectacular find ever made on Harmony. An ancient computer housing a database loaded with the secrets of the Aliens. The researchers back at

Foundation headquarters are going to go wild."

"Zara Tucker was right about one thing," Harry said. "In the long run, this thing will be worth a fortune. No telling what technological and medical breakthroughs may come from it."

Pride sparked in Alice. "And it was my great-grandfather, Nicholas North, who not only discovered it but also the tunnels that make it possible to navigate the territory inside the fence."

Charlotte laughed. "Don't forget the best part: that, thanks to your great-grandfather being a very clever pirate, you own half of whatever this computer turns out to be worth."

Drake looked at Alice, his silvery eyes heating. "As well as half of everything else that remains to be discovered on Rainshadow."

"The money will be nice," Alice said.

Drake smiled. "But it's not the best part about your inheritance here on Rainshadow."

"No," Alice said. She tightened her grip on the diary and looked around at the others. "The best part was being involved in this discovery. Just knowing that I have some history here on the island and now some history with you three and Jasper and Fletcher and some of the others in Shadow Bay — that's the best part."

"Welcome to the family," Rachel said.

CHAPTER 46

"You can't blame me for my conclusions, Ms. North." Ethel Whitcomb removed her reading glasses and closed the folder Drake had given her. She looked at Alice across the width of a First Generation antique desk. "I had every reason to believe that you were involved in the murder of my son. Frankly I'm not inclined to change my mind. Aldwin Hampstead and Zara Tucker may have confessed to the actual act, but as far as I'm concerned you bear a great deal of the responsibility."

"How can you say that?" Alice demanded.

They were in Ethel Whitcomb's study. Alice was seated in a chair near the window. Houdini was huddled on her shoulder, fully fluffed but watchful. She knew that he had picked up on her tension. The Whitcomb butler had tried to insist that dust bunnies were not allowed inside the mansion, but Drake had fixed the man with a single look, saying nothing. The butler had mumbled something about making an exception for helper animals and hastily showed them all into the study.

Drake had ignored Ethel's cool invitation to take a seat. Instead he had walked across the room and placed the folder containing the confessions and a record of the various criminal charges on Ethel's desk. Then he had stayed out of the way. Thus far he had remained silent, watching Ethel through his mirrored glasses.

Alice knew that the only reason Ethel had agreed to the meeting was because she had expected that only Drake would be present. She had been shocked when Alice had walked into the room at his side. Now Drake's icy stillness and steady, unreadable gaze were making Ethel nervous. She hid her unease very well but Alice was not deceived. In his present mood, Drake would have made a specter-cat nervous.

"I don't care what the police and the FBPI choose to believe," Ethel said. "I know that you seduced Fulton into an MC as part of a plan to convince him to finance your search for a treasure on Rainshadow."

"Fulton is the one who set out to seduce me," Alice said. "And for the record, he offered a full-blown Covenant Marriage, not an MC. The Marriage of Convenience was my idea."

"I don't believe that for a moment."

Alice raised her brows. "Well, to give him his due, he never expected that the marriage would last very long because his partners had assured him that after he inherited my share of whatever was discovered on Rainshadow, I would suffer a convenient accident. But in the end he lost his temper when I told him I wanted a divorce and he tried to murder me."

"That is an outrageous lie," Ethel said. She pushed herself to her feet. "What he saw in you, I'll never know. There is no doubt in my mind that my son is dead because of you. Get out of my house or I will call the police."

Alice looked at Drake. "I told you this meeting was a waste of time."

"The meeting isn't over yet," Drake said. He did not move, but the atmosphere heated with dangerous energy. "We aren't going anywhere until we have all reached an understanding on a couple of points."

Ethel glared at him. "There is nothing more to understand, Mr. Sebastian."

"You will stop harassing my wife."

"You mean your mistress."

"Alice is my wife," Drake said. His voice

was lethally soft. "In our family, we take marriage very seriously."

"It's an MC, not a real marriage," Ethel said, her voice very tight.

"It's a real marriage as far as I'm concerned, and that's all you need to know. If you continue to send your goon squad investigators after Alice, you will find yourself dealing with me."

Ethel's jaw clenched. "Goon squad? I have no idea what you are talking about."

"I'm talking about your deliberate campaign of harassment, intimidation, and attempts to destroy my wife's reputation."

Ethel stiffened. "That's ridiculous."

Alarmed by the cold energy radiating from Drake, Alice jumped to her feet.

"I don't think . . ." she began.

But no one was listening to her. Even Houdini was ignoring her. He was sleeked out and ready for battle.

The blood drained from Ethel's face. "How dare you threaten me and my family?"

"It's not a threat," Drake said. "It's a solemn promise. You've been running Whitcomb Industries long enough to know your way around the business world. You are aware that I can do what I say I can do."

"That little whore murdered my son."

"This meeting is over," Drake said. He started toward Alice. "You might want to contact your people who are working on the Morgan project, Ethel. As soon as we leave here today, I'm going to call Paul Morgan and tell him that Whitcomb is having some serious financial problems that have not yet become known to investors. The deal you're doing with him will be dead by five o'clock tonight."

"But Whitcomb isn't having any financial problems," Ethel whispered, shocked.

Drake gave her an icy-cold smile and took Alice's arm. "You know how it is when it comes to rumors in our world, Ethel. When word gets out that Morgan stepped back from a deal with Whitcomb, the gossip will spread like wildfire."

"No," Ethel said. "You can't do this to me and my family." She pointed a shaking finger at Alice. "Not because of . . . of her."

"Because of my *wife*," Drake corrected. "And, yes, to protect her, I will destroy you and everything you have built."

Ethel sank slowly down into her chair. She stared at Drake. "She's hypnotized you, just like she hypnotized my son. Don't you see?"

Drake's mouth twisted in a humorless smile. "I see more than you can possibly imagine, Mrs. Whitcomb."

"Enough," Alice said. She stepped between Ethel and Drake. "There is no need to crush the entire Whitcomb family, not that I don't appreciate the gesture. I mean, no one has ever offered to do anything like that for me before and I'm touched, really I am."

Ethel looked at her, evidently speechless. Alice smiled and then turned back to Drake.

"But we need to keep in mind that stalking me was Ethel's idea —"

"I am not a stalker," Ethel shouted.

"And it was a perfectly understandable reaction, if somewhat over the top," Alice concluded.

"What?" Drake asked.

"She honestly believed that I murdered her son and that there would be no justice." Alice turned to Ethel. "In your shoes and given your resources, I would have gone looking for a little rough justice, too. But it would have been nice if you had first made sure you had the real killer."

"Don't you dare lecture me," Ethel snapped.

"Just sit down and read the contents of that folder," Alice said. "After what you did to me this past year, it's the least you can do. You're an intelligent woman. Look at the evidence. And then, please, just leave me alone. That's all I ask. If you stay away from me, I promise you that Drake won't go after Whitcomb Industries."

Ethel appeared nonplussed. She looked at Drake.

"Do I have your word on that?" she asked.

Drake's mouth hardened. He gave the question some thought and then he shrugged. "What the hell. All right, it's a deal. But if I suspect at any time in the future that you have inconvenienced my wife in any way — if she even gets a parking ticket — I will assume that you are behind the said inconvenience. I will use all of the Sebastian, Inc. resources available to me to take down Whitcomb Industries. Do we understand each other?"

"Yes," Ethel said. She collapsed back into her chair. "Please go now."

Drake took Alice's arm and steered her toward the door. Neither of them spoke until they were back in the car. Drake sat quietly behind the wheel for a moment.

"I should have known that you would go soft on me," he said.

"I told you, I didn't want revenge," Alice said. "I understood her anger. All I wanted was for her to leave me alone."

"She will." Drake smiled his coldest smile and rezzed the car's flash-rock engine.

"Ethel Whitcomb won't bother you again. She knows that if she does make trouble for you, I'll take her company apart piece by piece."

"You'd really do it, wouldn't you?"

Drake turned his head to look at her. Light flashed on his mirrored glasses. "In a heartbeat."

Alice took a deep breath. "She believed you."

"Yes."

"Hopefully, she'll believe the evidence in that folder, as well."

"Don't count on it." Drake eased the car away from the curb. "Can't expect a mother to believe the worst of her son. But maybe, in time, she'll accept the fact that he wasn't the man she wanted him to be. Or not."

A wistful sensation wafted through Alice. She smiled a little and reached up to touch Houdini.

"Family," she said. "Sometimes the rules are different."

"Yes," Drake said. "When it comes to family, the rules are always different. You're my wife. I'd bend every rule in the book for you."

Warmth rushed through her.

"Drake, there's something I need to tell you, something important."

He started to turn his head to look at her, but at that instant his phone buzzed.

"Damn," he said. "That's my emergency number. No one uses it unless there's a real problem."

He hit the speaker button. "Drake Sebastian."

"There's trouble at the para-psych hospital, Mr. Sebastian. Zara Tucker has escaped to the roof with a hostage. Tucker is asking for a helicopter, a lot of money . . . and you."

"I'm on the way," Drake said.

Alice groaned. "I knew she was going to be a problem."

CHAPTER 47

Alice stood with Drake in the doorway of the rooftop stairwell. Together they looked out at the scene unfolding on top of the twelve-story hospital.

Zara Tucker stood at the edge of the wide circle that marked the helicopter landing pad. She was dressed in the oversized green scrubs that she had stolen from a supply cupboard. Her blonde hair was blowing in the snapping breeze. She held a mag-rez pistol on her hostage, a middle-aged woman named Dr. Harriet Metford.

Drake glanced back over his shoulder at the small crowd in the stairwell. The hospital administrator, two para-psych doctors, a couple of strong orderlies, and the guard who had lost his weapon to Zara were crammed into the space.

"What's the status on the helicopter?" Drake asked the guard.

"The chopper is on standby on the roof

of Sebastian, Inc. headquarters, as you ordered. The FBPI negotiator and his team are on the way."

"Trust me, she won't wait long enough to allow you to get into extended negotiations," Drake said. "Tell the pilot to take off and hover over the hospital. Tell him to be ready to land as soon as I raise my hand."

The guard asked no questions. Responding to Drake's cool air of authority, he immediately turned away to speak into his phone.

Drake looked at Alice. "Ready?"

Who was ever actually ready to confront a madwoman with a gun? Alice wondered.

"I might have a mild touch of stage fright," Alice admitted. "But they say that sharpens the act."

"No kidding?" Drake looked grim. "What about a case of stark terror? Does that work? Because that's what I've got."

Alice gave him her best stage smile. "Don't worry, this trick never fails. The audience goes wild every time."

"I'll take your word for it," Drake said. "You're the magician this time. I'm just the box-jumper."

He moved out of the stairwell doorway. The sharp sunlight sparked and flashed on his mirrored glasses.

"You always had a flare for the dramatic, Zara," he said. "But you've definitely outdone yourself this time."

"I thought you would appreciate the theatrics," Zara said. "Where is your lovely new bride?"

Alice moved out of the shadows of the stairwell to stand beside Drake. "I'm here."

"Excellent." Zara smiled. "Wouldn't be the same without you. Stay right where you are. One wrong move and I will start shooting Dr. Metford in various parts of her anatomy."

"I understand," Alice said.

The *whap-whap-whap* of a helicopter's rotor blades sounded in the distance. Zara tipped her head to one side. Then she gave Drake a glowing smile.

"Sounds like our ride is here," she said. "Time for us to fly off into the sunset together. Take off your glasses."

Drake did not move.

"Take off your glasses," Zara screamed. "I want you totally psi-blind, you bastard."

Slowly Drake raised one hand and removed the sunglasses. Alice glanced at him and saw that he had closed his eyes against the blinding radiation of normal sunlight.

"That's better." Zara looked at Alice. "Your turn. Pick up his glasses and throw them over the edge of the roof."

Alice hesitated.

"Do it now or Dr. Metford pays the price."

Alice bent down and picked up the sunglasses. She moved slowly to the side of the roof and tossed the glasses over the edge. The mirrored lenses caught the bright light in one last flash before they fell out of sight.

The helicopter cruised toward the rooftop and started to hover.

Zara looked at Alice. "Come here."

"Me?" Alice said.

"Don't worry, we're going to make a trade, but it's not quite the bargain that Drake expected. You're the one who is coming with me, not him. And don't even think of pulling your disappearing act or I will kill Metford first and Drake second."

"No," Drake said. "That wasn't the arrangement."

"It wasn't?" Zara smiled. "How forgetful of me. Come here, Alice North."

Alice walked slowly toward her. When she was a couple of feet away, Zara shoved Dr. Metford aside. The doctor stumbled and went down hard on her knees.

Zara aimed the pistol at Alice. "I'm holding the gun on your bride, Drake. Signal the pilot to land the helicopter."

"There's no need to take Alice," Drake said.

"There is every need to take her," Zara snapped. She took a syringe out of her pocket. "As long as she is with me you won't try to do anything stupid. Call in the helicopter."

Drake raised his arm. The helicopter eased in closer to the rooftop and started to descend. The downdraft from the blades whipped Alice's hair into a froth. The roar of the engine swamped all other sound.

"Magic time," Alice said quietly.

Houdini leaped from her shoulder where he had been perched. He sprang straight at Zara's throat, becoming visible the instant he lost physical contact with Alice.

For Zara, the moment must have been surreal, Alice thought. Without warning, a fierce creature with four eyes and a great many teeth was suddenly flying at her out of midair. She screamed and stumbled backward.

Houdini landed, drawing blood.

Zara screeched and clawed wildly at him.

"Down, Houdini," Alice said. "Now."

Houdini bounded out of reach of Zara's flailing arms, landing nimbly.

Drake was on Zara before she could aim the pistol. He snapped the mag-rez out of her hand. She crumpled, screaming in frustrated rage. She pounded her fists against the rooftop.

Drake looked at Alice.

"Good trick," he said.

"Thanks," she said. Her pulse was pounding. She scooped up Houdini. "But I think I prefer the old knives-in-the-box routine. You always know where you are with knives. Bullets, not so much."

"We'll keep that in mind for our next trick."

Three men wearing FBPI jackets charged out of the stairwell, heading for Zara.

Zara rose slowly to her feet. She stared at Drake in disbelief. "You're blind in daylight. You can't see without your special glasses. You're day-blind, damn you. I destroyed your talent."

"You altered my talent," Drake said. "You didn't destroy it."

"You're psi-blind!" Zara shrieked.

She flew at him. Alice watched, cold with shock, because she knew what was going to happen next.

Drake waited until the last possible instant and then he stepped out of Zara's path. She shrieked again and tried to change course, but it was too late. Carried forward by her own momentum, her knees struck the edge of the low parapet. She toppled forward and flew over the edge of the roof.

Her scream echoed forever, a shrill, keening counterpoint to the drumbeat of the helicopter blades.

And then it was over.

The helicopter settled onto the roof. The pilot shut down the engine.

Alice hurried to Dr. Metford and peeled the tape off her mouth.

Metford took several deep breaths. "There was a heavy sedative in that syringe. She said she planned to use it on you so that you wouldn't be able to pull any of your tricks. Once she was in the clear she was planning to push you out of the helicopter. She wanted to use you to hurt Mr. Sebastian."

"Yes," Alice said. "We assumed that might be her plan." She reached down to help Metford to her feet. "Are you all right?"

"Yes, I think so."

Metford stood, clearly shaken. She stared at Drake.

The guard, the hospital administrator, and the two orderlies who had emerged from the stairwell stared at him, too.

"Sorry for staring," Dr. Metford said. "But we were under the impression that you were day-blind."

Drake fixed on her with his silvery eyes. "Hasn't anyone ever heard of contact lenses?"

"Crystal contacts?" Dr. Metford said, dumbfounded.

"Something the techs in the Sebastian labs have been working on for me for a while now." Drake's jaw tightened. "They're prototypes. Not the most comfortable things in the world to wear. If you don't mind, I need to find a nice dark place where I can remove them."

He went toward the shadowed stairwell.

Dr. Metford looked at Alice.

"He's going to remove the crystal contacts and put on the other pair of special sunglasses that he brought with him today," Alice explained.

Dr. Metford's brows rose. "He knew that Zara Tucker would demand that he destroy his first pair?"

"He knew how she would stage her big scene today. He's got a talent for business negotiations."

"Obviously there's a reason the business world calls him the Magician," Dr. Metford said.

Alice smiled. "Yes."

CHAPTER 48

"You knew that if she saw one last opportunity to take revenge that she would try, even if it meant her own death," Alice said. "That's why you stood so close to the edge of the roof."

"I thought there was a high probability she would risk everything at the end, yes," Drake said.

He drank some of the whiskey in his glass. Alice swallowed some more of her wine. They were on the sofa in the living room of Drake's town house in the Old Quarter, feet propped side-by-side on the low black lacquer table in front of them.

It was late. Midnight was approaching. Drake was not wearing his sunglasses. The glow of the Dead City Wall was at full force, illuminating the narrow streets and rooftops of the Quarter. The eerie green radiance flooded the living room with paranormal shadows. The only other light came from the fire that burned in the hearth.

The remains of the rich, chunky soup and the sandwiches that Drake's housekeeper had prepared earlier were on the table in front of the sofa. Houdini had done his best to deal with the leftovers but now he was sprawled flat on his back on the sofa between Alice and Drake.

"You could have been killed," Alice said. She took a meditative sip of her wine. "You were standing very, very close to the edge."

"I should have done something permanent about Zara on Rainshadow," Drake said. "But it would have involved too many other people. Harry, Chief Attridge, Charlotte, Rachel, you."

"We would all have kept your secret."

"I know," Drake said. "But I did not want to put that burden on others who have enough secrets of their own to protect."

"Now I'm the only one who knows for sure that what happened to Dr. Z was not entirely an accident."

"Are you okay with that?"

"No," Alice said. "No, I am not okay with that because you could have been killed with that damn fool bit of strategy out there on the rooftop."

Drake looked briefly startled by the fierceness of her reaction. "It wasn't that risky."

"Yes, it was, and I want your promise that you will never, ever do anything that dumbass again."

"Dumbass?"

"Yes, dumbass. I'm sure there were other ways of taking out Tucker. You did not have to put your own life on the line."

"It seemed like the simplest and most effective strategy at the time."

"Don't you dare talk to me about strategy. We were staging a trick. Magicians don't like it when the box-jumper decides to improvise."

"When I saw Tucker there on the roof, I knew that she would keep coming at you until she was stopped," Drake said. "She realized that if she could hurt you, she would have her revenge against me. Sooner or later she might have been successful. I could not allow that."

"I realize you felt an obligation to protect me. I appreciate that. However —"

"Don't say that."

She frowned. "Don't say what?"

"Don't say that you appreciate my need to protect you."

"But I do appreciate it," she said earnestly. "It's very nice of you."

"Nice?"

"Gentlemanly. Heroic. Whatever. You feel

a sense of responsibility toward me, and you are the type of man who takes his responsibilities seriously. I admire that, really."

Drake took his feet off the table. He leaned forward and put his whiskey glass down with enough force to make a loud *clink*. He reached out, took Alice's wineglass from her unresisting fingers, and set it down beside his.

"Something wrong?" Alice asked, bewildered.

"I do not want to hear that you admire me," he said. His unshielded eyes burned. "I did not do what I did today because I am nice. I did it because it was necessary. That's how I work, Alice. I examine a situation, define the goal, and then design a strategy to achieve that goal."

Alice stilled. Something had changed quite drastically in the atmosphere. She was not at all certain where things were going.

"I understand your approach to life and business," she said. "Why don't you want me to admire you for it?"

"Because I want you to love me instead," Drake said, "the way I love you."

A great sense of warmth and wonder welled up from some place deep inside Alice. She looked into Drake's silver eyes and saw the silver fire that burned in the depths.

She touched his cheek.

"I thought you knew," she whispered. "You're the one who sees what others don't see."

"What did you think I saw?"

"That I love you," she said. "That's what I was going to tell you today when we left Ethel Whitcomb's mansion. Took me a while to recognize the feeling. I've never been in love before."

"Alice."

He started to pull her into his arms.

Evidently fearing that he was about to get squashed, Houdini stirred abruptly and bounded down to the floor. He whisked across the room, heading for the open slider. At the door he paused for a cheerful chortle before dashing out onto the balcony and hopping up onto the railing. Alice caught a glimpse of his small, furry frame silhouetted against the green light of the Dead City Wall before he took off into the night.

And then she stopped thinking about Houdini because Drake was kissing her in the luminous psi-and-fire-lit night.

A long time later they lay together, stretched out on the sofa in front of the fireplace. They were both still fully clothed, although Alice's pants and blouse were rumpled. Her initial sense of wonder had worn off. Reality came crowding back.

"What about your family?" she said quietly. "Will they accept me?"

"Accept you?" Drake laughed. "Get real. When they find out you've agreed to marry me, they'll fall all over themselves in gratitude. They were afraid that I was never going to get past what Tucker did to me, that I would never find the right woman."

Alice twisted a little in his arms. "When did you decide that I was the right woman?"

"I knew that the first night we met. Why in hell do you think I rushed you into that Marriage of Convenience the following morning?"

"What?" Alice struggled to a sitting position. "Are you telling me the MC wasn't about protecting me from Ethel Whitcomb?"

"I told myself that it was a good strategy for keeping her away from you. And it was true, up to a point. But there were other ways of handling people like Ethel Whitcomb." Drake tangled his fingers in Alice's hair. "From the moment I saw you in the alley behind the theater dodging those thugs, I wanted you. When you kissed me in that parking garage after we got the MC, I figured I had a chance. After we spent our wedding night in the cove watching each other's backs in that damn fog I knew I would do whatever was necessary to keep you close."

"I kept telling myself not to mistake sexual attraction for love," she whispered. "But I knew from the beginning that what I felt for you was not just physical in nature. It's as if I've been waiting all my life for you to show up."

Drake smiled. "We've both waited long enough. What do you say to a quick, quiet Covenant Marriage and another honeymoon on Rainshadow?"

"A third honeymoon on Rainshadow? Sure, why not?" Alice smiled. "A romantic island paradise teeming with escaped sea monsters living in flooded caves, giant mutant insects, and ancient ruins full of dangerous Alien technology — not to mention an underground labyrinth of uncharted catacombs. What could possibly go wrong?"

"We were made for each other. We can handle anything that comes along."

A sparkling tide of knowing and a sense of profound certainty flowed through Alice.

"Yes," she said. "Yes to everything, Drake Sebastian."

He kissed her for a very long time. After a while he got to his feet, picked her up in his arms, and carried her into the lingering shadows of the bedroom.

Houdini and the others played the new game of hide-and-seek among the ruins inside the great Wall that surrounded the Dead City. The centuries-old ethereal quartz towers glowed in the night, offering virtually unlimited hiding places for dust bunnies. They raced around, darting in and out of the ancient structures until shortly before dawn.

When the first light of the new day illuminated the sky, they left the long-abandoned ruins. They dined on leftover pizza that had been discarded in a trash container in the alley behind a nearby Old Quarter restaurant. A good time was had by all.

The ruins left behind by the long-vanished Aliens held many ancient secrets. But the future on Harmony was with the humans and their games and their pizza.

ABOUT THE AUTHOR

Jayne Castle, the author of *The Lost Night, Canyons of Night, Midnight Crystal, Obsidian Prey, Dark Light, Silver Master, Ghost Hunter, After Glow,* and *After Dark,* is a pseudonym for Jayne Ann Krentz, the author of more than fifty *New York Times* bestsellers. She writes contemporary romantic suspense novels under the Krentz name, as well as historical novels under the pseudonym Amanda Quick. She lives in Seattle.

The employees of Thorndike Press hope you have enjoyed this Large Print book. All our Thorndike, Wheeler, and Kennebec Large Print titles are designed for easy reading, and all our books are made to last. Other Thorndike Press Large Print books are available at your library, through selected bookstores, or directly from us.

For information about titles, please call:
  (800) 223-1244

or visit our Web site at:
  http://gale.cengage.com/thorndike

To share your comments, please write:
  Publisher
  Thorndike Press
  10 Water St., Suite 310
  Waterville, ME 04901

LP CAST
Castle, Jayne.
Deception Cove

APR 2 8 2014

No longer the property of
Boynton Beach City Library
Boynton Beach City Library

Books may be kept two weeks and may be renewed up to six times, except if they
have been reserved by another patron. (Excluding new books and magazines.)
A fine is charged for each day a book is not returned according to the above rule.
No book will be issued to any person incurring such a fine until it has been paid.
All damages to books beyond reasonable wear and all losses shall be made good
to the satisfaction of the Librarian. Each borrower is held responsible for all items
charged on his card and for all fines on the same.